Books by Gwen Masters

Sexy Snax

After All These Years

Single Titles

A Week in the Snow
The Green Room

The Green Room

ISBN # 978-1-78651-926-9

©Copyright Gwen Masters 2016

Cover Art by Lyn Taylor ©Copyright 2016

Interior text design by Claire Siemaszkiewicz

Totally Bound Publishing

Published in 2016 by Totally Bound Publishing, Newland House, The Point, Weaver Road, Lincoln, LN6 3QN, United Kingdom.

Printed in Great Britain by Clays Ltd, St Ives plc
1

THE GREEN ROOM

GWEN MASTERS

Dedication

For Patrick Jane...
The crystal ball is still crystal clear.

Chapter One

The first time I saw him, I knew he was the one.

He was on the dark side of thirty, blessed with the kind of good looks that made people say he looked younger than his age. Shots of Jack Daniels poured out of the bottle and into the glass and into him, a constant circle. The bottle was sitting on the amp and rocking gently with the vibration. He held a guitar in his hands as if it were a wounded lover, cradling it, leaning so far over the instrument that he could almost peer at himself in the polish. The strings were golden in the stark lights of the stage.

"Who is that?" I asked my boyfriend.

He squinted through the smoke, over the five yards that separated patrons from guitar man.

"I think his name is Anthony. The blues guy." David took a long drag of his cigarette and flicked the ash into his empty glass. The bartender shot him a look.

"He doesn't look like a blues guy," I said.

Blues guy closed his eyes and began to sing. The voice that came out of him surprised me so much that I upset my soda. David muttered to himself as he went to the bar to get a towel that smelt like liquor and stale chips.

I used it to clean the table, watching the blues guy all the while, listening to the sound of a deep southern drawl. David puffed his cigarette and laughed with the blonde to his right. Blues guy met my eyes once and looked away.

There were no lyrics then, only his hands flying over the fretboard in such a way that a collective murmur began to grow. I stared even as I elbowed the tall man to my left. Keith was tapping his foot on the floor while his fingers drummed out a beat on the table. He hadn't had too many drinks. This was work for us.

He nudged me back, grinning.

"What do you think?" I asked.

"He's got it."

"I think so." I picked up his drink. Keith glanced at me while I drank the rum, both of us pretending that the flush in my face was only the liquor. The blues guy in the centre of the stage had my whole attention, and Keith knew it.

"Looks like a guy on the cover of a romance novel. Tall, built, sexy."

I shrugged with what I hoped was nonchalance. I tried to ignore the thrill that ran through me, but to say that I didn't want blues guy from the get-go — well, that would be lying.

The number ended and the man onstage smiled with just the right mixture of arrogance and humble satisfaction. My boyfriend watched with interest as I stood and pulled a card out of my pocket. Blues guy noticed me but pretended he didn't. I met him at the bottom step as he came off the stage.

"Evening."

"Hello." His voice was deep and rough.

"I've been watching you up there."

"I've been watching you, too."

"You like what you see?"

"That your boyfriend with you?"

"Yes. The other guy is the head honcho of one of our little record labels."

His smile faltered a little. Wariness flickered in his eyes.

"And?"

"We're impressed." I flipped the cream-coloured card towards him, holding it between two fingers. When his hand brushed mine, I didn't move away. His fingers were calloused, the hum of the strings almost alive in them.

"And who are you?"

"I'm the woman who can get you in the door."

He held the card in front of his face, squinting to read it in the dim light. Laugh lines showed more clearly.

"Why would you want to get me in the door?"

"It's all about the music," I said, and he snickered, both of us knowing damn good and well that in the music business, the last consideration was always the music itself.

"Do you know who I am?" he asked.

"Not yet, but I will."

He stuffed the card into his pocket.

"Is there somewhere private we can talk?" I asked, knowing the only logical answer.

"Sure," he said with a shrug. "The bus is out back."

"Let's go."

* * * *

The bus had seen better days. It was an old Silver Eagle, painted blue. The dent in the side revealed its former colour in a slash of red paint. There was little doubt he was one of thousands of struggling musicians trying to make it on a measly income. His clothes were comfortable and not expensive, but he wore them as if they were.

A worn guitar safe stood to the side of the small sofa. The guitars inside rested neatly on their racks, carefully housed behind a wall of thick, durable glass. A cursory glance at the headstocks showed expensive names, making it clear where any extra money went.

But what I noticed the most was the space. Mirrors made it look larger. He needn't have bothered. The place looked lonely enough as it was.

"Are you married?" I asked.

"Yes. For seven years now."

There wasn't one picture, one homemade quilt. There wasn't a single sign of a woman's touch anywhere in sight. He wasn't wearing a wedding band.

"I'm going to need something to write on," I said. "I didn't bring anything."

I watched as he moved to the little room in the back and

opened one of the many small drawers on the headboard. He found a small spiral notebook and a pen. "Will this work?"

I nodded and reached to take it, letting my touch linger. He didn't flinch. I let my gaze trail down his arms, studying the muscles there, a habit I could never break. Something about a man's arms always got me where it counted.

"What's your name?"

"Anthony Keenan."

I raised an eyebrow. "Real name or stage name?"

"Real."

"That's a superstar name if I ever heard one."

I uncapped the pen, studying his biceps while I did so.

"You are doing quite a good job of examining me," he said. "Am I up to par?"

I looked him in the eye, taking my time, enjoying the deep brown, the lighter green underneath. Those were eyes the very definition of *smouldering*.

"I know enough about the industry to know what works and what doesn't," I said. "I know it's time for something new to hit. Your sound is promising."

He grinned, that easy smile that already had me unsettled, though I was determined not to show it. "I know I'm up to par for the industry, darlin'. I'm wondering, am I up to par for you?"

I dropped my eyes to the notebook. I wrote his name in flowing cursive on the first page, as if I needed a reminder.

"Definitely," I confessed.

* * * *

"I've heard about you," he said.

We were sitting in the bar long after it had closed. Our discussions on the bus had been less than businesslike, mostly flirtations that meant I didn't get a single lick of work done. We had come back to the bar in the hopes that being seen in public would keep us to the business side of things.

My boyfriend had left with a chilly glance in my direction. He had the blonde on his arm, so apparently all was well with the evening.

"What have you heard?"

He shrugged. "Rumours. The usual."

"The usual?"

"About men you've dated. Musicians you've…enjoyed."

He drew the word out, a slow, easy slide. He watched for my reaction.

"Do you believe everything you hear?"

He smiled. "That's not a very good dodge."

"Well, I could tell you all the rumours are true, and I'm the slut of Music City."

He took a small sip of his bourbon, savouring it, finally losing interest in preserving himself. "If you were, you wouldn't be sitting with the president of the record label."

"There's your answer. Now let's talk about you."

His hand rested on the back of my chair. I wanted him more with each passing minute, but I was trying hard to banish the visions of what he might look like under those clothes. It wasn't that I didn't pursue musicians. In fact, they were my conquest of choice. But I was truly interested in his talent, and that, I *didn't* mess with.

"How long have you been playing?" I shifted in my seat, putting some space between us.

He told me of New Orleans and St. Louis, no surprise. I pictured tiny stages in the corners of packed bars, the crowd more interested in their next shot than in the music. He mentioned little towns and big cities throughout the South, and the images in my head began to blur. They were really playing that often?

My interest was shifting. I was sure that was a good thing.

"How many dates a year?"

"Two hundred. Minimum. Last year, we ran closer to two-fifty."

He had to be kidding. Where had this guy come from,

and how had I missed him?

"All original stuff?"

The scepticism in my voice was clear. All teasing disappeared.

"Eighty percent, easy. All styles. I can play *anything*, as long as I like it."

His eyes flickered over my body.

"Anything, huh?"

"Anything."

"Where are you playing next? I have to see this. A real show, not a showcase."

He smiled that slow, easy smile. "Tomorrow night. Memphis. Two-hour show at Overton Square. The old pavillion? I would love to take you down there on the bus."

I raised an eyebrow. "I guess you do believe everything you hear."

"You could prove me wrong," he said. "But that wouldn't be as much fun, would it?"

* * * *

His body looked even better when he wasn't wearing clothes. I thought about my boyfriend as I stripped the shirt from a new man's shoulders. David was likely screwing that blonde by now. The fact it didn't bother me all that much was more unsettling than the thought of what he was almost certainly doing with her. It didn't matter, because I was going to be enjoying blues guy tonight regardless, but it was nice to do so without guilt towards a faithful boyfriend.

Anthony's sheets smelt clean and fresh. The fact he didn't have condoms told me he didn't do this often. I knelt before him. My tongue slid up his thigh, tasting denim and soap and just a hint of masculine sweat. He trembled. His hand touched my hair, moved away, then touched me again.

"Have you ever done this?" I asked.

"Been unfaithful? Not yet." There was the slightest hint

of a shake in his voice. For a long time, only the click of the cooling generators sounded in the tiny space. I was glad I was still partially clothed.

"Then maybe you shouldn't." I pressed my face to his belly, breathed deeply of his skin. I waited until his hands stopped shaking. Until his breathing calmed. Until we both knew he wouldn't do this, after all.

"Can you just sleep beside me?" he asked.

I looked up at him, surprised. For the first time, he blushed.

Of course I would just sleep beside him.

When his breathing was even and he was perfectly still, I dialled the number. David answered on the first ring, making it clear he was expecting the call. "I'm going to Memphis tomorrow," I said.

There was a moment of silence. The questions seemed to crowd the line, making it hard to breathe. His sigh was matter-of-fact. He wouldn't cause a scene.

"With blues guy, of course."

"I'm sorry," I told him.

"I'm sorry, too."

There was that crowding again. "Are you okay?"

I heard the drag of his cigarette, then a slow, long exhale. "Enjoy yourself."

* * * *

The gateway to the Delta was hot as hell. The air conditioning on the bus worked only half the time, but even then cooling seemed to be something the machine couldn't comprehend.

"The first thing we do is get a new bus," I said to him.

He looked up from his guitar. "All my money goes into overhead."

"That's what a label is for, darling."

I hit the air conditioner with a closed fist. It threw a blast of frigid air, then went back to blowing something far too

11

warm. One little blast wasn't nearly enough to pacify me. I needed something to cool my untouched skin. Lying beside him all night in that little space had done a number on my libido, and my hormones were suddenly all out of whack.

He had held me like a drowning man, making me wonder if he had nightmares like that all the time.

"Damn it to hell!" I shouted, and slammed the air conditioner one last time.

He chuckled. I looked out the window. We were closing in on the city. Behind us was one more bus, followed by one small equipment trailer and two SUVs. He definitely had the setup to carry two hundred dates a year.

"How long have you been doing this?"

"This?"

"Two hundred shows a year?"

He thought for a moment, counting back. In the light of the late morning, he looked young. He was thirty-five, he had told me. "Ten years?"

I nodded and watched him play. The old guitar had no name. It was the body of a Guild, the neck of a Gibson and the headstock of something unidentifiable. He practiced on the old pawnshop relics, he said. He played the good ones onstage.

Calling them *good ones* was an understatement. I had spied one particular Gretsch that cost more than a year's worth of car payments on my Lexus.

"Ten years. How long have you been in Nashville?"

"I can't afford to be in Nashville. It's not a place you can pay the bills, unless you're Vince Gill. Tim McGraw. Or someone like that boyfriend of yours."

I blushed at the thought of David.

"So, how does this work?" he asked suddenly.

"What do you mean?"

"Ever seen *Bull Durham*?"

I blushed with a very different kind of emotion. My silence made him uncomfortable.

"I'm sorry," he murmured.

"You should be."

His eyes met mine. "I trust too easily. It's part of why I haven't made it in Nashville."

"You just didn't know the right people. Now you do."

He looked down at his guitar and started to play again. He would be signed by the end of the month. I promised myself that.

Then I hit the air conditioner again.

* * * *

From the centre of the sold-out crowd, I yelled into my cell phone. "Keith! You have to see this guy. Can you meet us in Jackson tomorrow?"

"Which Jackson?"

"Mississippi."

"Let me listen."

I held the cell phone up. There were at least five thousand people around me, if the ticket counter was to be believed. For a guy who didn't have a label, he was cranking them out and reeling them in. His success on the limited budget left me speechless.

And the band! Holy Christ. The band was made up of men living on nothing but the joy of playing. It was so cliché—I hadn't thought they could really exist.

After the slide solo, I pulled the phone back to my ear. "Well?"

"Tell me when."

"Show starts at eight. Get here early—I want you to see the setup. How in God's name did we miss this guy?"

"Meet me at the airport at five."

I closed the phone and slipped it into my pocket, where it nestled in with a handful of guitar picks. I was no longer seeing dollar signs. I was seeing instead a man with a guitar, playing with his eyes closed to better feel the notes. A man who was pouring his heart and soul into the strings that would then take it to someone else. A man who cared more for playing the music than he did for fattening his bottom line.

It was virtually impossible.

I turned slowly to scan the crowd. It worked. Damned if it didn't work.

The guitars were polished. The equipment was perfect. The band was dead on, lick for lick. He was custom-made for a label, perfection in an eclectic package.

I watched his hand fly over the strings. His wedding band had come out of hiding and flashed on his finger under the stage lights.

"It keeps the groupies away," he had explained when I looked at it with a raised eyebrow.

"Groupies might be good for attendance."

"Groupies are nothing but whores," he snapped.

I stood silently and watched him dress. He turned to me and said he was sorry.

"Why? I'm not a groupie."

"Then what are you?"

"Ever seen *Bull Durham*?"

He kissed me then, his tongue sliding into my mouth with the ease of an old lover. He tasted like lemons. I kissed him back with slow exploration, enjoying every second.

"I want to make love to you," he whispered.

He picked up his guitar and left without a second glance.

* * * *

The Peabody in Memphis had seen more than its share of musicians, so hardly anyone noticed us as we walked through the lobby. He was surprised at the lavishness of the hotel. I decided he had dealt with enough long nights without air conditioning. Just one was enough for me.

"You don't need that other room," he said to me when I took two keys from the front desk. I simply shrugged and put one of the keys in my pocket. I handed the other to him. He didn't know how to thank me. I knew he didn't have to.

In the elevator, he asked, "Do you do this often?"

"Go on the road with strange men?"

"Am I a strange man?"

I snorted with laughter.

"I mean, how often do you give that little push? That foot in the door?"

"Only when I feel like someone hasn't had a fair shake. Which isn't that often. Most people who believe they have it really don't."

"And I do?"

"You have more than anyone else I have ever seen."

He looked at me, waiting for more. I looked right back.

"What?" I challenged. "Need an ego stroke?"

"No."

"Good."

"Seriously, though. Why are you here?"

I thought about it for a moment. "I chase what I believe in. I make no apologies, no excuses and no promises. But I can tell you this—you will have that foot in the door. The rest is up to you."

He reached into my pocket and took my room key.

"You won't need this," he said.

* * * *

The water in the Jacuzzi was too hot. The bubbles were on low, just enough to disturb the shiny surface. His hands under the water were slick and seductive, touching one place, then another. Then all the right places.

"God, yes," I murmured, letting my head fall back. My hair was wet. I clenched the smooth rails on the sides of the tub. His tongue was almost as hot as the water. The first orgasm he gave me was strong enough to make me jerk with surprise, hard enough to make water slosh out onto the tiled floor.

He came up for air, breathing hard.

I had to return the favour. His body was even hotter than

15

the water. I drank of him until I couldn't breathe, then I came up for air. His hands in my hair forced me down again.

So that is how he is, I thought.

We abandoned the Jacuzzi and made our way to the bed. I settled on my back and looked up at him. He lifted my legs high over his shoulders. He paused, taunting me. He held steady until I looked into his eyes.

"I'm going to fuck you every night that you're out here with me," he said. "I'm going to fuck you until we can't take any more of each other, then I'm going to tie you down and fuck you some more. I will make every moment of your investment worthwhile."

He thrust forward, impaling me completely. I cried out with the thrill of it.

"I don't need a return on my investment," I managed.

"You'll get one anyway."

He was thick and long enough to hit bottom. The twinge of pain every time was more than welcome. I raked my nails down his back, sucked on his fingers, yanked his hair and made him move faster. He threw his head back and let me have every ounce of power within him. The thrusts drove me up the bed.

The orgasm was building. I let it come. I let myself rock and buck and thrash under him until the intensity was too much, so much that I begged him to stop.

He didn't.

My scream was muffled against his hand as I came. He thrust a few more times and pulled out. When he straddled me, I closed my eyes.

He groaned deeply and thrust forward when he came, and I had the sudden thought that out in the world of notes and buses and labels and music, he held the guitar but I held the cards. In this world, the one of bodies and sweat and heated flesh, he could take over.

That sounded like a good deal to me.

I licked the salty drops from my lips. It slid down my

throat, my chest.

The leather of his belt circled my wrists. I let him bind me to the old-fashioned headboard.

I thought about the fact I had met him only two days before.

David crossed my mind, and I wondered when I had stopped caring.

"Welcome to the big time," I said.

* * * *

David had been the first. Anthony would be the second.

Anthony Keenan was a magnet of a man, quiet and shy enough to make one think he was a wallflower, but his eyes sparkled with fire that said he was definitely not. And those eyes, Lord have mercy — eyes that could be mesmerising, even from the tenth row. Brown as Mississippi mud, dark as Kentucky coal. There was a drawl as well — of course there had to be — deep and southern to the hilt, the kind of long twang that made women shiver.

The guitar was where he shone, and the slide was good to him. By the age of twenty he was playing every weekend around his hometown. By twenty-five, he was fronting a band with a set of equipment that would make old-timers envious. By thirty, his song catalogue was three hundred strong and swiftly growing.

By thirty-five, he had seen his fill of Music Row and no longer thought the politics were worth it. He had reached that point where a man simply threw back his head, took a long slam of disappointment right in the gut, chased it with Jim Beam, growled *the hell with this* and meant it.

That was where I came in.

You would never find a firm title on my business card. Titles served only to throw up boundaries where there was once wide-open space, and I liked my air fresh and free, thanks. I supposed I would have simply been known as that one person who happened to know everyone else — I was the three degrees of separation.

All this would have been fine and dandy, except for one little thing. I was delightfully weak. I had a weakness for beautiful men and their sexy guitars and their oh-so-cocky attitudes. I loved arrogance but more than that, I loved a man who had been beaten down a time or two, who had found it necessary to pull himself up by his bootstraps, so to speak, and make something of himself on sheer determination.

It was good for a man and absolutely essential for a musician. If he wasn't tested and scarred, then he wasn't worth a damn to the industry.

Once in a while, someone came along who had the talent, someone who had been beaten down just enough. A man who had been battered by those Nashville winds and somehow kept most of himself intact, someone who had just what it took and knew it, but damned if they were going to kiss ass to get the golden ring.

Fortunately, kissing corporate ass and fucking a sweet redhead were two different things, and so—like I'd said, that was where I came in.

I had always been mesmerised by those long-haired men who handled a guitar as if it were a woman, pulling every swell and moan from an instrument curvaceous enough to make any guy hard. I loved everything about it, and I dreamed of life on the road. I found romance in the grime and sweat and heartache, of the blood cried and tears shed over a dream that left you broken and with nothing but a bittersweet story to tell the grandkids. It was life lived in fast forward.

From the time I was no bigger than a guitar myself, I was hooked.

I wanted to be a songwriter.

As soon as I was eighteen and just as free as I was wild, I moved to Nashville with big dreams. I began dating a fellow songwriter, of all things. The first time I had sex, it was on top of a piano, which was about par for the course. I think I was sleeping with his reputation more than I was sleeping with him. He didn't mind, because he got the trophy girlfriend. Not the trophy wife, because I fancied myself far too sophisticated for that kind of mundane atrocity.

After that it was a string of men, all older and none the wiser. Usually they were married, because I had a seriously defiant streak curling inside me like a spiral of misplaced ambition.

I had a bit of success. In Nashville, that meant I wasn't popular enough to have my name in lights, but I was popular enough to hit the gossip columns. I was careful with money, and even more careful with the money of the men who loved to take care of their little mistress.

But that wasn't enough for me. Being a kept woman was nice, but the business was in my blood, and I wasn't entirely fulfilled without it. Eventually I signed on with Axton Records and started working in every capacity imaginable, and quite a few that were very unofficial.

I got lucky from the get-go. I signed a complete unknown. His debut album went double platinum. He thanked me in the liner notes, uttered the only four-letter word more salacious than *fuck*, and the gossip columns went crazy.

The money rolled in. I moved out of my shitty eastside apartment and into that big house in Brentwood.

I lived in the high-class part of town, the one where the beautiful starlets climbed gracefully into the limousines of men who have far too much money for their own good. If you went to the downtown tourist traps, you could buy a map of the stars' homes for an outrageous amount of money. A tour bus drove past my house a dozen times a day. I wasn't one of those stars, but I knew all of them. I was that woman you knew you had seen before, but you couldn't quite place. And that was just fine with me.

Because it wasn't about me. It was about them.

It was about those dark and handsome country boys and those slick overseas transplants who needed to learn the ropes. It was about those diamonds in the rough, those beautiful flawed men who knew their way around a guitar better than they would ever know their way around any woman. It was all about bringing them to your friendly local record store.

The game came down to who you knew. Anyone who said who you knew didn't matter—well, when their number was called, they were going to have a mighty quiet funeral.

I was the one who knew them all, knew all the secrets in the dark, all the nooks and crannies that were hidden away in the attics—and since I was the one who knew them all, I was the one who knew just who would fit in.

I could tell you from the first lick whether or not he had it. And to this day, I had never seen someone who had more of it than Anthony did. True music industry success wasn't in the strings or the voice or the pretty face. It was the attitude. No matter what the hierarchy said, it wasn't the conformist who ended up on the billboard. It was the rebel who had abandoned the cause.

Anthony Keenan was my new poster child.

Chapter Two

I regarded that new poster child as he changed the strings on his guitar. The guitar was an ancient Gibson. The binding was peeling and the veneer was worn away in all the right places. When he bent over the guitar, his dark hair fell to cover his face. He was barefoot and shirtless. His jeans fit him just right.

Old clothes, old guitars—everything old-fashioned seemed custom-made to fit him. That fact tugged at some sense of benevolence inside me until I reminded myself that it would make for a unique style, something that would serve him well in the wide world of music.

"What are you staring at, looking so dreamy?" he asked.

He had caught me looking at his arms again. I crossed my legs and my arms, feeling a slight pinch of annoyance. Dreamy, indeed.

"We're going to be meeting Keith in Jackson. I'm going to pick him up at the airport."

Anthony showed no reaction at all.

"I think he's going to offer you a deal, Anthony."

His eyes were unreadable as he sighed. "I've heard that more than once. They offer a deal, and then they want to change me. And I won't change, because what I do brings in crowds like that one last night. But they only want what is best for the label."

"Most of them think that way, I'll grant you that."

"Let me guess. He doesn't."

"Right."

He stood up and settled the guitar on the floor. I counted the four strings he had already replaced. "How do you

21

know that?"

He was looking for a fight, and we both knew it. I wouldn't rise to the bait. I would not allow myself to be a verbal punching bag.

"Maybe I don't want a deal. Maybe I've had enough."

This was the first place I had expected him to go. One cannot simply stop bucking the system on a whim.

"Then why are you still around?" I asked.

He stalked to the end of the bus, which wasn't a very long stalk. He surveyed his equipment, the bed, the ancient air conditioner. The mirrors on the walls needed to be cleaned. I was beginning to fear he would pace forever when he finally stopped.

"I'm still around because I have no other place to go."

He ran his hands through his hair, brushing it back from his forehead. It fell forward in a cascade of deep brown and the occasional silver strand. He wasn't a kid anymore, and he had been doing this for far too long.

I looked around the old bus. The guitars were expensive, yet many of them had seen better days. The air conditioner still didn't work despite the beatings I gave it on a regular basis. The only reason he didn't share a bus with the band was because this one was too full. Walking through the place where the six beds should have been stacked three to a side, there were instead amplifiers and cases stacked against a hatch that opened from the side of the bus. The clothes in his closet were old and worn. I began to wonder if his bohemian lifestyle was out of necessity, not a quirky sense of personal style.

"You really did put everything you had into this, didn't you?"

Anthony began to stalk again, refusing to answer.

I knew far too many good men who had burned out on this very dream, this very interstate. I knew what it could do inside a person, fostering a dream at every turn then dashing it with life in general. Hope was cruel and exhilarating enough to make you forget pain.

"My whole life is in this bus," he murmured.

I waited but nothing more came, and this did surprise me. He wasn't one to whine and bitch. Any regrets he held would be driven deep by the next chord, the next note, the next song. Leaving Nashville behind with nothing to show for it would slowly kill him inside. I wondered how many others there were like him.

It only renewed my determination to see him sign on that dotted line.

* * * *

If Memphis had been the gateway to hell, then Jackson, Mississippi was the seventh circle. The rental car was a convertible, thank Satan for small favours. I drove with the top down and the air conditioning on full blast.

The streets of Jackson were old and classy, rimmed with cobblestone walkways and the loveliest old elm trees I had ever seen. Only the slightest hint of ivy and Spanish moss was allowed to grow wild, but it was a beautiful sight. The humidity weighed down like a vice, but at least all the sweating felt like it was cleansing my body, so maybe it was worth it.

I wished my conscience could be cleansed as easily.

Anthony had given me his story the night before, as we lay awake in the little bed on the bus. He had asked that we not take another hotel room, since he didn't feel right about taking money he had not earned. This time, I did not protest. I simply undressed and climbed into the bed and into his arms. I listened to him talk with his warm breath against my forehead and my hand trailing idly over his chest.

Anthony came from a life of affluence and wealth, which was exactly why he was so hell-bent on making it on his own. From the day he picked up a guitar, his parents were against it, calling it a "frivolous mistake" that would eventually cost him his birthright as the heir to his father's medical practice. Anthony took the money that had been set aside for his expected tenure at Yale and spent it on a few secondhand vans and more than a few guitars. He hit the road with his father's angry words ringing in his ears.

"Your brothers went to Yale! Your sister went to Brown! Damned if I'm going to raise a boy to be some drifting harp-playing *vagrant*!"

He was never invited to come back home.

When he changed the subject and asked about my family, I found myself telling him what I rarely shared with anyone—that my parents had been the most supportive, wonderful people I had ever known. My mother had passed away after a long battle with breast cancer, and my father had followed soon after—dead of a heart attack at only fifty-five. I was twenty years old, and within six months I was an orphan. It had given me ample reason to throw myself into my work and try to ignore the pain.

It hadn't worked.

"You were lucky," Anthony said. "You didn't have them for very long, but you had the best of them. I envy that."

Then it was my turn to change the subject.

Anthony's wife was something he didn't talk about very often, and that was just fine. I didn't expect him to, nor did I want to know. She worked a steady job, keeping the bills paid while the overhead ate them alive. She supported him in every way she knew how. He told me this with unmistakable pride, and not without a little guilt.

I disappeared under the covers and made the guilt disappear with a few moans. We were getting very good at changing the subject.

The next morning I left him on the bus. I was headed to the airport and the roadies were setting up a show that would draw in around two thousand people. There was a producer and a record label president somewhere in the skies above me, their big black Lear circling in for a landing. That flight would pay off in the long run. They knew I didn't cry wolf.

I met them at the landing strip. The Lear taxied to a stop,

the black paint gleaming like a newly polished midnight sky. I looked at the gold letters on the fuselage as the engines died to a low whine, and wondered idly how much the plane had cost, and how many guitars it would buy. Every record the company produced, and every spin the gods of radio gave it, was a penny towards this plane before me. It was the way it worked, fair or not.

"Your boy knows we're coming?" Keith asked as way of greeting.

"He'll believe it when he sees it."

"He doesn't trust me."

"Does anybody?"

Keith smiled and bent to kiss me on the cheek.

One of the first powerhouses of business I had ever met in Nashville, Keith Axton had always been straightforward and honest. When his wife had left him for a man half his age, he had grieved in a way that made him entirely human and vulnerable. After a long stint in rehab and a brief forced vacation, Keith had rejoined the land of the living, though not without scars. He ditched his high-profile job at a vastly popular major label and started his own corner of the industry. That's where I found him, in a tiny little office on Music Row, determined to make it all about the music again. In Keith I found a kindred spirit.

Romance had never entered into our relationship. There was too little time for creating the stars we both loved to see catapult to the top. We always understood each other.

"Big bad label gonna want to change his religion, huh?" Keith drawled with that Alabama twang that somehow always made me smile.

"Don't you?"

The second man who stepped off the plane made me tingle in places I didn't want to think about. His blue eyes met mine without a flinch. I tried hard not to think about the way his body had felt when it slid inside mine.

"Jason," I said coolly.

"Janey, darling. Good to see you."

25

His eyes were as brilliant blue as that handsome silk shirt, expertly cut by some ridiculously expensive designer. His suit jacket was tossed over his shoulder in such a way that said he didn't care that it was worth as much as a small car. His Rolex was far too flashy and his shoes were too obviously Italian leathers. But his demeanour spoke of the man he truly was, a hard-working specialist who could focus completely on what had to be done and how to do it. I suddenly remembered why I had liked him in the first place.

Then he smiled that sly smile that said he knew what I was thinking, and I remembered even more clearly why I despised him.

Jason let his eyes linger on my hips, and even longer on my chest. "It's always good to see you," he said, talking to my breasts instead of my face.

"Your grey is showing," I said sweetly, and that was enough to snap his eyes back to mine, where they belonged.

Jason stepped back from the distaste that was so thick a blind man could see it. He reached up to touch the perfect black hair, slicked back with some unknown substance that still left it feeling smooth as silk. It wasn't actually black. I had spied a bottle of hair dye in his house during one of my short visits. He had never admitted his age, but I knew of the skills of his plastic surgeon, so Jason must have been ten years older than he looked.

Keith stepped in to keep the peace.

"Okay, kids, get in the car," he ordered.

I leaned close to Jason and took a deep whiff of his cologne. "You still smell good."

"Thanks."

"You always wear that cologne when you're not getting any. Tough times?"

"Fuck you," Jason shot back.

"Whatever."

Keith threw up his hands. "God, what's wrong with you?"

I slid into the driver's seat.

"We're here to work, right?" Keith reminded me. "Not pick fights like high school kids."

I started the car. The air conditioning hit me full in the face. "I don't want him messing with Anthony. He will kill the whole deal with all those fancy electronic mixes of his."

Jason settled himself in the back seat and made a point of ignoring me. Keith, on the other hand, looked me dead in the eye. "Last I checked, I was the president of the label."

I shifted the car into gear and squealed out of the parking lot. I adjusted the mirror so I could watch Jason, who was already looking pained. One swatch of hair came out of the carefully styled perfection and grazed his face. Keith looked down at the speedometer with barely concealed concern.

"Last I checked, Anthony wasn't with any label yet," I reminded them.

"No, but he's with you, which might as well be the same thing," Keith said, still looking at the speedometer. I didn't slow down.

"Why are we here anyway?" Jason sighed.

"Because he's a diamond in the rough," I said. "But that's exactly what he needs to be. He doesn't need the studio polish."

He knew better than to argue. When it came to raw talent, he knew I was to be trusted. "Tell us about him," he said instead, newly determined to be civil and adult.

"He's been playing the Southeast and some of the Southwest for the last fifteen years. He's a huge ticket in Louisiana and Texas. He's got that blend of Delta and Texas blues, with a little honky-tonk thrown in."

Jason raised an eyebrow, but I cut him to the chase.

"The usual, I know, but there's something there I haven't heard in a long time. Besides that, the man knows how to write a song that is his and his alone. His covers were okay, but his originals are the showstoppers. He's smart, not green in the least."

"That's always good," Jason offered.

"He's not going to be suckered. You throw out that polish

and he's gone."

"Is that your call or his?"

I was happy to answer that. "He is entirely his own man. Trust me."

Keith and Jason both looked at me in silence for the space of two miles. Keith was the first to speak. "Well. Looks like you know what you're doing."

And with that, he sat back and turned up the radio. The song was quite familiar, sung by one of the label's most popular artists. Keith rested his arm on the back of my seat and gave my hair a playful tug.

"You've been right before," he teased.

We talked about everything but Anthony on the scenic drive through Mississippi. Magnolias nodded their wide heads over the car as we passed. During a silence in which we admired the beauty, it occurred to me I was driving a car with two passengers, one a multimillion-dollar producer and engineer, the other the president of an independent, upstart label that had stunned the music industry with platinum artists straight out of the gate.

The men in that car could make or break a career with a single nod or shake of the head. Now we were going to see whether they would make or break Anthony.

We pulled up beside the old bus. I parked the shiny new convertible while we looked over the Silver Eagle in silence, all of us seeing something different. Jason saw a bus that he would never be caught dead riding in. I didn't have to look back to imagine the slight sneer of disdain on his chiselled face. Keith saw dollar signs leaving the label, knowing that old clunker would have to be replaced, also knowing that you had to give a little to get something back. I saw a machine that had faithfully crossed the steaming asphalt of the South to carry a man and his guitar to one show after another.

Keith was the first to speak. "Soundcheck?"

I smiled as we climbed out of the car. "You're going to be impressed."

The venue was cavernous for the seating capacity. The ceiling was high, almost three stories, and the seats were in the horseshoe array that was hell on a sound system. It took a band with a full-bodied voice and even fuller guitar licks to fill up that kind of space. I glanced over the Marshall half stacks on either side of the stage and the Peavey equaliser in the centre of the floor. Keith looked it all over with a low hum of approval.

"He's got a sound tech?" Jason asked.

"Yeah. He doubles as a guitar tech."

Keith slipped his hands into his pockets and walked closer to the roadies. He looked every bit the average guy, not the chairman of the board. He stepped over the lines on the floor. The black wires snaked in all directions, ominously complicated to the untrained eye. Within an hour those wires would hardly be visible, and the instruments would be tuned to perfection.

Mike, the guitar tech, caught my eye as he played with the strings of a Gibson 135. It was a beautiful guitar, a lazy grey colour that made it seem almost black in one light, and almost white in another. I watched the stage lights play over the sheen as he moved. Mike had sure and steady hands, and a kind of reverence that said he would be more than happy to be surrounded by guitars for the rest of his life. He wouldn't even need to be paid, which was why he was so good at what he did.

I pulled a thick bandana out of my pocket, wrapped it around my long hair, and bent down to power up one of the amplifiers. I picked up a guitar and plugged in. She was a lovely Taylor 310, tested and found true, as evidenced by the wealth of missing veneer in all the right places. I played the strings, strumming them one at a time, then in chords. Mike glanced up at me and grinned when I hit a squeal of feedback.

Jason watched me from the side of the stage. I pretended to ignore him. Most of what I knew about instruments I had learned from him, in the privacy of his home studio.

The research had taken on a decidedly more personal slant, and in the end we wound up making love on top of the mix boards. It had been a bitch to reprogramme the thing, but the long hour had been worth it.

As if conjured by my amorous thoughts, Anthony appeared at the side of the stage. He lifted a bottle of iced water in welcome, and I smiled back.

Jason's take on the situation was immediate. I could almost hear the hair on the back of his neck beginning to rise. His flashing blue eyes told a tale he couldn't hide.

"Well, well," I murmured. "Look at that."

I put down the Taylor and picked up a Fender. Anthony strolled over to me and watched as I plugged in and began to play.

"You want some company?"

"If you think you can hack it."

"You have no idea," he said with an arrogant wink.

"Place bets?"

"Sure. Winner gets to be on bottom."

I chuckled. He brushed his hair back, and his wedding band gleamed in the stage lights. I kept my eyes on it while he picked up the Gretsch, a fine 1964 Firebird. At least five grand had been sunk into that guitar, and I was sure the sound would prove it.

Anthony played a few chords and I matched him, both of us getting up to speed. I forgot about Jason's stare and Keith's prowling. I forgot about labels and Lear jets and old tour buses. Soon there was nothing but me and Anthony, standing there holding a few amazing guitars, fooling around with the music when we both should have been working to set up the stage.

Anthony suddenly cut loose with a series of riffs and squeals that made me laugh out loud. When he was finished, a sheen of sweat covered his forehead.

"I guess I lost," I said dryly.

"Later, you'll be glad you lost," Anthony promised in a whisper. I looked up. Keith was watching us with the ghost of a smile on his face. Jason was nowhere to be seen.

"Congratulations, my dear Anthony. You just auditioned for the label president."

Anthony's face turned white, but he recovered quickly. He unplugged the Firebird and set her reverently on her stand. That was my cue to step in and make the introductions. Anthony did not smile as he shook Keith's hand.

I moved away and let them discuss whatever it might be they had to discuss. I knew I would hear it all later, two versions of the same discussion, and I would pay attention to both. I would listen for discrepancies. I trusted Keith, but I didn't trust Anthony. It was nothing against him, for he seemed to be everything he claimed he was, and I had made a living out of seeing through tough-guy demeanours. Not trusting him was as natural to me as breathing. In the cutthroat music business, the only man I trusted was Keith. And even then, I sometimes questioned my sanity in doing so.

I sat on the edge of the stage and watched them. Wires coiled around my hand, one after the other, but I hardly noticed the little stacks I was making as I kept them nice and neat. I was too busy studying the differences in the two men. Keith and Anthony were about the same age, though Keith made over a million dollars a year, and Anthony was lucky to break even. Keith dressed in fine slacks and dress shirts that cost more than most men made working forty hours a week. Anthony's attire of choice was a pair of ripped jeans, a T-shirt and perhaps a button-down shirt for show time. Keith was clean-shaven, his hair professionally trimmed at salons that booked three months in advance. Anthony showed signs of a five o'clock shadow, wore his hair simply and probably cut it himself.

The contrasts were startling, especially considering the real talent was in Anthony. Keith did a good job of manning Axton Records, but that machine ran on the grease provided by those who really deserved the cash, those at the bottom of the food chain of profits, the artists themselves.

31

Anthony was right – he couldn't afford to be in Nashville. What guitar-slinger could?

I watched Anthony as he watched Keith, saw the wary flicker in his eyes and the determined set of his jaw. It was good to see him think on his feet, and he did it well. Keith was smiling, which was always a good sign. When Anthony bent to pick up a guitar and Keith picked up one as well, it was my turn to be surprised.

Keith strapped on and fiddled with the volume knob. Anthony kicked a pedal across the stage, and Keith caught it under his foot with the precision of a seasoned player. The amplifiers crackled to life. Then they were both playing, the sound blaring loud enough to bring Jason in from the back of the stage. His look of shock was priceless.

"Keith can play?"

For once I didn't have a smart comment in response. When the twang of the guitars finally ended, Jason sighed.

"I guess that means he just signed your fellow," Jason said.

"Apparently."

"Did you know Keith could play?"

"He used to front a band."

"No kidding?"

"He gave it up a long time ago."

"I wonder why," Jason mused.

We watched as the men settled the guitars back on their stands, talking quietly. A crowd was beginning to gather outside. Jason and I watched Keith as he saluted Anthony, then leapt from the stage with the vigour of a man half his age. One thumbs-up in my direction, and he was off to talk to the road manager.

A minute later, Anthony was standing before me. The smile was for me, but the curiosity in his eyes was for Jason. I made the introductions.

"So you're the new guy," Jason said without preamble.

Anthony was immediately at ease, knowing he had the upper hand. "I suppose that makes you the old guy."

"Something like that."

"Well, it's good to know what I'm up against."

"Who said you were up against anything? There is always a new guy."

I gave Jason a dismissive glare as he walked away. I would make no apologies for my behaviour, and he knew it. Anthony watched me closely, gauging my reaction against a metre only he understood.

"Welcome aboard Axton Records, Anthony."

He ran his hand along my back. I shivered despite the heat. He took my hand and slowly pulled me behind the tall amplifiers.

"Welcome me properly," Anthony demanded, and in seconds I was on my knees. I didn't care who saw. Propriety had disappeared, and I was never one for shame. When Anthony came in my mouth, his low groan was drowned out by the thumping bass guitar.

As I swallowed, I opened my eyes to see Jason at the edge of the stage.

Watching.

* * * *

The concert that night was nothing compared to the sex.

Anthony's hands were everywhere. He played me like a fine guitar, finding all the chords to strike deep within my most forbidden places. On my hands and knees, I braced myself on the rumpled bed. He slipped deep and I hissed in a breath of satisfaction.

"Is this what you want?" he moaned.

"For now."

The motion was steady and unbroken. We were both dead tired, but that didn't seem to matter. Nothing seemed to matter, not even when his cell phone rang from somewhere on the nightstand. My fingers searched the polished top until I found it. Feeling entirely inappropriate and loving every second of it, I flipped the phone open and handed it to him.

"Yes...yes, I'm here in the hotel room..."

It was his wife.

I bit my lip and thrust back hard. I was determined that he would not forget whom he was fucking, who had got him here, who had led the way to that recording contract he would sign in a few days. I swivelled my hips, reminding him who was really fucking whom. My lack of shame would bother me later, but right now I was too far gone with illicit pleasure to care.

"I miss you too, honey..."

He dipped one finger into the cleft of my ass. I pushed my hips up, inviting.

"No...no, I'm not sure..."

He thrust harder, and I reached under us to touch his balls. He struggled to control his breathing. He pinched my hip viciously, as if to warn me against acts that were far too indecent to carry on during a phone conversation. I squeezed with my inner muscles hard enough to make him stifle a moan.

It was a battle of wills, and I wasn't the one holding the cell phone.

I picked up the pace, merciless.

"The show went well... I'm going to be in Alabama tomorrow..."

I looked at him over my shoulder. "Sodomy is illegal in Alabama," I mouthed.

Anthony slipped out of me. He pressed hard against the tighter hole, the one that he hadn't sampled yet. I pushed back and felt the delightful sting as my body began to open under his. I swivelled my hips, trying to make it easier.

"The show was great. Lots of fans...the place was packed..."

He held perfectly still. I thrust back slowly. I would pay for my little ingenuity in the morning, but I didn't give a damn. I wanted to be as dirty and naughty as I could be while his wife listened to what she didn't know was happening. If I had stopped to think about it, I might have been appalled by my actions.

Lucky for me, I was too busy fucking to think.

I thrust back harder, and Anthony's cock slowly impaled me. I opened under the pressure with a burn and a moan. Anthony quickly covered my mouth.

"I'll call you in the morning, honey…"

We suddenly found the right angle, the perfect fit. He slid all the way home, his balls pressing hard against me, every inch of my body throbbing with heat.

"I love you, too," Anthony said to the Mrs Keenan as he began to move back and forth in earnest. He said goodbye, hung up the phone and tossed it to the floor. He grabbed a handful of my hair and thrust hard. Pain and pleasure shot through every pore of my body.

"Who's doing the fucking now?" he growled in my ear.

I looked over at the mirror on the wall. I watched everything — our bodies, his thrusts, and my own face, flushed and wild with passion. I watched as he pushed my shoulders down on the bed, the better for my fingers to reach beneath me.

"Touch yourself. Make yourself come when I do," Anthony demanded. I found my clit and began to play myself with the rhythm of his thrusts. The orgasm built from somewhere so deep it was almost frightening. I watched in the mirror until the pleasure of it made my eyes heavy, and I cried out into the comforter as I came.

Anthony followed right behind me, emptying himself with a harsh groan. For long moments there was no sound in the room, save our unsteady breathing.

"Oh, God," I whimpered when I could finally catch my breath.

He slid out of me. I collapsed onto the bed, exhausted.

"Is sodomy really illegal in Alabama?"

I laughed weakly. "Sodomy is illegal in lots of places. Especially in the South."

"What's the penalty if you get caught?"

"Castration, maybe."

I slowly climbed off the bed. Anthony came with me, one hand on my belly to make sure I didn't fall. My shaky legs came through admirably, and I wobbled towards the bathroom. Anthony watched me as I stepped into the shower.

"Is adultery illegal or just immoral?" he asked.

"It depends on how good your divorce attorney is."

The water cascaded over me. Anthony climbed in uninvited and reached for the tiny bar of soap. He lathered a washcloth and ran it over my neck, down my chest. My nipples hardened under his touch. He watched the soap bubbles catch on them before sliding down with the water. I closed my eyes and let the water run down the sides of my face.

"If you leave her now," I said, "she probably won't be able to take a cut of your profits."

Anthony became motionless. The lather made a plopping sound on the floor of the tub as he squeezed the washcloth.

"I can't leave her," he said.

"I'm not asking you to," I countered. "I'm just telling you the way it works. If you wait until you've signed the contract, she can take you for the next twenty years, easily. She might be able to anyway. But at least you would have the foundation for a fight."

Anthony began washing my belly with slow, circular motions. He was already hard again, his erection pressing insistently against my hip.

"And what if she leaves me?"

"She won't."

Anthony gently turned me around. The washcloth slid down my back.

"How do you know she won't leave me?"

"Because she's too set in her ways. She's so used to you being on the road, your absence doesn't faze her much. She will never admit that, but when you roll out again after a week at home? She's probably glad."

"How do you know that?"

I smiled and dipped my head under the water, remembering. "I used to be her."

Anthony gripped my hips. His hand slid up my spine. My hair fell over my face as he bent me down, until I was holding onto the side of the tub.

The first thrust made it clear what he wanted. With a twinge of annoyance, I tried to move away, but he hauled me back to where he wanted me. The water ran down my face and I gasped for air. The drops hit his chest and ran down between our bodies, washing away the lubrication. It was strangely like a dry fuck, considering the water coming full blast from the showerhead.

"That hurts, Anthony," I protested.

"Does it, now?"

He thrust again. He wasn't even hard enough to do a good job of the screw — this wasn't about sex. It was about power.

The son of a bitch had no idea what kind of mistake he had just made.

I held onto the side of the tub as he made short work of the act, coming too soon, without giving me a chance to catch up. The spreading warmth burned like fire. My pussy contracted hard around him, an involuntary response of woman accepting man. I began to shake with the magnitude of crossing an invisible line.

"Don't you ever talk about my wife again," he hissed into my ear.

The shock turned to anger, then to fury. The flare of rage started somewhere deep in my belly, spreading out like wildfire, just as fast and just as dangerous.

I shoved back hard, knocking Anthony into the wall of the shower as he lost his balance. I spun around before he had a chance to react. The sharp sound of my open palm hitting the side of his face was quite satisfying. He stared at me in shock as the handprint began to flare on his suddenly pale skin.

I stood toe to toe with him in the shower, the water

cascading down my back, the warmth of his semen running down my leg. I had the shakes, but now they took the form of rage.

"Threaten me one more time," I hissed, "and you can say goodbye to your career."

Anthony continued to stare at me. I almost felt sorry for him. He was playing in the big leagues now, and he had no idea that my slugger was bigger than his. He would learn quite a few things before I was through with him.

"I'm sorry," he said.

I barely heard him. I slammed the shower door behind me and headed for the bedroom. I swatted at my body with the towel, pulled my wet hair up into a haphazard ponytail and pulled on a T-shirt. I threw the rest of my clothes into the suitcase and slammed it closed. He could sleep alone tonight and wonder exactly what he had got himself into.

He was dripping water on the carpet as I walked past him. His expression was one of carefully banked terror.

I slammed the door in his face.

"Son of a bitch!" I railed as I punched the button at the elevator doors. I didn't bother to look back and see if he was coming to follow me or not. Surely he was smarter than that, and God help him if he wasn't. Why did I have to find the ones who became worse than unruly children when they caught wind of ink on a dotted line?

I didn't know what he was expecting, but in the world of the music industry, there were a few people who called the shots for you. Anthony would have to play by the rules.

My rules.

Chapter Three

Anthony stared at me through the glass. His long hair was caught up behind the headphones. They completely covered his ears and made him look like a housefly. The microphone in front of him obscured most of his face but nothing could dull those eyes. Uncertain yet determined, he latched onto me with a look that said we had a lot to discuss. I liked to think there was nothing to talk about.

This was business, after all.

I slid the bass level up just a hair. Jason glanced over at the digital gauge above it. "Perfect," he praised in a voice that was devoid of all emotion. I watched him move over the mix board like the professional he was. That was the true beauty of Jason—when it came to the music, there was nothing but the music. Period.

If only certain other people could be as mature.

I hadn't spoken a personal word to Anthony since I had slammed the door in his face three weeks before. I slept in my own hotel room and didn't darken the door of his. Sex was power, and damned if I would let pleasure of the flesh tip my scales. I had worked too hard to allow an upstart to ever believe he could have any measure of control just because he gave me an orgasm. It was easy to give lip service to the idea that it was all about the music, but everybody knew damn good and well it was about the politics, and sometimes sex was the lubricant that kept the machine rolling.

Anthony was not going to throw a wrench in the works.

"I think that's good for now," Jason said with a decisive air, and I pressed the intercom.

"Looks good, Anthony. Let's call it a day," I said.

He never took his eyes off me as he removed the headphones and draped them over the music stand. I glanced at the clock. We had plenty of time to get downtown to the Axton offices. Keith would be waiting for Anthony along with a bevy of legal eagles, all the staff an artist needed to take care of the royalties rolling in from every direction imaginable.

The cool, hushed rooms of the recording studio opened out into a world of humid air, squealing traffic, bustling shoppers and map-toting tourists. Many of those tourists looked hard at Anthony, trying to place the handsome man who had just stepped from the recording studio into the July sunlight. I cut to the inside of the sidewalk and pulled him with me.

"Let's walk. Leave the cars in the parking garage. We need to talk about some things."

"That doesn't sound good."

"It's not good or bad. It just is. Axton is going to want to take over your publishing. Who holds the songs now?"

Anthony told me, and I filed the names away in my memory.

"Okay. Some things you need to know. All right?"

"Shoot."

"Okay. We're going to sign you for a five-album contract. Keith is going to make damn sure it's airtight, because he's certain your first album will break black."

"Break black?"

"Yes. Five-hundred-thousand copies, after advances and such, will break even. Break black."

"Okay."

"Some of those advances are going to be big enough to get the ball rolling on a house and get your wife up here to Nashville. You are going to need to move pretty soon. Studio time is going to be leisurely, because that's the way Axton works with the first record. But once you hit the road, we're talking two hundred dates, easy. If you want to have a family at all, you have to get them up here."

I was a good five yards in front of him before I realised Anthony had stopped walking.

"I resent you mentioning my family," he said. "I thought I made my views on that clear several weeks ago."

I blinked in surprise. Jesus, were we really back to that? "You have a family, do you not?"

"You know damn good and well I have a wife."

"Then she is the reality of your life," I snapped. "What, are you expecting me to be a jealous suitor? If that's what you are thinking, Anthony, you are far, far off base."

"So I'm just a fuck, is that it?"

"You're a talent."

"I'm sleeping my way to the top."

Inexplicably, my blood ran cold. I felt the colour drain from my face before it was replaced with the flush of anger. Who the hell did he think he was? Did he think he was special?

"Your talent is enough to get you there," I said. "Which is a good thing, because your fucking leaves something to be desired."

Anthony didn't say a word in response to my gut-punch. Instead, he took my arm and led me roughly down the street, back the way we had come. Passersby stopped to look. I kept my mouth shut in front of all the gawkers, lest we make the weekly tabloids. I wrenched my arm away from him when we reached the studio. He opened the door hard enough to rattle the glass against the brick facing.

"Get in there. Now."

I hesitated, buying time. It was a delicate choice. I could argue with him and cause a public scene. I could watch Keith's golden boy slide away on the slickness of my own anger. Or I could play the role Anthony needed right then.

How strong was my pride? How strong was his?

We were going to find out.

I walked through the door without a word.

Anthony tried to yank the glass door closed, to make a

41

point. The door hissed a slow note of infuriating comfort as it bumped gently against the frame. I spun around and stared at him, waiting. Now that Anthony had me inside the building, he didn't quite know what to do or say.

"Typical," I said. "All talk and no action."

I knew the building very well. The small office on the right was unoccupied and always unlocked, now used for storage, and no one would ever think to go in there. It was perfect for those moments when a come-to-Jesus meeting was in order.

"In here," I said.

Anthony looked at me with fire in his eyes. Walking into the office behind me, he slammed the wooden door behind him with enough force to shake the platinum plaques on the walls. I turned and he caught my hair in mid-swing, making me cry out in surprise. When he tried to force me to my knees, I slammed an elbow into his gut. Air rushed from his lungs on a sharp grunt of pain. I stepped back and watched as he struggled to regain his breath.

"I won't suck anybody's dick unless it's on my terms," I hissed.

"I wasn't…"

"Yes, you were."

We watched each other in the silent room, standing at a crossroads.

I unbuttoned my jeans. Unzipped them. Slid them down and kicked them away with my canvas tennis shoes. I was wearing nothing underneath. Desire began to creep into the fire of Anthony's anger.

"What are you trying to do?" he asked, his voice a razor edge of quiet.

"I'm giving you what you want, Anthony. I always give you what you want. You just have to trust me." I unbuttoned his shirt. Unbuttoned his jeans. Pushed him down into the chair, hard enough that it rocked back on two legs before settling again.

"I can't be coerced into that contract," he said.

"No, you can't," I agreed.

"Then what is this?"

What *was* this? Maybe it was my way of making up for lying to him about his sexual prowess. Maybe it was my way of punishing myself for wanting what I knew damn good and well I shouldn't. If I was completely honest with myself, maybe it was my way of erasing the pain I had seen in his eyes when he spoke of his wife, or coming to terms with what he hadn't told me, news that the grapevine had already delivered — that the day after I slapped his face in the shower, he had filed for divorce.

I straddled him and slid down. He was hard and ready. "What do you want this to be, Anthony?"

I started to move. He thrust up at me, wanting more even though I was giving him all he could take. Nothing was ever good enough for him. He was just like all the others, wanting the world on a silver platter then acting all indignant when you handed it to them. He was minutes away from signing a contract that would bring him the fame and fortune he had worked so hard for, yet he was still finding reasons to bitch.

"I don't know what I want this to be," he said softly.

I stopped moving, overcome by the surprise turn of emotion. Anthony wrapped his arms around me and carefully pushed us both from the chair. The desk was cool under my back. He slipped my legs over his shoulders and slammed me hard. I bit my lip and moaned despite myself. A fingernail snapped when I clenched the edge of the desk, sending a shaft of pain up my arm, bringing me back to reason.

"Don't get attached," I warned. "You're the talent."

Anthony gave me the slightest smile as he called my bluff. "Keep telling yourself that."

He buried his head in my shoulder and went at me hard, relentless. I let him. I knew that in a few minutes he would sign a contract and his world would change overnight. He would never forget about me but he would move past me.

I would become a footnote in interviews, the infamous "friend" who was never named. It was where I was most comfortable, the anonymous thank-you on the CD liner and the nameless face at the awards shows.

It was romantic to him. It was all business to me.

Anthony came without me. I wasn't even close, and this time it was my own fault, not his. He growled with pleasure, and I closed my eyes while he pulled out and zipped up.

"Get dressed," he instructed, then walked out the door.

"Son of a bitch," I growled, but he didn't hear me.

I stood up and his essence slid down the inside of my thigh. Platinum and gold mocked me from the walls. Who the fuck did he think he was? I grabbed tissues off the desk and stared at my reflection in a platinum plaque as I cleaned up what he had left.

My hands shook when I tried to button my jeans. The breath left me in a rush. I fell to my knees there beside the big desk, the desk where he had just fucked some sense into me, whether I liked it or not.

Keep telling yourself that, he had said.

"No," I whispered to the platinum plaque on the wall.

Long moments passed while I sat there on the floor. I sat there until my knees hurt. I suddenly remembered the way it felt when I first came to Nashville. Young and scared, I thought everyone who showed kindness towards me was my friend, and the only enemies were the others with their guitars and dreams in their eyes, too much like mine. It didn't take long before I realised just the opposite was true. The dreamers were the ones who gave you a break. The rest had already seen thousands of starry-eyed girls fresh from innocence, and knew exactly how to play the game.

I looked up at the desk again. It was the same desk where I had done unspeakable things for a label executive who promised me the world, not to mention a recording contract. He had sat in his big leather chair and looked down at me while the floor made my knees hurt. The next day I came back with a cassette tape full of songs and a heart full of hope, but he acted as though he didn't know who I was.

"But we did things last night," I had said, sounding pathetic to my own ears.

"You were one of the three?" he had asked, and even years later I wasn't sure he really remembered, after all. In the end it didn't matter. I had been initiated into a world where nothing was ever what it seemed.

Anthony had dodged that. Anthony had a stubborn streak born in him, one I had been forced to cultivate within myself during those first long, depressing months in town. It had become a matter of survival for me, and I would do good to remember it now, now while I knelt on the floor where I had first sank to my knees, in the office where I had first given myself ten years ago and had just done it again, only on a much grander scale.

This time, I knew exactly what I was doing.

I stared at the platinum as I stood. My jeans snapped under fingers that were steady as rain. I ran my fingertips over the names on the plaques, names any country music fan would recognise. I stopped by the door and looked up at the plaque that heralded my ex-boyfriend.

David McGregor. Double platinum. The photograph on the CD cover was one I recognised, for I had been standing beside the photographer when it was taken. It was during a time when we both conveniently forgot I was the foot in the door. That smile was for nobody but me. We thought we were in love.

"I will not go there again," I told the photograph, but David didn't answer.

* * * *

Anthony was waiting for me in the lobby of Axton Records. I walked up to him with eyes that were clear, focused, giving no indication of the cataclysm that had passed through me ten minutes earlier. He looked at me with more concern than anger, and that was the one thing I

45

couldn't take. If he showed too much concern, I just might collapse into the comfort of it.

"Have you seen Keith?" I asked curtly.

"Not yet. I was waiting on you."

"Good. Listen, we didn't finish talking about what to expect in there."

"I'm listening."

"There are going to be lots of people. Attorneys. A publicist. A few managers, including yours. What's his name again?"

"Richard."

"Richard. He's likely already working numbers up there with them. Everything has already been taken care of— that's what you pay these people for, so let them do their jobs. Don't interject your ideas on the contract. You already discussed it all with the powers that be, correct?"

"A million times."

"Then you have nothing to do but smile for the photographer while you sign on the dotted line."

"Where will you be?"

I took a breath and looked around the lobby. "Do you want me there?"

"Yes. I want you there."

"It's basically a photo op."

"Janey."

"What?"

"Shut up."

I glanced over at the front desk, where the secretary was minding her own business, completely oblivious to us while she answered a phone. I watched her laugh, watched her earrings flash.

"We will talk when this is over. Okay?" Anthony's voice was gentle and careful.

"Do you want to go out to dinner?" I asked.

"Yeah. Let's get this done, and then you can slow down and take your time while you tell me all I need to know. Fair enough?"

I looked up at him. His eyes were dark.

"Where did the attitude go?" I asked bluntly.

"I think you fucked it out of me."

"That wasn't the intent."

"Yes, it was."

I had to look away. The elevator dinged and I watched a tall drink of water in a cowboy hat saunter out. Anthony watched him walk away, recognition dawning in his eyes.

"That's—" Anthony said, then stopped.

I said hello and nodded at the face that had seen hundreds of magazine covers. He dipped his hat. Anthony and I stepped onto the elevator and I pushed the button for the eighteenth floor.

"Yeah, that's him," I said.

"Holy shit."

The reverence in Anthony's voice made me smile. "A year from now, he won't hold a candle to you."

* * * *

The office was rather crowded for such a large and luxurious space. As the master of Axton Records, Keith had his own corner office of the high-rise, a suite of rooms that took up a whole quarter of the eighteenth floor. He would have taken the top floor, but he claimed he was afraid of heights.

Keith met me at the door. He was one of the few hands-on label presidents, one of the few who didn't delegate near as much as he probably should have. On the other hand, doing things his way was what had moved a small independent label into holding its own with the big dogs. Today he spoke quietly into my ear, told me it had all been done—all they needed was that final signature. It was nothing more than ceremony, but it was the way things were done around here. I nodded while I stared at Anthony.

"Hey." Keith took my elbow and gave me a gentle shake. "What's up with you?"

47

"Nothing," I lied.

Keith wheeled me around and pushed me through the closest door. It was a boardroom, completely empty and silent as a tomb. In the centre of the room sat a table long enough to seat thirty people. Keith pulled out two of the chairs and plopped down into one of them.

"Talk to me," he said.

I ran my hands through my hair and squeezed my temples. I sat down on the table with a frustrated sigh. "I'm getting *really* tired of being ordered to do things today."

Keith looked at me for a long moment. "Is Jason getting to you?"

I snorted with indignation.

"Look," Keith said, getting up from his chair to stand in front of me. "We've been friends for a long time. We've seen the best and the worst of each other. Right?"

I nodded and stared at the pattern on the carpet.

"I know you're sleeping with him."

Of course he knew.

Keith stepped forward a bit, his hips bumping my knees, and trailed a hand down my back. The touch was not sensual or untoward in the least. It was comforting and easy, that of an old friend who knew me far too well, almost like that of a father. "Didn't you know that you would eventually fall in love with one of them?"

I shook my head vehemently as tears stung my eyes. "I'm not in love with him."

"Oh, Janey." Keith's voice was gentle and filled with too much concern, damn him. "If you're not, you're going to be. He's not like the others."

I sniffled and ran the back of my hand over my eyes. "Not like the others?"

"You know he's not."

"Explain. Why is he not like the others?"

Keith thought about that for a moment before answering. "He's the real deal."

"The real deal," I repeated.

48

"He's it, Janey. We don't talk about it because we don't want to jinx it, but let's be honest here, just you and me and the walls. He's not just a hitmaker, though we both know he's going to churn them out by the dozen. There is something else there."

"Something else."

Keith nodded. "Star power. Is that a proper term for it? He will be the kind of artist who moves platinum units a week after release. He will be in demand everywhere. Star power sounds like a good description for that, you think?"

"Yes."

"Well, that's Anthony."

"Yes, it is."

Keith moved so he could see my face. He raised an eyebrow. "Yes? Miss Jaded and Cynical? You're saying you think Keenan is the real deal?"

"I'm saying Anthony is going to make history."

Keith smiled and shook his head.

"Janey," he said reasonably, "how could you not fall in love with a man like that?"

I lowered my face to my hands and started to cry. Only in front of Keith would I ever let that carefully placed façade crack. He was the only one I trusted enough. Keith's suit jacket was soft against my cheek as he pulled me tight against him and rocked me like a little child.

"It's okay," he said.

"No, it's not."

"I know it's going to be hard."

"Don't you see?" I whispered. "I'm only the beginning. He's going to have women swooning over every move he makes. Every word will be scrutinised. I'm special now because I brought him to that dotted line but he doesn't know, Keith. He doesn't know the hurricane that's bearing down on him right this second, and he doesn't know how much his life is going to change."

Keith watched me as I stood up and wiped my eyes. I took deep breaths to get myself under control.

"The man out there is dead once he signs on that dotted line. Once that spin machine cranks into gear and fame gets her claws into him, he will never be the same."

"Did you ever stop to think," Keith countered, "that maybe you can change that?"

"I can't stop him from signing. I would never."

"Then don't let it end there."

"What do you mean?"

"I'm sending you out on tour with him."

My heart sank in my chest, even as my belly flipped over with anticipation. "No."

"Yes."

"You're insane!"

"Keep your voice down."

"I'm not going."

Keith reached to fix my hair, smoothing the strands that had gone awry during my crying jag. "There. You look presentable again."

"I'm not going out on the road," I said again.

"You're going to see this one through."

We glared at each other, two strong wills meeting at a crossroads.

"I don't work in that capacity," I reminded him. "You can't pull me out like that."

"Little missy," he sighed, and my heart softened at the old nickname. "You work in more capacities than the paperwork implies."

"I'll quit."

"You'll quit because you're in love with somebody? You're more professional than that."

"I'll quit because I'm being bullied."

"Bullied? Fine. Here's some bullying for you." Keith planted his hands on the polished table on either side of my thighs and leant forward, his eyes only inches from mine. "You'll go on that tour, whether you like it or not, and you won't complain. You started this ride, and you'll see it through to the end, because after all the bells and whistles and contracts and fans and radio spins and little details, that's what you do, Janey. You see things through. *That's what you do*."

I tried to think of a protest, but I knew he was right. Keith stared me down, and I was the first to look away. I fixed my eyes on the mother-of-pearl button on his deep-blue shirt until his next words shook me out of my daze.

"This business is going to be yours one day."

I shook my head. "You didn't just go there…"

"I did."

"Keith. Stop this."

"You know it, and I know it."

"You don't have to guilt me into this."

"I know."

I wiped one last tear from my eyes and took a deep breath. "This is what I do, huh?"

"You know it."

"Do I look okay?"

Keith nodded. He put his hand on the doorknob. "This is what both of us do, Janey. So let's go out there and do it."

We walked out among the throng of businessmen, attorneys and assorted other people who had one reason or another to be here. Anthony was seated at a table on the far side, smiling for a photographer. I watched the flash glance off his dark eyes, watched the smile that wasn't practiced, but genuine. Millions of pictures would be taken of him in the coming years, and I hoped he never lost that easy smile.

I hoped he never lost anything at all to the hands of fame, but I knew she was a vicious bitch, one who would hand you a dream in exchange for your life.

When the photographer was done, Anthony's eyes searched the room. His eyes met mine, and he flashed another smile — this one was a little sultry, a little filled with promise, meant entirely for me. I couldn't help but smile back.

At a word from Keith, Anthony picked up the pen. I had seen artists go from nothing to everything overnight, so the surge of pride was nothing new. After all, like I had told Keith, I was the one who had brought him to that point of no return...

The flash of possessiveness flickered through me like lightning, sudden and unexpected. My mind reeled to a halt and it was suddenly hard to breathe. I watched as Anthony began to sign.

Laughter and cheers accompanied the flourish of the pen. "God help us all," I whispered.

Chapter Four

The buses were sleek rolling mansions. The groupies would be hounding the buses soon enough, so the exterior of all three were identical. They matched the two tractor-trailers that sat in the corner of the lot. Anthony stood in silence for a long time, looking at them.

"Want to go inside?" I asked when I had heard enough of the quiet.

"They are the same colours as my favourite guitar," he said.

"It didn't cost any more to get those colours."

"Janey, the cost wasn't my concern."

I looked away. "Ready to see the inside? They fit in all your specs, with the exception of the shower. They couldn't make it as big as you wanted, but they got close."

"Janey."

"Come on. Take a look at your palace."

The door opened with a whoosh and we stepped inside. My smile was a thousand megawatts and did nothing to hide the fact I was suddenly nervous as hell around him. Any conversation he wanted to have was lost when he caught sight of the interior of his rolling home.

The leather couch sidled up to one side of the bus, directly under the wide window that appeared completely black from the outside, but was completely clear from the inside. The television was larger than those found in most homes. The flat screen looked down upon the couch with an expensive air. Another small couch sat on the other side, framing the narrow walkway and butting up against the small countertop. The kitchen was next, with everything needed for a bachelor on the road, and a table that seated four. The bathroom was impressive, just as nice as that found in a four-star hotel, even if it was extremely small.

Anthony opened the door to the bedroom and sucked in a breath. "Wow."

A full-size bed sat in the centre of the small room. Mirrors were everywhere. Another flat-screen television looked down from the corner. The headboard of the bed was a bookcase with several small cubbyholes, perfect for the little things that would probably otherwise get lost in the shuffle of a busy tour schedule. The closet was roomy and already had some of his clothes hanging on the bar. Anthony touched them. We watched them rock gently before settling down to their calm, everyday place.

"This is all for me?" he asked in awe.

"Most artists don't start out in something this nice, but Keith went all out with you."

"But it's so…" Anthony gestured helplessly, looking for the words. "Big."

"But you haven't seen the half of it yet. There's a desk that pulls down from the side, right over there, and there's a switch in the living area that extends the bus out by another five feet once the brake is engaged. Perfect for jam sessions. The kitchen is amazing, how they have everything fit in there just so, and the whole area under the bed is storage, the couches open up into storage space, and look at the skylight—"

Anthony shut me up with a kiss.

His lips were warm and supple and made me weak in the knees. I had spent long weeks in the studio with him, watching his every move while he recorded the album that was guaranteed to go platinum. I had made a point of not touching him after the last time in the studio office. Since he had signed the contract, I tried hard to think of him as the talent, and nothing more. I had spent long hours denying the very thing that he pulled from me with one touch of his lips.

"Janey," he whispered against my lips as he smiled. "What does this do?"

He touched the switch on the wall. The door whooshed closed.

"That," I said inanely.

"That's what it does, huh?"

"Privacy…"

"Perfect."

Anthony's mouth was on mine again and still I hesitated. This was not smart. The day he signed the contract was still too fresh in my mind. So was the fact he had finally mentioned what the gossip columns had been ranting about for weeks — that he had filed for divorce. I wasn't sure why it took him so long to mention it to me, but I convinced myself it didn't matter.

Oh, but it did matter, for reasons I understood all too well. While he wasn't free, he was safe. I still had an out. I could always blame his wife for the fact our relationship — if that's what it was going to be — couldn't move forward. Now I was quickly heading to the point of no excuses, and the way the man kissed wasn't helping one damn bit.

"Anthony…"

"I want you, Janey."

He ran his hands into my hair and pulled my head back. His lips played over my throat. He found the top button of my shirt and gently pulled on it with his teeth. I sucked in a breath and when I touched his shoulders, my hands were trembling.

The bed was just right, not too soft, not too hard. The blinds and curtains were open, and sunlight streamed through to warm the deep-blue bedspread. Anthony's weight above me was thrilling but a sense of panic began to rise, clouding out the part of me that begged to just give in. When his hand slid down my hip and pulled me tight against him, I couldn't take any more.

"Anthony…stop."

He hesitated. "What did you say?"

55

"Stop."

He froze. He didn't move away, but he didn't push things, either. He just hovered there above me, his breath coming slow and steady against my jaw.

"Things have changed," he said.

"Yes."

"Tell me, Janey."

"No," I choked out. I could not possibly be crying. There was no *way* I could be crying.

"Janey."

"Stop saying my name," I snapped.

His voice was a whisper against my ear. "Janey, sweet Janey. I've watched you fight it for weeks. Aren't you so tired?"

I pushed hard against his shoulders. He was off me in an instant, and I was left feeling bereft, even though I wanted him gone. What the hell did I want, anyway? No wonder he was so confused by my attitude—I didn't even know what I was doing, so how could he possibly have a clue?

I buried my face in my hands. We faced each other, me on the rumpled bed in a pose of despair, him standing over me uncertainly. What a portrait we would have made—*Study of Janey's Earthquake*. I laughed once, harsh and bitter, and Anthony shifted his weight from one foot to the other.

"Talk to me," he implored, but there were too many memories, too many thoughts of the future. Too many things I simply didn't know how to handle. I grasped at the one thing I knew for sure.

"The single is released today. Are you excited?"

"What?" Anthony was startled at the sudden change of topic, his voice tinged with the slightest edge of panic.

"The video shoot is tomorrow," I said.

"Janey, don't—"

"Do you want to talk about it?"

"You know what I want to talk about."

"Maybe you should just discover it all for yourself when you get on the set. Only word of advice, do what she tells you to do. The director. Even if it sounds crazy and it probably will. Trust me, it will work. She's an artist in her own right."

"Don't put on that armour again," he pleaded, and I stood up to face him. My eyes met his and I knew he could read everything. I hoped he could read the pleading in them as well.

Please don't make me say it. Please give me time.

"Janey?"

"Don't," I murmured. "Please, don't."

We stared at each other. I held my breath. He let his out in a resigned sigh.

"What time should I be there tomorrow?"

My knees went weak again, this time with relief.

* * * *

The sun was shining through the early morning clouds when I showed up on the set. I found a parking space near the back of the warehouse, tucked in between a big flatbed truck and a sleek convertible whose vanity plates proclaimed LUVTUNES. The engine of my little car ticked as it cooled. Dead leaves tumbled on the breeze and brushed over the cherry-red hood.

Outside the old warehouse, people moved back and forth, one carrying a long black loop of wire, another carrying a camera. A man appeared holding a strange item that looked for all the world like a royal crown. I stared at it until he went out of sight behind a trailer. I had almost forgotten how insane making videos could be.

I found Anthony standing in the corner of a makeshift room, looking at a blue screen. He heard me come up behind him but he didn't turn around.

"I saw one of these once," he said. "On a movie set. It was in California. My parents took me to Universal Studios when I was a kid and we got to look at a real movie set. Now I hate to watch movies."

"Why?"

"Movies…they aren't real. Right? They're just characters speaking lines that are written down for them. But I didn't know that *nothing* was real. Even the water that moves behind two people while they're on a beach, that's probably not real. Or a house. A whole house, made up out of cardboard and plywood. It's pure make-believe."

"What's wrong with that?" I asked. Anthony turned to face me, and his eyes were dangerously dark, heavy lidded.

"Because even in make-believe, you have to have something to hold onto. You have to be able to look at something and ground yourself. Did you know that they can even create those characters? They might not even be real people. They might just be made up. Created on a computer screen."

"Maybe—"

"Now *I'm* the one in front of the blue screen. Made up and moulded for the camera."

A small grey camera was running on a track. The technician tested it as we watched. The little camera spun around, then rode on its silvery path like a car on a rollercoaster. It came to a stop and turned, focused on us. We suddenly appeared on a monitor to our left, and the image startled me.

So that is how we look together, I thought.

"Is it real?" Anthony whispered from just behind my shoulder.

I stared at the monitor. Anthony was stunning. His hair had been brushed back from his face in casual waves. The jeans he wore fit his body just right, and the T-shirt rode his muscles, smoothing over them like a lover's touch. He stood with an air of aloof confidence that would come across on camera as downright sexy. A bad boy, a touch of darkness, and the kind of introspection that would make women stop their chores in houses all over the world, the kind of look that would make them pause and daydream a while whenever that face appeared on their television screens.

"You are very real," I said, looking at his image on the screen.

"You are beautiful," he said abruptly.

I smiled. "I was just thinking the same thing about you."

The director came around the corner of the blue screen, all business and rush. Anthony's attention turned towards her. I watched as they talked, her fast northern clip and his slow drawl an almost laughable combination. He was starting to focus on the task at hand. His eyes were taking on that intense distance that he got when he was playing his guitar, the look that said he was fully present yet his mind was working in a dozen different ways. I could see the wheels turning and locking onto a course of action.

The single was the one I had heard him play that first night at the club. The first words I ever heard Anthony sing would now be shared with millions, courtesy of radio and television. I watched as he sang those words into that microphone in front of the blue screen, as the voice track boomed from the overhead speakers, as his hands played over the guitar like they had played over me. I remembered the way they felt, and the way his voice sounded when he made love and whispered my name, that deep growl. Even the way he took a breath was sexy to me.

Anthony. Dear, sweet Anthony, I'm falling in love with you.

The thought popped into my mind, completely unwelcome and startling. I turned and walked quickly away, headed for the car I had left five minutes before. Once inside, I took deep breaths to keep from crying. I locked the doors. I stared at the steering wheel and bit my lip.

I will not cry, I told myself, over and over.

So I did the next worst thing.

"Damn him!" I hollered in the small space. A crew member walked past and bent to peer into the car. I glared at him until he went along his way, with more of a hurry to his step. God knew what that insane woman back there in that car might have to say to him if he lingered too long.

David popped into my mind then. I had been avoiding

thoughts of him for weeks.

"Avoidance," I mused, looking at myself in the rearview mirror. "So, how's that going for you?"

I had never fallen in love with David. Oh, I had fancied myself in love. I had made myself believe that someone so handsome, so successful, could be the love of my life. I ignored the fact I didn't feel those butterflies in my belly every time David looked at me. My heart didn't leap into my throat and my eyes didn't sting with tears when he told me how much he loved me. I said those three little very important words and I meant them, but not in the way I should have. In the end he was the talent and I was the springboard, and I convinced myself his love was nothing but gratitude. I even managed to convince David.

I sat there behind the wheel and stared at the dashboard. I had never been in love before. How did I know this was it? Maybe this was just the thrill of finding that diamond in the rough. Maybe it was the rush of the next big thing.

Someone pushed open the doors of the warehouse, announced it with a squeal of rubber on metal. I looked up to see Anthony standing in front of those doors. They moved behind him and made me feel as though he were the one in motion. I clenched the wheel and looked at him until he looked at me.

He grinned, just the slightest motion of his lips, so quick I almost didn't catch it.

My stomach flipped over like a fish out of water.

* * * *

The steady whomp of the helicopter's blades cut through the conversations and the late afternoon heat. The wind from it was a welcome respite. I watched as the helicopter gently hovered to a standstill and the engine geared down. That whomp became a high-pitched whine. Anthony stood in the corner with the director, listening to last-minute information about editing and such. The door of the chopper opened and the co-pilot gave me a look that said we had a schedule to keep.

I looked at Anthony and tapped my watch. Within seconds he was trotting up to me, guitar in hand, the wind from the blades making a mess of his hair.

"Where are we going?"

"Memphis," I said into his ear. "Radio promo. Remember?"

He nodded and climbed into the helicopter. I watched him as he buckled the seat belt, brushed his hair from his face and surveyed the small cabin.

I'm in love with him.

He watched intently as the chopper lifted from the ground, staring down until the people became like ants and the buildings became like a child's playland.

"I've never been in a helicopter before," he said.

"Ever?"

He nodded and looked over the pilot's shoulder at the dials and gauges. For the first time, I looked too. How daunting it seemed. I was suddenly afraid of the physics of it all, of the impossibility of staying up in the sky. How could something so big possibly sustain flight?

My stomach lurched. I lunged for an airsickness bag on the back of the co-pilot's seat. The men in the front of the chopper glanced at one another and I felt a strange shift, as if they were decreasing speed. I didn't get sick, but sweat popped out on my forehead and the world grew slightly dim. Anthony put his hand on the back of my neck.

"What the hell is wrong with you, Janey?"

"What does it look like?"

"I never pegged you for one who gets sick in the air," he chuckled.

"She doesn't," the pilot said helpfully.

I closed my eyes and tried to breathe. Anthony's hand slid up and down my neck, under my hair. His touch made me shiver, even as my stomach threatened to rebel for real this time.

"Then it must be me," he said into my ear.

The helicopter shifted and Anthony's guitar shifted with it, ending up against my leg. I wrapped my hand around the neck, squeezed hard and felt the strings cut into my fingertips. I traced each one carefully. I didn't dare open my eyes, even though that seemed to make the sickness worse. I didn't want to look at Anthony. He was too persistent, too caring and too devastatingly handsome.

"We're going to do a promo," I said. "You'll just go in there and basically answer a few questions. We'll give away CDs to caller number ten or something. You'll play a song if you want and sing it live. Callers will probably ask about you and they can ask some off-the-wall things, so just go with the flow. The easier you laugh about it all, the more they will like you."

"Then autographs," he added. "And pictures with the crew and things like that."

"Yes."

"And will you be under the table, blowing me while I talk to caller number ten?"

I laughed, despite the fact that I still felt terrible. "You wish."

Anthony looked at me with mock seriousness. "Yes, I do."

I smiled, despite feeling for all the world like I had just gone through a terrible ride on a faulty rollercoaster. I watched the skyline of Memphis grow closer and closer. I took deep breaths and tried to calm my body, but there was nothing that could calm my heart.

I'm in love with him…

We didn't say anything else, but we sat there holding hands.

Chapter Five

Anthony began a whirlwind promotional tour. That new tour bus racked up the miles. Planes sometimes took us to three states in a day. Once we had breakfast at a radio station in Miami, Florida, in the morning, then dinner with a radio crew in Portland, Oregon, that evening. It was insane. It was necessary.

It was working.

The song was climbing the charts like a bat out of hell, a slam dunk for Axton Records and a constant reminder of the first time I ever saw Anthony Keenan. I could not listen to those first chords without being drawn to the memory of him playing them, half-drunk on Jack Daniels, cigarette smoke curling lazily around his throat as he sang into an old microphone. I saw him the same way every time. No matter how many photo shoots he did, no matter how many times I saw him in a different light, my thoughts always returned to that little bar and to the man who made my heart skip a beat the moment he opened his mouth.

We were in Santa Cruz when Keith called. I snatched up the cell phone while watching Anthony through the window of the small recording booth. He was strumming on an acoustic guitar and singing one of the ballads off the record. The DJ had a genuine smile. The phone board was lit up like a Christmas tree.

"How's he doing?" Keith asked.

I watched Anthony sway to the music, his eyes closed, lost in it.

"Great to fantastic," I assured him.

"He will be even better in a few minutes," Keith said, and

I turned away from the window so I could pay attention. Anthony was far too distracting.

"Do tell?"

"We're moving the release date up, from July to April."

"*April?*"

Keith wisely stayed silent, allowing me time to take in the news. A three-month jump? It was usual to have delays that lasted at least that long, but to move an album up in the release queue? What the hell were they thinking?

I must have asked the question out loud, because Keith began to talk, spewing out information on charts and tour dates and the latest *Billboard* magazine article. "They want him, Janey. Nobody can get enough. This week the single is the fastest mover in the history of country radio."

"In the…" I closed my eyes. The room began to spin. Hadn't I been the one, just a few weeks ago, to tell Keith that I believed Anthony would make history? Here it was.

"Oh, Christ."

"I told you he was the real deal, kid."

I turned to look at Anthony. He had finished the song and was smiling at something a listener had just said. He nodded when the DJ made a comment. He glanced at me, saw my gaze and gave me the thumbs-up sign. I smiled back.

"Find somewhere nice to tell him," Keith said. "No need to do it right now. Make sure it's something he will remember for the rest of his life."

I didn't miss the note of longing in Keith's voice. "You want to tell him yourself?"

"No," he replied, and I heard both the pride and the sadness. "I was just thinking of what you said. That he doesn't have a clue what's coming."

I said nothing.

"Make it special and make it count," Keith said. "Over the next year or so, he's going to need those little moments to hold onto. So will you."

The line went silent. I slipped the cell phone into my

pocket and looked at Anthony through the glass. The train had been pushed out of the station and now it had picked up enough steam. It couldn't be stopped. Looking at Anthony as he began to play another song, I finally accepted the fact the train wasn't just carrying him. It was carrying both of us.

Anthony finished the number. The disc jockey was laughing. The little lights on the call centre were going crazy. The programme manager walked into the hallway and stood beside me. Together we watched as Anthony fielded a few phone calls then began to strum his guitar again, playing a special dedication for a listener.

"He's our top request," the manager said to me. "That song is infectious. The interesting thing is that the majority of the listeners have never even *seen* this guy. Wait until they do."

I nodded and watched him through the glass. His hair fell over his face in a most appealing way. His eyes were dark and sultry. Every motion of his body made me think about what he looked like when he didn't have any clothes on. The man projected sexuality without even trying.

"They won't know what hit them," I agreed.

"Men will envy him and women will lust after him."

"There's the formula for a number one star."

"I want to book him again. Get in good now, before the bigger stations snatch up all the time. Can we do some interviews this afternoon so we have something in the can?"

I glanced at my watch. "Want to do lunch? He's got to eat. He forgets and then wonders why his head hurts."

She grinned. "Welcome to the whirlwind, huh?"

"This is just the headwinds of the hurricane," I promised her. "It only gets worse from here. Getting to the eye is going to be a bitch."

She nodded. "I worked in A&R for years. I remember."

"Then you also remember that an artist makes a pittance even after a few major hits," I said with a wink. "You're buying."

* * * *

The hotel that night was an oasis in a sea of commitments. Anthony walked into his room, dropped his duffel bag and collapsed onto the bed with nary a word. Within two minutes he was completely out, snoring with his face pressed against the comforter at an odd angle. I pulled his shoes off, tugged on his shoulder just enough to make him straighten out his neck, and pulled the heavy drapes together to block out all the light from the streets below. Anthony didn't move.

Back in my own room, I looked at the cell phone and the list of calls I had to make. I scanned the schedule and saw we had to be on a plane by eight in the morning, and it was already eleven at night. My credit card was almost at the limit. The luggage was filled with clothes that needed to get to the laundry service. We hadn't eaten anything since lunch.

I lay back on the bed and traced the swirls on the popcorn ceiling with eyes that were so tired they burned. Not too many years ago, I could go for days without a wink of sleep or a bite of food. Now I was ravenous, my stomach growling loud enough to hurt, and my body was exhausted.

Christ, I was too old for this shit.

The phone rang and jerked me out of a dream. I sat up and shot a glance at the clock, my mind already racing again, tallying up the things I had to do.

It was midnight. Another hour lost. I snatched at the phone and closed my eyes again.

"Yeah."

"How did it all go?" Jason asked, and I lay back with a moan.

"Absolutely wonderful," I said. "I'm so tired."

Jason laughed, a warm sound that made him seem right there in the room rather than over a thousand miles away. We had come to an uneasy truce, and now I could listen to his laughter without thinking the most ungenerous thoughts imaginable.

"Why in the world are you calling me?"

"Keith told me the news. I wanted to say congratulations."

"But it's…" I tried to calculate the time in my head and couldn't. "Hell. It's late there. Or early. Don't you ever sleep?"

"You're the night owl. I figured this would be prime time for you."

I rolled over on the bed and yanked a pillow from under the comforter. I curled up in a ball and drew my knees to my chest. "My timing is all messed up," I admitted. "I don't even know which way is up anymore."

"You take on way too much, Janey."

"I was kinda forced into this one, you know. Keith told me I was going, and so I'm here."

"You're not all that upset with him," Jason said.

"No."

"Besides, it gives you plenty of opportunity to sleep with the star."

"Shouldn't you be getting your beauty sleep?" I snapped.

Jason sighed, but it was a sound filled with more affection than exasperation. "That's my girl. Get some sleep, and I'll see you in Nashville. We have an album to produce and the schedule just kicked into high gear."

"Adios."

I clicked off the phone and lay there in silence. The streetlights made a thin sliver of golden colour between the drapes. The room smelt of cigarette smoke. The bedspread smelt faintly of detergent. The digital clock on the nightstand ticked off long minutes. The numbers began to blur as sleep overtook me again. I wasn't even hungry anymore. This was my prime time, just as Jason had said, but I had never been this tired.

My eyes flew open.

"Oh my God. No."

My voice sounded just as shaky as I felt. I sat up and the world began to spin. I lay right back down and stared at the ceiling, at the line of light that cut across it. My mind raced as I racked up all the moments that didn't make any sense. But suddenly, they *did* make sense, made more sense than I wanted them to make.

It just wasn't possible. Not now.

Maybe not ever.

Around five in the morning I let myself into Anthony's room. Unable to sleep for hours, I had taken the laundry down to the all-night service, made minor adjustments to the schedule and called the grave-shift jockeys at the radio stations to let them know we would be visiting in just a few hours. I had turned on the television, watched the news until I felt as though things could be worse, and refused to give in to the urge to cry.

By the time the sun was peeking over the horizon, I felt more in control.

Anthony was sleeping on his back. He hadn't bothered to get undressed or even to get under the blankets. Sometime during the night he had apparently woken up to see he was lying at the foot of the bed and had crawled to the top of it. His hair was messed up and he was still snoring. I stood at the door and watched his chest move up and down. I tried to match my breathing to his. He was so calm, so serene, and I wanted some of that for myself.

When I closed the door there was nothing but darkness. I couldn't see a foot in front of my face, but I knew where the bed was. I made my way to it without incident and sat down when I felt the mattress bump my knees.

Anthony stirred. I found his ankle in the darkness.

"It's me," I whispered.

"Who is me?" I could hear his smile.

"Someone who should know better."

Anthony's hands fumbled on my shoulder before he found my hair. His sigh was filled with relief.

"You're here," he said.

My knee slid over his thigh. His lips found my forehead, then my nose, and finally landed on my lips. His hands sought and found the buttons of my shirt. Soon the cool air was washing over my body and I was lost, spiralling in a vortex of sensation as his hands and his lips explored every inch of skin he uncovered.

The desire took the place of everything else, a hunger that was frightening in its intensity. The sensation swept away all thought, all doubt, all sense of time and place. "Don't wait," I implored, and Anthony's laugh went straight through me, to the core that was already aching.

"I want to wait. I want to savour."

He slipped off my jeans. His hands were reverent and gentle. By the time his tongue slipped over my thigh and his breath slid over my belly, I was crying.

"Things are different," he said, and I remembered when he said that weeks ago, the first time he looked over the new tour bus. How much could change in so little time...

"Nothing will ever be the same again," I whispered.

To Anthony's credit, he didn't pause. He didn't slow down. He just kept doing what he was doing and let me cry, until the tears turned to gasps of pleasure and the sobs turned to moans. By the time he slid into me, I was digging my nails into his shoulders and begging him to let me come.

"Tell me," he whispered.

"Make me come, please, please..."

"Not that."

"Anthony..."

His lips settled on my throat. "Say it," he whispered against my skin.

Still, I hesitated, unsure of what to say, what to think, what to do.

"Janey, say it. Say you love me. Say it because you know I love you, too."

The tears were gone, and the heaviness in my heart was gone too. "Yes," I murmured.

"Say—"

"I love you."

Then Anthony was the one crying, the tears silent and

shocking. I kissed them away in wonder. Soon there was nothing but his gasp and my moan, followed by the silence of the dawn.

* * * *

Afterwards I lay in the crook of his arm. His chest rose and fell under my ear. The lamp had a very satisfying, understated glow. With one finger I traced designs on his broad chest. The clock on the bedside table read six-o-four.

"I've missed doing this with you," he whispered.

I smiled and burrowed deeper under the covers. His body was warm as a furnace. It felt good to be near him but what felt even better was giving in to what I had fought for so long. I was in love with him. He knew it. Why deny it any longer?

He kissed the top of my head and worked a tangle out of my hair with his long, slim fingers.

"I have something to tell you," I said.

"Tell me you love me again. I want to hear it."

I laughed. "We know that already."

"So today is going to get even better? I might not be able to stand it."

I rose up on one elbow and looked at him in the light of the bedside lamp. I traced his lips with my fingertips. The laugh lines weren't so deep now. The little lines around his eyes seemed almost gone. He looked ten years younger in the quiet of the morning.

"Think you can handle being even busier?"

Anthony rolled his eyes. "It isn't possible."

"It is."

"What now? Keith is sending me overseas?"

"Not yet."

"Oh, wait. I know. Keith wants me to do every radio station from here to Saigon and back."

"Well, there is that…"

"Okay, stop teasing. What is going to make my day better

70

than it already is?"

"How about an album so in demand, so highly anticipated, that the label is moving the date up instead of back?"

Under my hand, his heart began to speed up. His eyes were wide and filled with the kind of fire that reminded me of why I was out there living a crazy life on the road.

"By how far?"

"Oh, about three months."

"Three…"

He hauled me against his chest, planted my head firmly under his chin and squeezed me so hard I could barely catch my breath. He let out a whoop of happiness.

"Let me go," I begged. "I can't breathe!"

"It's happening, isn't it?" he said. "It's finally happening."

"Are you ready?"

Anthony shook his head. "No."

"Me neither."

"Too late now," he said.

The alarm on his watch went off, an annoying little beep.

"Another day," I said, and didn't tell him the rest. It could wait. Right now there were interviews, then a photo shoot, then tonight there was a concert.

And it was sold out.

* * * *

The screams of the crowd were constant. They were loud enough that it was hard to hear ourselves think, even in the back of the bus. Anthony sat on the end of his bed, going over the set list. Mark, the drummer, listened intently while Anthony talked about last-minute changes. From the living area, two players bickered over strings.

"I cannot believe you are still using Ernie Ball, man. They got too much twang."

"And that shit you use ain't got enough twang, dude. What you think we're playing here, thrash metal?" No response came, and that obviously pissed him off. "I oughta thrash *you*," the one with the deep voice threatened.

"Grow up," came the bored reply.

Someone knocked on the door of the bus. No one bothered to answer. From just under the window, feminine laughter pealed. The driver sat on the couch and watched a basketball game on television, earplugs in, oblivious to the chaos around him.

A tall, thin woman in a business suit put a stack of glossy photos on the table along with a box of Sharpie markers. She looked around until she found me.

"He needs to sign those," she said. "At least twenty of them for right now. For the radio promo guys. I'm not sure why they need twenty, but they insisted."

Angela Moore was the publicity manager for Axton Records. She had been with Keith since the very beginning, and to say she knew what she was doing was an understatement. She could put a spin on a story so fast it would make even the principal characters dizzy. She could convince anyone of anything, and it was a skill that served her well in the lean days, when Axton was struggling to find a foothold.

Angela took her charges very personally. She was genuinely interested in Anthony. Whatever it took to get him to the top, Angela would do it.

"It's insane out there," she said.

"It sounds like it." I picked up the glossies. A gorgeous Anthony looked out at me from under the fall of his dark hair. In the photograph, his hands were stuck deep in his pockets. He looked almost shy, approachable, and entirely sexy.

"Maybe it would be a good idea to get him off the bus for a minute," Angela said. "Let the fans see him. They are lined up outside."

"Think he would come back in alive?"

"We have a barricade."

I blinked at that. "Barricade?"

"It's groupie central out there."

Anthony walked up behind us, grabbed a Sharpie and slipped into the chair next to the table. He grinned up at Angela as he grabbed the first glossy from the stack.

"Heya, good lookin'."

"Heya, guitar man. Wanna sign for me?"

"Anywhere, anytime."

They leered at each other. They had become fast friends over recent weeks, and now they had graduated to the point of teasing each other mercilessly. Whoever blushed first, won.

"For my adoring fans," Anthony intoned as he started to sign the picture in front of him. "May you always find an extra bottle when you thought the liquor was all gone. Love, Anthony."

Angela chuckled. Anthony thought for a moment before signing another one. "Dear So-and-so," he said. "Don't forget that mustard sex leaves stains. Cheers, Anthony."

"Mustard sex?"

He winked at Angela and fixed me with a sultry gaze. "Wanna?"

Angela looked at me with nothing short of glee. "Oh, wow, the two of you? This is great. When did this happen?"

"Oh, hell…" I buried my face in my hands.

"How many times?"

"Enough," he said, and she beamed ear-to-ear.

"Is there video? Please, God, let there be video."

Anthony laughed.

"You have groupies," I said, trying to change the subject.

"You mean, other than you?" His eyes were mischievous. Angela let the silence hang there for a moment, let the teasing sink in and marinate, then saved me.

"There are hundreds of women outside. We erected a barricade."

Anthony sat very still. "Well…hundreds of women certainly would erect something, I suppose."

"You need to go out there. Touch hands, sign autographs, let them touch you a little. Look the part of the benevolent

73

superstar. Then leave before all of them have a shot."

Anthony looked at me for guidance. I nodded. "Make them want more."

"That's a bit harsh, isn't it?"

Angela shrugged. "That's the way it works. Always leave them wanting more. You should know that, you didn't just fall off the turnip truck, did you?"

Anthony grinned and wielded the Sharpie on another glossy photograph.

"Dear Turnip," he intoned. "Beware asphalt. Much love, Anthony."

The groupies screamed with delight when the door of the bus opened, and they hollered even louder when Anthony bounded down the steps. Women dressed in halter tops and shorts cut off far too high leaned over the barricades. Women with plunging necklines and bare midriffs shook their chests at any man who might be part of the band. They were all made up, dolled up and salivating for the handsome bodies on the other side of the barricade.

Anthony had dealt with groupies before, but the look on his face said he had never dealt with this many. He smiled and waved, then reached for a pen to sign an autograph. The woman immediately reached out to touch his hair, and Anthony drew back in surprise. I watched from the window of the bus as the women fought for autographs, pushing and shoving one another until the lone security guard began to look more than a little worried.

"Get more security at the bus," Angela ordered into a tiny walkie-talkie, and within seconds burly men in bright yellow shirts appeared from all directions. They hung back behind the crowd, watching warily.

"Anthony, I love you!" The shout came from a girl in her middle teens, a child made up to look like an adult. I wondered where her parents were until I saw the woman behind her with the dark lipstick and the miniskirt, the spitting image of the girl, and I remembered that sometimes being a groupie ran in the family.

A few band members wandered off the bus, their eyes wide. The women were distracted by Anthony, but they certainly noticed the other guys. Autographs were signed, and the women started to chat them up. I watched Chris in particular. The handsome guitarist slipped his hand into his pocket while talking to a woman young enough to be his daughter. When he pulled his hand out of his pocket, his wedding band was nowhere in sight.

"It's going to be a long night," I murmured to no one in particular.

And oh, it was. Groupies were a dime a dozen and there were so many of them to go around, there was never any doubt everyone on the tour would have ample opportunity to get laid. That's the way it was that first night of the tour, and it set the tone for weeks to come.

But first there was a show to do.

By the time Anthony hit the stage, the crowd was on their feet, hollering his name in chants that rolled like waves up and down the throngs of people. The intro music was blasting from huge speakers, the bass throbbing hard already, the lights low and flashing idly across an empty stage. Girls in skimpy clothes lined the front of the stage, their makeup too overt and harsh under the lights that were meant to subtly enhance.

Anthony's T-shirt skimmed tight over his body, showing the definition of hard, honed muscles. His belly was flat and his shoulders broad. He sauntered onto the stage with a wicked grin. With a practiced flip of his head, his hair fell from his forehead in waves. One unruly strand came down over his eye as he played the first lick. Even from a good distance, I could see how brilliantly the hue of the guitar set off the deep colour of his eyes.

The crowd went crazy when he stepped to the microphone. There was that voice, that sound they had fallen in love with, and there was the man who created it, the man who brought it to them. And my goodness, wasn't he wrapped up in a pretty package?

A groupie in the front row vaulted onto the stage. She ran her hand up Anthony's leg. He shot a startled glance at security, who hauled her off, as her arms pinwheeled like those of a rag doll.

"I love you, Anthony!" she screamed. He had never seen her before in his life.

"Jesus Christ," Angela murmured from beside me. The look on her face was one of pure, naked lust. She reflected what I saw in dozens of women at the front of the stage.

Then the spotlight shone down, and those women were nothing but shadows at Anthony's feet.

* * * *

After the show things weren't any less rabid. The women were all over the band members. They were all over the crew. They were all over the drivers. Besides that, management team members weren't doing their jobs, and my threats to pull them off the tour fell on deaf ears. They were, instead, spending time locked with female bodies around every corner of the venue. It was the first night of the tour and it was sold out. Why not celebrate?

"This is chaos," I said to Anthony, but he couldn't possibly hear me. The screaming was too loud, too close. We were both being hustled to the tour bus amid a throng of screaming fans. There wasn't enough security to go around. The burly men provided by the venue were overwhelmed. How did all these people get backstage?

It took two tries to open the door of the bus. There were women leaving lipstick all over Anthony's face and clothes. They were leaping at him, showing their cleavage as they panted, pushing papers and pens in his direction, telling him how much they loved him. Anthony was tired, sweaty and riding on an adrenaline high, but that wasn't enough to hide the spark of fear in his eyes.

"Where is security?" he demanded.

"This is it, man," the burly guard next to us said. He shoved a woman out of the way. She squealed with indignation, and he shoved her harder.

"This is dangerous for you," I shouted to the guard.

"It's more dangerous for you. Get on that bus." The woman was coming at him again, and this time she was furious. The guard slammed her against the side of the bus with a beefy forearm, glaring at her and shoving Anthony up the bus steps. "Now!"

The door whooshed closed behind us. Someone was pushed against it, or threw their weight on it. The security guard started yelling at the groupies, and it was clear from the tone of his voice that he meant business. It was utter insanity.

"This is like the Beatles," I said.

"That's blasphemy," Anthony told me as he peeled off his shirt.

The windows were tinted black and the fans couldn't see in. Thank God for small favours. The sight of Anthony taking off his shirt would send the women into convulsions of lust. He was covered in sweat and his hair hung in almost unattractive strings around his face. He needed a shave and a shower.

"Come here," he said.

His body still hummed with the power of the amplifiers as he slid into me there on that couch. The leather squeaked against my back. The taste of the strings was on his fingertips. I could feel the hum as he touched my thigh, could rise on the notes as he slid those fingers across my overheated skin. He watched my face as he did it, then raised his fingertips to my lips, one at a time. I sucked them clean. I tasted like guitars and stage lights and dust and sweat and him and only a little bit like myself.

The bus rocked. It wasn't until after we both came, until after Anthony sank his teeth into my shoulder and growled out his release, that I realised it wasn't our motion that made the big bus rock. It was the throng outside.

Even as the orgasm faded, I felt the first stab of true fear. I had never seen anything like this. There were more shouts from security, and the rocking lessened, but did not cease.

Anthony and I didn't say a word. We both headed to the back of the bus, to the shower, where he stepped in and turned the water on. We didn't turn on the lights, lest the fans see our silhouettes and go even crazier. The only illumination came from the lights along the baseboards, giving the inside of the bus an otherworldly glow. I leaned against the wall and watched tops of heads out the tinted windows. The sun was setting. Would they get rowdier with the darkness, or would they finally go away?

As I watched, slow strobes of blue lit up the bus. A siren pealed. The relief was enough to make me weak in the knees. The bus suddenly stopped moving, and the security guards stopped yelling. The water in the shower cut off and Anthony looked out at me, water dripping from his lashes.

"The police are out there?"

"Thank God. I was getting nervous."

Anthony stared at me for a moment. "I'm not sure I'm ready for this," he said.

I didn't know how to respond. I opened a towel for him and he stepped gratefully into it. Water from his hair dripped down his back as he went into the bedroom and pulled out a fresh shirt and jeans. I stepped into the shower and made quick work of cleaning up. When I got out of the shower and came to the bedroom, Anthony had his jeans on but nothing else. I dropped a kiss on his forehead and shrugged into one of his fresh, clean shirts from the closet.

"Do I have to do the meet and greet right now?" he asked.

"I'm not sure it's a good idea."

"But it has to be done, right?"

I looked at my watch and shook my head. "We'll give it another twenty minutes or so. See if this mob clears out a bit."

The bus rocked again, as if on cue.

"Good Lord," Anthony breathed, and sat on the bed. His jeans were unbuttoned. He was wearing no underwear.

Looking at him from this angle, I realised I could see his ribs under his tanned skin.

"You're too thin," I said.

Anthony shrugged away my concern. His mind was filled with a million things, and his next meal was not exactly his first worry. He studied the shirt in his lap for a moment before he put it on. He buttoned it slowly while looking out the windows. More blue flashing lights joined those already there, and the colours washed over Anthony's face in the dim light, etching every laugh line a bit deeper, making him look older than he really was.

"This is insane," he said.

"Yeah."

"You tried to warn me."

Then it was my turn to shrug. No amount of warning could prepare anybody for this, could it?

We stood in front of the windows in the bedroom. The groupies couldn't see us, but we could see them. It was a strangely powerful feeling. Anthony pulled me back against him and ran his hands under my shirt. He pinched my nipples and I turned my head, moaned against his throat as I kissed the little spot he had missed when he shaved.

"They can't see us."

"No."

His hand slipped down. His fingers found the place he had been so interested in ten minutes earlier. He gently stroked and squeezed until I was breathless, my knees weak and my hands tight on his arm.

"They can't see me make you come," he whispered.

I arched back against him. His fingers delved deeper. The thrill of being with a man who caused so much chaos, the tension, and the fear made it fast. I came with a cry against his throat.

"You have what they want," he murmured into my ear as the orgasm began to fade. "The man they all want just made you come. How does it feel?"

The sense of power was almost frightening in its force. I

looked down at the groupies just outside the windows and for the first time felt something very akin to anger.

"You're mine," I said, shocking myself.

Anthony bowed his head and kissed my neck.

"How does it feel?" he whispered.

Chapter Six

The landing gear thumped under my seat as the Lear rose into the skies over Dallas. We had three hours to get to Nashville, then the hard work would begin. The album had already taken shape on the stage, but how would it translate to the studio? It was the usual battle that every good record went through, the normal birthing process.

Anthony sat in the seat opposite mine. His eyes were closed, his head leant back against his seat. He gripped the armrest, knuckles white.

"We're in the air," I said softly.

"Yeah?"

"Yeah."

"Physics still work, then."

"You should be used to this by now," I said.

Anthony sat up and opened his eyes. He unbuckled his seatbelt and carefully stood, as though he was afraid the plane would lose its balance with his shifting weight. In the minibar he found all sorts of liquor, but not what he really wanted.

"In the cooler, underneath the table," I said.

Anthony cracked open the beer as he sat down. He pulled the low desktop out from the side of the plane. It swung around and hugged his body. His paperwork was still on it, right where it had been left when the plane took off. Anthony looked at the convenience of it all and shook his head as he flipped through the pages.

"Absurd," he said.

"Money always is."

He flipped me a copy of the upcoming schedule. "So is

that."

I carefully avoided looking at it. I stared at the Texas sky instead.

"I read about flaps," I said. "On airplanes? They help keep the plane in the air. You know, one mistake with one flap and we could plough a crater in the ground a good fifty feet deep."

Anthony stared at me.

"Sorry."

"Jesus Christ, Janey. What the hell is wrong with you?"

"What the hell is wrong with *you*?" I fired back.

"Don't do that."

I sighed and flipped through the schedule. What *was* wrong with me? Perhaps the better question was what wasn't?

"I'm just tired," I said, and it was the truth. "I'm bone-deep tired, and this train hasn't hit its full speed yet."

"You're anticipating too much," he said. "Just go with the flow."

"That's your job. Mine is to plan for everything else."

Anthony plucked the schedule from my fingers.

"Tell me, Miss Mills. Are you a member of the Mile High Club?"

I laughed despite my darker thoughts. Anthony dropped to his knees in front of me and looked up from between my thighs. His hands slid over my jeans and a smile played along his lips. He pulled my shirt from my waistband with agonising slowness.

"Are you?"

"No."

"You're lying," he said, giving me his best leer.

"God's honest truth."

"Swear?"

"Pinky swear."

Anthony slid his hands up the inside of my thighs. One of them stopped at the apex of my legs, where he found the heat of me. The other slid up my belly and under my shirt.

I arched into his touch just as a voice came from behind my seat.

"Mr Keenan?"

Anthony's hand slowly crept out from underneath my shirt. He laid his head on my thigh with a frustrated sigh.

"What?"

"I have a few papers I need you to look at before we land."

Anthony slowly pushed himself away from me and settled back into his seat. His eyes were bright with desire, and his cheeks were flushed with the certainty that we had been caught. Someone I only vaguely recognised put another sheaf of papers on the pull-out desk.

Anthony glanced through the paperwork. His frustration quickly changed to confusion.

"Who is this guy? This Anderson guy?"

"Tom Anderson?"

"Yeah."

"That's your new manager."

Anthony looked at me, not understanding. "But I *have* a manager. What happened to Richard?"

"Your manager now has a manager," I said. "That's simplifying it a bit, but that's how it is."

"Does Richard know this?"

"He will."

"Richard has handled everything for years. We started this whole thing together. He knows how I work, inside and out. He controls more than you think."

"Sometimes change is good," I said carefully.

Anthony dropped the papers to the floor. They fluttered down, held together by a staple. The white pages looked like the wings of a dying bird.

"And what, exactly, do I control?"

I opened my mouth to speak. Anthony waved me away with an angry hand.

"At least I can still breathe for myself," he said.

"It's not as bad as that."

Anthony looked out the window. Neither of us really

knew what else to say, so we just watched the world fall away beneath us.

* * * *

The jet landed on time. We had left Dallas in the sunshine, and we landed in Nashville right in front of a massive cold front. Tornado warnings were all around us, and though the Lear had flown through the clouds with nary a shudder, the clouds looked ominous.

We taxied to a stop near the hangar of the private airport. A long black limousine sat idling, waiting to carry Anthony to the studio. A smaller car sat nearby, waiting to take me to my home in Brentwood. Anthony grabbed my arm and stopped me in midstride as soon as he noticed the second car.

"Where are you going?"

"I'm going home to work. You're going to the studio to work. We'll see each other again in a few days. You've got my home number, right?"

Anthony shook his head. "I want you there with me."

"I have paperwork to do. I've been neglecting it."

"Can't you do it in the studio?"

I sighed. I wanted to be with Anthony more than I could ever say, and he knew that, no matter how much I might try to hide it. But I did have a ton of paperwork, most of it relating to him, and it was all sitting in an office that was gathering dust. There was only so much I could get done while I was on the road with him day in and day out, and now it was time to pay the piper for all that travelling. I had to do some of that work.

I also had to do some thinking.

"Call me," I said, and walked away to the waiting sedan. I didn't wait for what Anthony might say. I didn't look back, for fear he might take it as an opportunity to change my mind. I climbed into my own car and by the time I settled into the seat, Anthony was behind the dark windows and the limousine was pulling out into the main road.

The heavens were opening up, and a fine mist had already settled over the windshield. The driver turned on the wipers. They made lazy streaks of wet against the glass. The brake lights of Anthony's limousine flashed, flashed again, then turned west. My car turned east. It took a lot of willpower not to turn around and watch them drive away.

It wasn't ten minutes later that the driver opened my door and ushered me up my front steps under the shelter of a huge umbrella. He refused to leave until I had opened the door and safely closed it behind me, and for some reason the consideration made me want to cry. I watched the car drive away then I was left in the big house, all alone for the first time in weeks.

It was quiet, far too quiet for a place so large. Thunder rumbled outside and rain peppered the floor-to-ceiling windows in the living room as I walked across the hardwood floors. During those long weeks on the road, the house had been sealed up, without even an occasional housekeeper to lift the silence, and now the air seemed stuffy and stale. I slid up windows in one room after another, raising them just enough to let the fresh air and the heavy scent of rain flow in. I took deep breaths of the cool air and walked through the house, looking into every room, reacquainting myself with the space I called home.

In the kitchen, the tiny red light on my answering machine was steady and not blinking, telling me that the recording was full. I pressed play and listened to one message at a time, all of them wanting something, all of them needing a corner of my time. I opened the fridge, looked in at virtually nothing, and pushed it shut with a slam and a sigh.

I touched my belly and closed my eyes.

I hadn't given myself time to think about what was really happening, that one little secret that even Anthony, with all his intuition, had not guessed.

It was time to find out for sure.

Several times over the last few weeks I had thought about

85

the contents of my medicine cabinet, about the pregnancy test that was still in there from long, long ago, when I had missed a period and got nervous. It was negative then, and I was relieved. The boxes always came with two tests nowadays, and I had only used one.

I searched through the medicine cabinet. The test wasn't there. I looked under the counter, in the plastic bins that held everything from extra toothpaste to the mascara I hadn't used in years. I found the little trash can next to the sink—it actually had dust on the lid—and started throwing things out while I searched.

Finally, there it was—in the back of one of the bins. I looked at the box. It was still good, according to the date. I had missed the expiration by a month.

I unwrapped the little white stick and pulled a Dixie cup out of the dispenser. There was dust on that, too. I gently blew over the top of the cup and watched the dust go flying. "I've got to get home more often."

Five minutes later I had my answer. I was not surprised. I sat on the side of the tub and looked at the stick, as though those two pink lines might merge into one, as though this might not be happening.

So much for birth control pills.

I tossed the stick into the trash and walked down the hallway, feeling out of balance. I thought I might be sick. I touched the wall, leaned against it, and that wasn't enough. I pressed my forehead to it, and the coolness seemed to seep through me, calming me from the head down.

"It's going to be all right," I said. My voice echoed in the great vault of a house.

I stood there for a long while. I looked at the pristine paint, at the picture beside me, a pastoral painting I had picked up somewhere along the way. I touched the frame and wiped the dust away and looked at the grey smudges on my fingers.

Under the kitchen sink I found dust rags and cleaners. In the utility closet was a broom and mop. I started working in the hallway and made my way through the house. I was getting drunk on the fumes, which was better than getting lightheaded over the facts.

I went to the bathroom to empty the trash. Right before I dumped it into the larger bin, I stopped. I carefully pulled the pregnancy test out from between old tubes of cosmetics and ancient, useless razors. I looked at it for a long time.

I put it on the back of the sink. I wanted to keep it for a while.

* * * *

I was down on my hands and knees, scrubbing the kitchen floor. My knuckles were red and irritated from all the chemicals, and I was developing a headache. My whole body ached with the unaccustomed physical work, but my mind seemed to be healing with every clean swipe. I was so intent on my cleaning that I didn't notice the knock on the door, nor the beep of the code or the sound of the door opening. I looked up to see familiar black boots on slim, sexy legs. "You're actually home!"

I looked up into the smiling green eyes of my best friend, Kristin. I hadn't seen her in…months? Was it really that long? We had talked on the phone and caught up on things when I had a spare moment, but those moments were fewer than I would have liked. Seeing her in the flesh brought a wave of happiness that made me forget all my troubles.

Kristin was a looker, one of those women who turned heads while minding her own business and stopped traffic when she was so inclined. Her blonde hair was expertly cut and fell on the side of her face in appealing waves. Her skin was lightly tanned and her smile showed perfectly white, even teeth. She was slim and tall, and wore her black sweater like it was a second skin. She was as gorgeous as ever.

She looked around the kitchen. "Somebody has been busy, busy, busy."

"Somebody has a lot of things on her mind."

Kristin opened her arms. "Come here, honey."

I stood up and wrapped my arms around her. The feeling was just like home. Much to my shock, I began to cry.

"I figured that was coming," Kristin said. She ran her hand over my back in small circles, like I had seen her do so many times with her children. The thought of children made the tears stop, and I sniffled as I stood up straight and looked at her.

"I need to talk," I said.

"I'll just bet you do," Kristin replied, and her smile was filled with reassurance. No matter the situation, Kristin was the kind of woman who could roll up her sleeves, narrow her eyes and take care of business. "I've got all day. Let's go get Mexican."

"Food or men?"

Kristin laughed. "Maybe a bit of both."

The restaurant was one of our favourites. The music was authentic and so was the food. The waiters hardly spoke a word of English but Kristin spoke enough Spanish to order for both of us. I looked over the menu, suddenly ravenous. I hadn't eaten since early morning, and even then it hadn't been much more than a few bites of oatmeal and a small glass of orange juice. My stomach growled even as the waiter set the chips and salsa on the table, and I reached for them before he turned away.

"You worked up an appetite, cleaning like that," Kristin said. "What got into you? Where did you learn how to use a broom?"

"Very funny."

"Cleaning like a scullery maid is a sign of deep psychosis," she said, pointing at me with a chip. "Or something like that."

I shrugged. "There are many things on my mind."

"Like what?"

The waiter came around and Kristin ordered drinks. I cut her off when she pointed to me and mentioned margaritas.

"I don't want one today."

She gave me an odd look and ordered Pepsi instead.

"Something must be *really* wrong if you don't want your top-shelf tequila," she joked.

"Have you seen Anthony's video?" I asked.

"I caught it on CMT the other day."

"You didn't watch the promo I sent you?"

She shrugged and bit into a chip. "I like to be surprised."

"You sold it on eBay," I said, and when she carefully dipped into the salsa without an answer, I grinned at her. "How much did it go for?"

She laughed, her earrings flashing in the light. The men at the corner table stared.

"More than enough to pay for this lunch, let's put it that way."

"Good thing I'm a cheap date without that top-shelf tequila, huh?"

The waiter returned with our drinks and took our order, writing so fast on his little pad that I had no idea how he could keep it all straight. I swirled the straw and made the ice spin in the glass. Kristin took a sip of her margarita.

"He's a looker," she said. "I won't lie to you, babe. He looks like the bad-boy type who is going to break your heart."

"He does look like that. It's his appeal."

"Is he?"

"A bad boy?"

"Is he going to break your heart?"

My hunger for food disappeared. I looked at my best friend, the one I could never hide anything from, the one who saw through every lie, even the ones I told myself. There was no point in pretending she couldn't read the truth about Anthony by just looking into my eyes.

"I have no idea," I admitted.

Kristin studied me for a moment, a smile dawning on her face, and I knew I didn't have to say the words. She knew I was in love with the man, knew it just as well as I did, and probably got wind of the news long before my own heart had a chance to catch up. She didn't need to be told, but there were other things I had to say, other words I had to hear come out of my own mouth before I would believe them at all.

"I'm pregnant," I said.

And just like that, the dreamlike fog disappeared. It was real.

Kristin's eyes grew wide. She stared at me, her margarita completely forgotten. My face burned with a blush that rose up as suddenly as a rogue wave. I buried my face in my hands, certain I was going to cry. What came from me instead of a sob was a loud peal of laughter. The men at the corner table now had another reason to stare.

Kristin shook off the shock like the practical woman she was. She took a long gulp of her margarita and watched me carefully, gauging my reaction and what might be appropriate to say. "Is this a good thing?"

I couldn't manage to answer. I was laughing too hard. I put my head on the table and gave in to it. The waiter came over to refill my glass and Kristin waved him away.

"Honey?" she asked tentatively, and I slowly got myself under control.

"I guess it has to be a good thing," I said.

"What are you going to do?"

"I'm going to have a baby."

"You're going to have it," she repeated.

"You know I don't believe in abortion. And how could I give it up, when I know I have the means to provide for it?"

"You wouldn't want to give it up anyway," she said. "It's his."

I thought about that. "I think it's more about me. That might sound selfish, but it's the truth. The baby is part of me."

Kristin nodded, and now her eyes were filled with tears. She reached over and laid her hand on mine. Her smile was still there, but this time it was so motherly that it took my breath away.

"Things happen when they are supposed to," she said.

The waiter came again, this time with our food. I dug in with relish, thinking about how things had changed in the last few months. I had ridden the rise with the hottest new superstar in the business, got romantically involved — against my better judgement, granted — and now here I was, pregnant with an unexpected baby and feeling surprisingly okay with that fact.

"I really do want this baby," I said again. Kristin had drained half her margarita.

"Good. Does he know yet?"

"I'm not sure how to tell him."

She dropped her lime wedge into the margarita and licked salt from the rim. "How do you think he will take it?"

How would Anthony take the news? The ink was barely dry on his divorce papers. His career was on a mercurial rise, and he might look at a child as a hindrance rather than a blessing. Nothing would tarnish that sex appeal faster than a kid on his hip and a woman on the sidelines.

We might be in love with each other, but I knew how the world worked and so did he. We didn't have much of a commitment that wasn't tied to the record label, and either one of us was free to walk.

"I have no idea how he will react to this," I said. "I'm still not sure how I'm reacting to it. Honest to God, sometimes I think I'm going batshit crazy."

"Not a far leap, sweetheart."

I grinned at her. "I'm just following your lead."

She snorted with laughter. "When are you going to tell him?"

"Soon." I dipped into the salsa. "Today."

I hadn't expected to do it today, but now that the words were out of my mouth, I knew I would. From the moment those two little pink lines showed themselves and confirmed what I already knew, the thought of telling him had been in the back of my mind, slowly pushing its way forward.

"Tonight," I said.

"Oh, to be a fly on that wall."

"Jason could probably rig up something to let you listen."

"He would require payment in sexual favours. No, thanks." She sat back in her seat and simply smiled at me, ignoring her meal, her drink, the waiter and even the men who were staring at her like she was the next coming of the Goddess.

"What?"

Her green eyes twinkled with pleasure.

"You're going to have a *baby*," she said.

"I'm going to have a baby."

"I'm…wow. I'm Auntie Kristin!"

"Your kids are going to be thrilled," I said. Justin was six and Destiny was eight, at the perfect ages to love the hell out of a new baby.

"I have to tell you, Janey, I know this hasn't been easy for you, and I know it's not the best time or the best circumstance…but you're going to have the most beautiful baby in the world, and I can't wait to meet her."

"What if it's a him?"

"I'll spoil the hell out of it either way. Imagine! Auntie Kristin!"

She reached over the table to squeeze my hand, and suddenly it all seemed very simple indeed.

* * * *

After a long dinner and more than a little discussion on the future, Kristin dropped me at my door with a kiss on the cheek and the assurance that I would do the right thing. I waited until her car was out of sight before I picked up the phone and called Anthony. He answered on the first ring.

"You missed me," he said in his friendly, arrogant way.

"Where are you and why aren't you here?"

"I thought you would never ask."

The speech I had prepared disappeared when Anthony

showed up on my doorstep. He climbed out of his truck and walked towards me without an umbrella. The rain drenched him as he made his way up to my wide front porch. Droplets fell from his hair. His T-shirt clung to him like a second skin.

"We have to get that off you before you catch cold," I said, already breathless.

Anthony grinned. "That's the idea."

I stripped the shirt from his body. Wetness from his hair dripped on my freshly polished hardwood floor. He brought with him the scent of rain and something else, a low and musky scent that was undeniably masculine. I buried my face in his neck to breathe in more of it. Anthony's hands were strong and broad against my back as he lowered me to the floor, right there in the open doorway.

I struggled out of my jeans. He pushed his own down just enough. He thrust deep and I rose up as we both cried out in pleasure. Then I was rolling with him and watching him from above as I rocked back and forth. My hands took their time in learning his body all over again, as if it had been months instead of just hours since I had last touched him. He lay back against the hardwood and watched as I explored every inch of his chest, as I rocked harder. When I finally exploded over him in a fury of pleasure, he was staring at my face, taking in every nuance of my passion and filing it away in his memory.

I slumped over him, almost spent. His heart thudded hard under my ear. He thrust up underneath me, and within three strokes he was over the edge. I both heard and felt his shout as he emptied himself into me.

"That was fast," I murmured when I got my breath back.

"I don't think I've done the two-minute thing since high school."

"Want to try the twenty-minute thing?"

"In about twenty minutes, sure."

"Welcome to my house."

He chuckled. "What a way to be introduced to it."

I cuddled close to his side. The door was still open and the wind was blowing water across the porch, but it wasn't blowing hard enough to reach us. I looked out at the driveway and the trees beyond, most of which were obscured by the grey cloud of rainy fog. Twilight was quickly giving up the ghost.

"How crazy our world is," I said softly.

"Why do you say that?"

I shrugged and his hand came down to caress my shoulder. "We work in a cutthroat business that threatens to drown us at every turn, but we both love it."

"And we love each other. Don't forget that most important part."

I sat up and looked down into Anthony's eyes. What I saw there was total trust. The jaded man I had met months ago had turned into an even more cynical one, but at the same time he had given me one chance after another to come through for him. And I had. In the world of the music business, we had found that almost impossible balance between the personal and the professional.

I hoped that would never change.

"How much do you love me, Anthony?"

Where I expected to see wariness flicker in his eyes, there was nothing but that trust and acceptance I had grown so accustomed to seeing. "More than you know," he said.

Tears stung my eyes. "I hope so," I whispered.

He was immediately alarmed. He came up off the floor to sit facing me, his hands on my arms, squeezing so tightly it almost hurt. He stared right into my eyes. "What's wrong, Janey? Has something happened?"

The words were there, but they wouldn't come. I shook my head.

"What's wrong?"

"Nothing is wrong," I said.

"You're crying…something's wrong!"

The panic in his voice shook me back to reason.

"I'm pregnant," I said.

The words hung between us for what seemed an eternity. Anthony stared at me without comprehending what he had just heard. He didn't react for a long moment, and when he did respond, he seemed almost disoriented with the shock.

"What did you just say?"

"I'm pregnant," I whispered.

Slowly the news sank in, and amazingly, the alarm in his eyes changed to something downright puzzling.

Anthony looked *relieved*.

"Thank God that's all," he said, and pulled me into his arms. He held me so tight it was hard to breathe. His knee nestled against my belly, right where his child was growing inside me. I struggled to loosen his grasp and stared up into his face.

"That's all?" I asked, incredulous.

"My God, I thought you were going to drop a *bombshell*. I thought something had happened to you, or you were sick, or something…just something horrible."

"This isn't horrible?"

Anthony threw his head back and laughed. "Hell, no! We can deal with this."

Sudden trepidation flooded me. "Deal with this?"

"Well, yeah."

"What do you mean?"

Now the wariness came over his features. His lips tightened and he took a deep breath. "What exactly were you planning on doing, Janey? We can't have it, for God's sake."

"Why not?"

"Because…" He paused and looked around the living room, as if the answer might be sitting on an end table somewhere. "I'm barely divorced."

"That doesn't matter," I said.

"We're not married."

"That matters even less."

"Then — well, what —"

"What did you expect, Anthony? For me to just scrape it

95

out like so much trash?"

He winced and pulled away from me. "Must you be so crude?"

"That's what we're talking about, isn't it? We're talking about getting rid of it."

Anthony stood and started to pace the living room. He angrily zipped up his jeans and shoved his hands into his pockets. I stayed where I was in the doorway and looked at him while he came to grips with the reality of the situation. Finally he stopped at the picture window and looked out at the rain.

"I've always been honest with you, Janey. I'm going to be honest now. It's about my career. It's about this thing I have been working so hard for all my life. I finally have it. I can feel it growing. It's my baby. I don't want any other baby taking the place of the one I already have."

All those things had gone through my head too, and I couldn't blame him for reacting in such a way. It was what I had expected, truth be told, but I hadn't expected him to come right out and say it. The fact that he had made me respect him even more.

"I appreciate that you are honest with me," I said.

"Then it's your turn," he said, still looking out the window. "What do you want to do?"

I watched him — the defiant set of his shoulders, the uneasy way he shifted his weight from one foot to another, and especially how careful he was about not looking in my direction. Anthony was much more frightened than he would ever admit.

"I want to keep it," I said softly. "This baby is part of me, and if that sounds arrogant, then so be it. I don't want to kill a part of me."

Anthony's shoulders suddenly slumped, as though all the fight had gone out of him when he heard my words. He covered his face with his hands and his voice broke. "I don't want to kill a part of me, either."

I rose from the floor and came to him. Anthony dropped

to the nearest sofa and I went with him, not touching him yet, letting him make the first move. His hands found mine and squeezed, then the sobs broke free. When he buried his head in my shoulder, I cradled him like a child and whispered into his ear as he cried. I felt entirely helpless as I thought about what I could say to ease the situation and came up completely empty.

"Nothing is mine anymore, Janey," he managed to say. "No decision is mine. I have everything I want and everyone else controls it. What is mine?"

I had wondered when this would come, the emotional backlash of sudden success. There was a reason those who seemed to have it all were the first ones to burn out. It was entirely possible to have everything and nothing at the same time. It was a lesson Anthony was quickly learning, no matter how much I had tried to shield him from it.

"Your life is yours," I said. "We can stop all of this right now, if that's what you want."

"No." He took a deep breath and tried to get himself under control. "That's not true. We can't stop it. This whole damn machine is moving along with or without me, and if I back out, it will cost me more than I can ever repay. I'm stuck, don't you see?"

I did see, but I would never let him know that I agreed with him. For the first time, my loyalty to Keith and to Axton Records was shaken by my loyalty to someone else.

"You can have a life and have a career," I insisted. "They don't have to be one and the same."

"Do you really believe that?"

"Yes."

"Why?"

I caressed his bare shoulder as I thought about it. "My life is separate from my career."

"Yeah, but what life?"

"What do you mean?"

"You're home now. When was the last time you were here, in your own house, your own space? You probably

97

know the inside of my tour bus better than you know your own house."

Redness crept over my face. He was right. I hadn't been home in months. I thought about the frenzy of cleaning, and even as I took a breath now, the scent of cleaning supplies filled the air.

"That's my fault," I admitted. "I work too much."

"You think a baby will change that?"

I was stung by his assumption that a baby would make everything better, as if I were a lost and lonesome teenager who just wanted someone to love, who would love me back. I wasn't a statistic. I was a full-grown woman making the choices that a woman sometimes had to make.

"Would slowing down be so bad?" I asked.

"Do you think it could change me, too?"

I took a deep breath. "We're going to find out."

"Are you sure?"

"I'm not going to get rid of it, Anthony."

He nodded and sniffled once before he kissed the back of my hand. "Good."

"Good?"

"Yes. How far along are you?"

I had given it quite a bit of thought. "About ten weeks, I think. I need to see the doctor as soon as I can get an appointment."

"Can I go with you?"

"Of course."

"Whatever you need, Janey, I'm there."

"I want you to know, I don't expect anything from you. I have my own money…"

"Don't go there," he said sharply. "This isn't just you. It's you and me. I don't tell a woman I love her and then walk away at the first sign of things getting tough. I'm better than that, and you damn well know it."

I smiled against his back.

"But I have to tell you, Janey," he said with a resigned sigh. "About all the rest of it. If this is the big time, I'm not sure I want it."

"Don't say that," I whispered, though I was thinking the exact same thing.

Chapter Seven

I woke the next morning with Anthony beside me. The phone was ringing on the bedside table. From somewhere in the front of the house, the merry ring of his cell phone chimed in. I rolled over and my body immediately protested, all the vigour of cleaning the house the day before coming back with a vengeance.

I groaned and stared at the caller ID through a haze of sleep. When I recognised the number of the studio, I flicked off the ringer and looked over at Anthony. He was awake and smiling at me like I had just done something ridiculously funny.

"What?"

Instead of answering, he rolled on top of me. He pulled the covers over us, completely blocking out the sunlight with a cocoon of cotton. From the far distance that was the living room, his cell phone began to ring again. He chuckled and nibbled at my ear. Already his hands were busy playing with other places. I stretched luxuriously under him, still warm and supple with sleep.

"I was supposed to be working last night," I said. "I still haven't done a lick of paperwork."

"You poor thing."

His tongue made its way down the centre of my chest. I reached up and grasped the headboard with both hands. My legs fell open to him as he worked his way down. His hands caressed my thighs as his breath fell over every secret part of me. Then his tongue followed the way his breath had gone, and I sighed with the pleasure of it.

"So much for work," I said with a laugh.

The buzzer sounded in the living room. The security panel beeped. There was someone at the outer gate, hoping I would open it up and allow them inside. I closed my eyes and tried to focus on what Anthony was doing, but my brain wouldn't let me. It was already moving in a dozen different directions.

"Anthony."

He hummed a reply. The vibration of it went right through my centre and I gasped in surprise. I reached down and twined my hands through his hair. When I lifted my hips to him, he slipped his hands under my thighs, pulling me up higher and holding me steady for what his tongue was doing. And that tongue was doing a lot—he had spent plenty of time learning just what I liked, and those lessons had paid off in spades. He flicked his tongue back and forth until I was on the verge of an orgasm, then pulled back to tease me with his soft, full lips.

"Don't stop," I whimpered the third time he did it. Anthony looked up from between my thighs. His eyes were bright. He watched every reaction of my body as he brought his fingers up and slid two of them inside me. I ground against him.

"Come," he said quietly, and I did, clenching his hair in my hands and howling as the pleasure rocketed through me. Before the orgasm was gone, Anthony was sliding up between my thighs, slamming himself into the place that was already so wet and throbbing.

"Maybe if I come deep enough, I can make you pregnant," he teased.

I weakly punched his chest and laughed as he started to move. There was no lingering—I had mine, now he wanted his, and that was just fine with me. I wrapped my legs around his waist and played with his nipples, kissed his neck and whispered naughty things into his ear until he threw his head back and came, uttering my name through gritted teeth.

He collapsed beside me and hauled me into the warm

spoon of his body. Now that passion had been sated, the only thing on my mind was sleep. I was almost there when Anthony's cell phone chimed from the living room.

"Again?" I sighed.

"Make them go away," he moaned.

We listened until the chiming stopped. I stared at the clock for a moment while Anthony stretched behind me. I watched the numbers change.

"We've got work to do," he mumbled, sounding like a petulant child who didn't want to go to school. He lay there for another long moment before he resigned himself to a long day and pulled himself out of bed. He walked into the bathroom and flipped on the light. I watched his tight buttocks through the doorway and smiled.

"Towels are in the cabinet to the right," I said. "Shampoo and everything else, too."

He got what he needed and started the shower. When I thought he was already under the water, he poked his head out the door and looked at me. "Well? What are you waiting for?"

I climbed out of bed and joined him under the too-hot spray. I watched as he washed his hair, the muscles in his arms moving under his smooth, tanned skin. Once he was done, he started to wash mine. I leaned in to him, gave myself over to it, my eyes closed and my body limp. The massage of his fingertips on my scalp was like heaven.

"Remember the first time we were in the shower together?" he asked.

"Mmm-hmm."

"You slapped me."

"You deserved it."

He kissed my nose and gently pushed me away from him. "Get under the water and let me get this shampoo out."

The time for leisure was over. We quickly finished our shower, dressed – Anthony's clothes were still slightly damp, but he didn't seem to care – and got in his truck to go to the studio. I took along my laptop and some paperwork that was begging for attention. The fun part of my job was out on the road, but the tedious work still had to be seen to while I was jetting all over the country. I was determined to get that work done. If Anthony proved to be too much of a distraction, I would come back home.

When we opened the door to the studio, we were met by a very angry Jason.

"Where the hell were you?" He ignored me completely and instead homed in on Anthony. "Our work today began at eight. Eight sharp. Not nine, or ten, or whenever you found it convenient to drag your lazy ass out of bed."

Anthony settled a bored stare on Jason. There was no love lost between them, and already he knew how to push Jason's buttons. "I'm here now. Are we ready?"

"We were ready an hour ago," Jason reiterated. "You lost a bundle of money today, buddy."

"So are we going to talk or are we going to work?"

Jason glared at him and for the first time, glanced over at me. I blushed as Jason's gaze took in the dishevelled clothes, the wet hair and the fact we had both arrived in one vehicle. He gave us both a sneer that spoke volumes, but his words were directed towards me.

"You look like you've been rode hard and put up wet."

I refused to justify his jab with a response. When he didn't get a word out of me, he turned his ire back to Anthony. "I hope the tumble was worth it."

"It was," Anthony shot back.

Jason turned on his heel and walked into the studio, not bothering to hold the door for either one of us. It swung closed in Anthony's face.

"I would love to beat the shit out of him right now," Anthony said.

"I'm sure the feeling is mutual."

"He's just in a jealous snit."

"But he's right." I suddenly found myself in the position of being an advocate for the very thing we had shunned only an hour before. "You should have been here on time.

It's bad for the bottom line and bad for the reputation if you don't keep the commitments."

Anthony shot me a look, and I shrugged. "Hey, I'm at fault too," I admitted. "I wasn't exactly gung-ho about answering the phone or even setting the alarm, was I?"

He smiled. "That means you wanted me too much to think of such mundane things."

I chuckled and pushed my way through the door before him. The studio musicians were sitting in their seats, waiting. They all greeted Anthony with cheer, and why not? His lateness was of no concern to them—they got paid by the hour, regardless of whether he showed up or not.

Anthony walked to his booth and pulled the headset off the stand. Sheet music lay in disarray on the chair. His guitar sat in the corner, gleaming even in the muted overhead lights.

He put on the headset, adjusted the mic and picked up the guitar. The first few chords rang out, and the other musicians sat to attention, their instruments primed and ready.

"Play me a song, music man," one of them said, and at the tiniest signal from Jason, the parts began to fall into place. I set my laptop and paperwork down on the already cluttered counter and watched through the glass. Jason ignored me completely. Every bit of his attention was focused on the soundboard in front of him. He adjusted one level after another before stepping back and listening to the sound with a critical ear.

I sat back in the chair and watched, mesmerised, as the magic began to happen.

It took a long time to get the tracks absolutely perfect. Jason was meticulous about pitch, speed, tone. He wasn't one to hand out praise, so when he said nothing, a player could take it as a compliment. Anthony could hold his own with the other men in the room, which Jason seemed to appreciate. They worked for over an hour on the bridge of a tune, then moved to something else when they were all reaching a point of frustration. Jason had a knack for keeping their mindset in the right place. When he said it was time for lunch, I was surprised to find that two hours had passed. I hadn't glanced once at the clock.

"I'm going to have to go home to work," I told Anthony out in the parking lot. "I'm too enamoured with this whole process. I'll never get any writing done while I'm sitting here watching."

Anthony nodded. He opened my door and I climbed into the truck. Jason was walking down the sidewalk, and he turned to drop one last comment. "Don't keep him away from what he has to do, Janey. You can always fuck later."

Anthony slammed the door before I could answer. He walked to his side and didn't give Jason a second glance, but he put the pedal to the metal as he tore out of the parking lot.

"Slow down."

"He pisses me off," Anthony said by way of explanation.

"Okay, so he does. Do you have to kill us because of it?"

The needle on the speedometer edged back into the land of sanity.

"Does he have to be so fucking anal?"

"He's got a tight ship to run, and this morning didn't help."

"Just as long as he lays off you," Anthony said. "I know what he's thinking."

"It doesn't matter," I said, and put my hand on his thigh as he drove. "Things are different now, don't you think?"

"I don't want him thinking he's going to take you away from me."

I looked at Anthony in surprise. He stared straight ahead at the lunch-hour traffic until he was stopped by a red light, then he glanced over at me. His hand landed on top of mine and he squeezed it gently.

"I'm not going anywhere," I murmured.

"Good."

Back at home, I fired up the laptop and settled in to finish a report that had been sitting idle for weeks. I listened to the messages on my machine and made notes on who to call back and who to ignore. I paid bills online then started writing again. By the time I stopped, it was almost dinner time and my stomach was growling.

I laid my hands over my belly and leant back in the chair. I wasn't showing yet, but soon I would be. Would Anthony be proud to see that? What would we say to people who asked the inevitable questions about our relationship and our future plans? I had made it clear that I wasn't going anywhere, and Anthony seemed to feel the same way. But a baby suddenly gave everything a sense of urgency, a need to know exact plans.

There was nothing in the refrigerator, so I made a call to the Chinese place. While I waited, I sat down to make a grocery list. I had to spend more time at home, no matter how much Axton Records needed me to be out on the road. When the baby did come, my work for the label would shift to accommodate that. I would take on more paperwork to justify my salary. I had already decided I didn't want to raise my child on a tour bus, rumbling from one city to another until I wasn't sure where we were anymore. Some people did it and made it work, but I didn't think I would be one of them.

Chinese arrived and I dived right in. I went through the General Tso's chicken like it was nothing, then munched on a fortune cookie while I sat in front of the laptop again. I had done the work I needed to do for the day; I could spend a few minutes having a bit of fun.

I logged on to the Internet and did a Google search on Anthony's name. Hundreds of entries came up, most of them reviews of the single, but there were a few that seemed to be from message boards. One of them in particular was going strong already, and Anthony's own board hadn't been completed yet. I looked at the member stats and uttered a laugh of surprise.

Nine-hundred-and-forty-one members.

Young and old, they couldn't get enough of him. And they were overwhelmingly women, with screen names like *MrsAnthony* or *AnthonysMuse* or *All4LuvAK*. They might have been silly names with little more than a lot of silly things to say, but those message boards were an appropriate gauge of how popular he was becoming.

One particular message caught my eye — *New York tickets already sold out?*

They had to be kidding. I opened the message and scrolled. My scepticism turned to shocked disbelief. Sold out? Already? But those tickets for the New York show went on sale today, didn't they? I looked at the calendar then back at the message board in amazement.

After a bit of research, I realised it wasn't just the New York dates. There were dates all across the nation, Anthony's first tour, and a small one at that. The venues were selling out within hours. More dates would surely be added within days of a sell-out like this.

I looked at the calendar. The days he was home were highlighted in yellow. I counted them, which was easy enough to do at a glance. Five days during the month of June. I flipped to July. Six days.

I sat back in the chair and watched the posts pile up on the message board.

I was waiting for him that night when the session was over. I had a hunch he would come back to my house instead of his, and sure enough, I was right. He pulled into the driveway and only then did I push the button that would close the gates and lock away the rest of the world. It was a curious feeling to watch his truck pull right up to the steps, as though he were comfortable here already, and I gave myself a moment to indulge in the fantasy, Anthony coming home to me, to his child, all of us a family without any worries about tours, albums, charts and when the next flight left the airport.

Anthony pulled a duffel bag from the back of his truck and smiled at me as he came up the stairs. He must have been reading my mind.

"We've got to get a place that is ours."

I raised an eyebrow. "Ours, huh?"

Anthony walked right past me into the bedroom, where he dropped the bag. Then he turned and took me into his arms. He kissed me with enough passion to take my breath away. We stood there for the longest time, kissing and swaying and kissing some more, letting the fire build. Just as I had enough of the teasing and pushed him back towards the bed, his stomach growled. We both laughed at the unexpected interruption.

"How hungry are you?" I asked.

He gave me an apologetic look. "Starving. I couldn't eat anything for lunch."

"Me too. But there's nothing in the house to cook."

"We have to fix that problem, too."

Anthony walked into the kitchen and stopped dead in his tracks. He took in the stainless steel appliances, the wide slate counters and the glassware in the open-faced cabinets. His eyes lingered on the enormous island in the middle of the room, the copper pots creating a chandelier of sorts above it all, and the table suitable for eight. "Wow."

"Too bad I don't have enough time to use it all," I said. "I've been on the road for the last six months with some guy who needed a babysitter."

Anthony snorted in amusement and walked around the kitchen island. He touched the copper pots and watched them gently sway. "We're going to have to make some changes, Janey. I can't imagine having a baby out on the road. That's not where a child should grow up, don't you think?"

I sat down on one of the high bar stools that surrounded the island. "You read my mind. I was thinking the same thing earlier today."

"Some people can do it, but I don't think I'm in that position yet. But where does that leave us? I want you there with me, but I know someone has to take care of the baby. And even that bothers me, because it should be a joint effort. I don't want to go out on the road and leave you as the only one here to take care of our kid."

I shrugged and played with a salt shaker. "Sometimes that has to be the way it works, Anthony. My job allows me to stay home, but your job calls you out across the country. I appreciate that you want to be here, but we'll just have to make sure you get home as often as you can." The word *home* tasted warm and sweet on my tongue.

"How often is that?" he asked. "Seriously, Janey. Things are different now. There's more than just me to consider. What do you see happening with my schedule?"

I watched him as he looked out the window. "Your shows are selling out," I said softly. His back stiffened as he took in the words. Even a day ago this news would have been reason to rejoice, but now his happiness was tempered by things that mattered more. He turned to me with eyes that gave away nothing.

"You sure?"

I nodded. "I spent some time snooping around your fan message boards," I said.

"I actually have those?"

"You would be amazed."

His lips curled into a grin. "Stalking me online. Awesome."

"I think they probably know things that even the label doesn't know yet. The tickets for the New York show were sold out in hours. Keith probably has a machine full of messages that he hasn't had time to check, but once he does, more shows will be added."

"You know that for sure?"

"It's too much of a gold mine to not make that move. Strike while the iron is hot, so they say."

"You know what's funny? I spent years wanting to hear something like that. Shows sold out. Tour a massive success. Groupies swarming like flies. Too busy to breathe. Now that I have it, it's different than I imagined."

"You didn't imagine a kid in the picture," I said. "It

changes things."

Anthony gripped the edge of the counter and leaned over it. "I'm going to be on the road nonstop for the next six months, at least, Janey. What can we do?"

"We make it work," I said. "I fly out as often as possible."

"I don't fly in?"

"How can you?"

"It's not fair that you are the one doing all the work here," he said.

I understood his need to be noble, to do the right thing, and that included doing his part. But there were realities of the situation we couldn't deny. I wasn't the kind of woman who had to have him around all the time, and I wasn't a shrinking wallflower who couldn't handle a baby on my own. I had been prepared to have the child with or without his help, and that would serve me in good stead, I was sure. Being in a relationship with a musician on the road was, in fact, quite like being a single mother. I had seen other women go through it, and I knew it was no picnic...but I also knew there was only so much Anthony could do.

"It's both of us," I said. "If we want to make this work, it's going to be hard. Really hard. You have to be on the road, and I have to take care of this child. It means we have to make decisions we might not want to make. I don't mean to insult you, and I hope I don't — but I don't think you have any idea of how hard this is going to be."

He nodded, deferring to my experience and opinion. "Was it like this with David?"

I thought back to the way things had been with David. It was a constant whirlwind, jets going from one city to another, the convoy of trucks following, the two-day setup in arenas when he hit the big time. Even when he had an open space on the schedule, it was usually filled with radio interviews and photo shoots and lunches with people the label considered very important to his career. His free time didn't happen until just hours before the show, then he needed to sleep to make up for the time he would miss that night, when the show ran long. Then he had so many obligations afterwards, before he climbed onto another plane and went to yet another city. The only time we'd had together was during those brief hours when I was alone on the bus with him, and those vacations we managed to sneak in whenever he had a three-day break in the middle of the madness.

"David and I didn't have a baby," I said, and Anthony shook his head.

"But his life. It was too chaotic to even think about having a child. Mine is going that same way, isn't it?"

I reached over and took his hand, yet said nothing. What could I say?

He shook his head again. "Be careful what you wish for, huh?"

"We'll make it work."

"Let's get dinner and talk more. I need to talk about this. I'm scared, Janey."

I looked up into his eyes. I wasn't surprised at all that he was scared, but I was surprised he admitted it so freely. I appreciated that he knew when he needed help and that he wasn't afraid to ask for it. We would do a lot of talking in the days and weeks ahead, and I was scared of how we were going to make things work, too — but at least we knew we were on the same page.

"I want Mexican. I'm craving Mexican like crazy right now."

Anthony boosted himself away from the counter. "My pregnant woman gets whatever my pregnant woman wants."

I laughed. "That's a good way to look at things."

111

Chapter Eight

The plane touched down in Seattle and I watched as Anthony jogged across the tarmac and slipped into a waiting car. He was two hours behind schedule and had to either catch up or cancel something, and cancelling was a last-resort option. I stepped off the plane into fifty-degree weather and pulled my jacket closer around me.

Anthony had been going hard and solid for the last two months, and I was starting to wonder if he could possibly keep up the insane pace. He fell into bed at night in some hotel room and slept hard, but then was up at an ungodly hour to do the local morning show, wherever that might be. Then he pressed the flesh until the hours began to wind into one another, and that was all before it was time for the show to start. He wouldn't lay his head on his own pillow for at least another month, assuming all went well.

Lately he had been acting more and more distant, an expected result of being burned out. But on the stage every night he seemed to remember what he was there for, and delivered a show that put the first ones I had seen to shame. He finally knew his music was a hit, and it gave him a groove that was missing before, a confidence that was a thrill to watch. The album was ready for release, the single was at the top of the charts, and the video was the highest requested on country music stations for the third straight week. It gave Anthony's music a razor-sharp edge that glistened under the stage lights.

I had been on the road with him for three days this time. This was the last day I could afford before I had to board a plane that would take me back home, away from wherever

Anthony was going next. He had good people around him—Tom, his new manager, was superb at handling the little details and giving Anthony as much time as possible to rest between obligations—but it wasn't the same as me being there and taking care of him. Taking care of him had suddenly become much more important than taking care of the interests of the label.

I watched the scenery roll by as the car took me and two others to the hotel. Angela sat in the far seat, working through notes and phone numbers written on a little notepad in front of her. Joey, the publicist, sat in between us, talking quietly on a cell phone. I had a pile of magazines in my lap and a dozen thank-you notes to send to journalists, but I wasn't thinking of that. I was rubbing my belly and watching the industrial park roll by while I thought about the many years it would take before Anthony could settle down a bit more and spend time with his family.

Family was a concept I was just beginning to grasp. That meant not being alone anymore, giving up some of my independence for want of something more. I had always felt that being the strong, solid woman who could handle herself and everything around her was the place I truly belonged, but since my body had begun changing I had been looking at things from a completely different perspective. I no longer saw my solitude as the best way to live my life. I wanted Anthony in so many ways, but the dearest longing was to simply share everything with him. For someone who had been aloof to relationships even when she was in one, it was both a heady and frightening thing to realise.

I looked back at the two people beside me. Joey was a confirmed bachelor, going on forty with no plans to settle down—ever. Angela had a husband, but I never saw him. Considering how often she was home, she probably never saw him, either. She didn't have children. Suddenly I wanted to ask her why she hadn't, and had she ever regretted it?

My thoughts were cut short when the car turned into

the parking garage underneath the hotel. We went from sunlight to darkness in an instant. The car went down, around a curve, then abruptly stopped. A well-dressed man opened the door and ushered us to an elevator. We were taken straight to a suite of rooms, where a dozen people were milling around. Half of them were busier than they could stand and the other half seemed bored out of their minds. Quick introductions were made, and I struggled to remember names.

I ducked into the nearest bathroom as soon as I could gracefully break free. I had somehow managed to avoid most of the nausea that so often came with early pregnancy, and I was thankful for that—but I hadn't managed to miss the boat on the constant trips to the bathroom. Sometimes I felt as though I were growing a water cooler in there instead of a child.

Staring at myself in the bathroom mirror, I rubbed the bump of my belly—still small yet—and listened to the jumble of voices just outside the door. I used to be right in the thick of such discussions. Now I knew what would happen. They would shut their mouths as soon as I opened the door, because I was no longer one of them. Now I was the woman who was sleeping with the talent, and furthermore, I was the woman who was carrying his baby.

Sure enough, the conversation became awkward when I emerged from the cocoon of the bathroom. I excused myself, found a quiet corner and sat with my laptop, studiously ignoring everyone around me. I fired up the email and began sending out thank-you notes, each one of them with a personal touch, something I had learned early on was the best way to make a busy journalist remember you.

I was halfway through the stack when I looked up to see a woman in a business suit. She was leaning over the counter of the kitchenette. With a rolled-up bill, she snorted a line of white powder from a compact mirror. She took a deep breath, licked her lips, then snorted another one. She shook her head, snapped the mirror closed—it was now clean as a whistle—and slipped it into her pocket before walking away.

I watched the place where she had been. Cocaine and other drugs were the mainstay of big tours, no matter how hard the principal players fought to keep it all clean. It wasn't unusual to step into a room and inhale the sweet aroma of a freshly smoked joint, or to see the story in the dilated, wild eyes of a band member. Most of the time the drug use was never mentioned. How else could mere mortals make it through a schedule that tried to kill them at every opportunity?

I thought about Anthony and the unbelievable schedule he was on, the nights when he only slept two hours or so, and the way his eyes looked right before he went onstage. He was dead tired but still, he kept going. Going and going and going.

Like he had a battery inside him, revving him up.

I looked out the window at the city street below. The people buzzed along the sidewalk, in a hurry to get somewhere, each one with their own individual lives, their own hobbies, their own fears and doubts and joys. I found myself wondering how many of them were pregnant. How many of them were uncertain of their futures. How many of them were snorting a line now and then, or shooting up with something that made their heart race and their eyes go glassy.

I pulled my eyes back to the computer screen, but all I could see was Anthony.

It was possible. Wasn't it?

An hour later Tom came rushing into the room, followed by an entourage of the management team. Anthony was right in the middle of them, ushered along like a golden prize. He was trying hard to ignore all that was happening around him—his iPod buds were stuck deep in his ears and he was trying to avoid eye contact. He looked tired. The laugh lines around his eyes and mouth were deeper than they had been in a while. But when he saw me, his whole attitude changed.

"Janey." Anthony took me into his arms and kissed me. He pulled the earphones out of his ears and kissed me again. His hand dropped to my belly and he teased the little spot where my innie belly button had started to become an outie.

"How was it?" I asked.

"They loved me."

"They aren't the only ones."

Anthony grinned down at me. His eyes gave away nothing but how tired he was. I watched Tom as he talked on his cell phone, always keeping Anthony within his sight. Angela was waiting patiently for us to finish our little reunion. She had a stack of photos in her hand—it had almost become her trademark—and she was twirling a pen between her fingers. The others in the room kept sneaking glances at Anthony, as if they were trying to pay attention to business and were fighting the presence of the giddy fan that still lingered deep underneath the polished appearance.

"You've got more work to do," I said gently, and he turned to Angela. She smiled and patted his shoulder as she laid the glossy photos on the table.

"You can put her in your lap while you sign these." She gave me a coy wink.

Anthony did just that. He opened a new box of Sharpie markers. The smell hit my nose and made me pleasantly lightheaded. Anthony signed the photos with his usual flourish. His signature was starting to come apart a bit— months ago every letter in his name was clear, and now it was disintegrating into longer lines and illegible scribble.

Anthony finished signing another one and held it up. We both looked at his image. This one was of him standing against a wall, dressed sexy and pouting with insolence, giving the camera the kind of look that said he was ready for anything, especially if that anything included a nice shot of liquor and a warm, soft woman.

"How many of those do you think you've signed?" I

asked.

"More than I care to count. Sometimes my hand hurts."

"Really?"

He shrugged. "It never hurt from playing guitar, so it must be from signing so much shit."

"Anthony," Angela chided from the window, where she was listening intently to someone on the other end of her cell phone. She was biting on a nail when she wasn't writing something down.

"It's true. It's your fault."

Angela rolled her eyes at him. Anthony flung a glossy her way, and she caught it neatly in the air. She gave it a cursory look and flung it back. It sailed like a Frisbee onto the floor at Anthony's feet. "You forgot to sign that."

Anthony grinned and bent back to his work. Angela was one of the few people on the tour who didn't treat him with kid gloves. In fact, she treated him more like a little brother than someone she was responsible for handling, and he loved that about her.

Anthony finished the stack—including the one Angela had flung onto the floor at his feet—then someone handed him a cell phone. He had a ten-minute interview with a journalist in Atlanta. Would he like to make the call in private? Hangers-on were ushered out of the room and I listened as Anthony answered all the usual questions. It was all the same, every single time, and I wondered how he stood the constant repetition.

"He must dream about those questions in his sleep," I told Angela.

"I don't know how he does it, either."

We were standing near the window, watching Anthony. No one else was around, which was definitely a small miracle. If I was going to talk to her about anything on my mind, now was a good time to do it.

"I wonder about you sometimes," I said. "I wonder how you handle it all."

Angela smiled. "I knew this was coming."

117

"Why?"

"Because you've got that lost look about you. What's on your mind?"

I decided to give it to her straight instead of trying for finesse. "How do you handle being married and being on the road all the time? Your husband never sees you."

Angela thought about that for a long moment. "No. But we talk all the time, three or four times a day. And we live for the times when I am home."

"What does he do?"

"He's a schoolteacher. High school."

"So that's why he doesn't travel with you."

"Yeah. He works all the time, even when he seems to have a break. When it comes to time, most schoolteachers have just as little of it as we do. He even picks up a few summer classes at the universities in town."

"How long have you been married?"

She smiled. "Ten years, this fall."

"I worry about me and Anthony," I said.

"You two are solid," she answered firmly, as though there was no doubt.

"Yes, but…"

The silence hung in the air as Angela looked at me. Her eyes were wise. "It's different when he's out here," she admitted. "You know he's busy. But once this dies down, he's going to realise how much *else* is out there. The groupies can be a problem."

I knew she was being just as straight with me as I had been with her, and I knew about the danger of groupies just as well as she did, but hearing the truth of it still stung. I watched Anthony as he walked around the room, talking on the cell phone and acting like the journalist had just asked him the most interesting question, even though we had heard him answer it a hundred times before. The thought came, completely unbidden, of what he looked like naked, of his strong muscles and flat stomach and broad chest. I remembered the first time I had seen it — that was only hours after I first met him.

I shook my head vehemently, knocking the memories away.

"I'm not saying it will happen," Angela said. "I'm saying, it's going to take a lot of trust and a lot of communication to make sure it doesn't."

"Has it happened to you?" I asked directly.

Angela winced, but didn't back away from the question.

"Things happen."

"You've cheated?"

Angela looked out the window and bit her lip. "No. It wasn't like that. It wasn't…it wasn't me."

"And you stayed with him?"

"We learned to accept and to compromise," she said. "I was never around. I was always out on this jet-setting life, and he was at home alone most of the time. No matter what the marriage counsellors like to tell you, it's almost impossible to sustain certain aspects of a relationship while one person is not present to make it happen. It's like those men who went away for years during World War II. Did the women at home really think they had been faithful all that time?"

I sat heavily in the chair. Anthony walked by and ran a hand through my hair, distracted by his phone call. When he was on the other side of the room again, Angela looked at me as though she had something to say. I beat her to the punch.

"It's not just groupies," I said. "I worry more about the rest of it."

"The rest of it."

"Don't tell me you don't know what I'm talking about."

Angela considered for a moment. "I know what you're thinking."

"He's not sleeping. He's not eating. But when it's show time, he's hitting on all cylinders and then some. The energy has to be coming from somewhere."

Just then, Anthony closed the phone and came to me,

where he got down on his knees and laid his head in my lap. Angela turned away, but not before I caught her look of motherly concern when her eyes landed on Anthony.

"I'm so tired," he said.

* * * *

The show that night was loud and rowdy. The radio station had offered a contest with the prize being a helicopter ride to the venue, and rumours went through the crowd that Anthony would show up in the helicopter, too. All eyes were focused on the sky while the disc jockey made grandiose introductions. Anthony sat quietly in the back of the venue, watching it all on a big-screen television and eating chips methodically, one at a time, two bites for each one. I watched him, unduly fascinated by this, when three members of the security team ran past us, their radios squawking with panicked tones. Another security guy stood guard at the door to the room where Anthony and I were sitting.

"What's wrong?" I asked the guard, and he gave me a look that said it was none of my business, that they would take care of it all and no one would ever be the wiser.

I turned back to Anthony and watched as he downed half of his water bottle in one gulp. His eyes were bright and glassy.

"Anthony?"

He looked at me. It seemed to take a moment for his eyes to focus—only a split second, and I wondered if I had imagined it. His gaze was sharp and alive.

"What?"

I stared at his eyes. "Nothing."

He grinned and kissed my chin.

"You're so cute," he said, and went back to his chips. He watched the screen intently. The helicopter was landing in the middle of the field outside the venue, and the crowd was going wild. Their disappointment when they didn't see Anthony emerge ran through the crowd as a long, low moan. Then everyone turned to the stage again, and there was a sudden forward rush that made security scramble.

Anthony stood, grabbed his guitar from the stand in the corner and reached for me. He kissed me, long and hard, and held me against him for a moment. He was rock-hard behind his jeans, and I suddenly realised it had been over a week since we had made love.

"I'll wait for you on the bus after the show," I murmured into his ear, and he pulled me even closer.

"Good. I've got something to give you."

Anthony winked at me and was out the door. I watched on the big screen as the crowd built themselves up to a fury of anticipation. Security rushed to the front and sides. The lights went down and a spotlight came up. Anthony's voice, beautiful and clear, soared out over the crowd. For a moment, they all stopped and stared in awe, and a lull overcame them as Anthony sang into the microphone.

Then the drums kicked in, and the crowd went insane.

I watched from backstage as it all happened out front. Anthony was everywhere, prowling the stage like a cat in heat. He grabbed the microphone, swung the guitar behind his back and hit his knees at the edge of the stage. Women screamed and reached for him, running their hands along his denim-clad thighs. He stayed there just long enough for them to get the feel of him into their memory, then he was up and wandering to the other side of the stage, dancing as he went. His body was in constant motion, his voice now and then breathy with the effort, but the occasional missed word simply made him seem sexier.

Cameras flashed everywhere, a blinding sea of light.

Then Anthony was at the centre, putting the microphone back in the stand. He swung his guitar up with one smooth, fluid motion and started playing lead. The other guitarist fell back into rhythm as Anthony took over. The men in the crowd stared at Anthony's hands, watched as they flew across the strings. The sound wailed from the speakers stacked at the back and sides of the stage. The crowd sang along and clapped their hands over their heads. It was a rally of music and lust. Anthony swung his hips and the guitar swung with them, throwing glints of light off the polished red sheen. His hair grew damp. His shirt pulled tight across hardened muscles, rode up his arms, especially when he stopped to throw a guitar pick into the crowd. The fine sheen of sweat on his body shone with a soft glow under the stage lights. His smile was infectious.

I found myself staring at the screen, breathing hard, my whole body alive and singing with desire. "My God, you're beautiful," I whispered.

The women swayed with the love songs and danced with the fast ones. The audience was dotted with blue light as they opened up their cell phones to let faraway friends listen. Anthony pulled up a stool and sat down in a mellow spotlight, just him and his guitar, and the crowd quieted enough to hear the subtle nuances of his deep voice. He poured everything he had into the songs, and by the time the last note sounded, everyone listening was in the palm of his hand.

He looked at the crowd, leaned close to the microphone and smiled.

"It's so good to be here," he said.

I watched through the entire show. The encore proved he knew his music and he had the chops to play it all. He swung from Johnny Cash to Ricky Skaggs to the Rolling Stones and back to Ronnie Milsap. Most of the crowd was too young to follow the lyrics to those golden tunes, but they weren't too young to appreciate the skill with which Anthony delivered them. By the time the lights went down for that final bow, he had turned them into believers.

The band came down the aisle just outside the door. I slipped out and ran to the bus, where dozens of women were already waiting. When they caught sight of me, the rumbles of dissatisfaction were loud and clear. When security let me through without even looking for my pass, a wave of anger and speculation rose through the crowd. The questions of who I was and what I was doing there were loud enough that I could hear them through the blackened windows. Once behind the door, I breathed a sigh of relief. I walked to the bathroom, flipped on the light and stared at myself in the harsh, unforgiving glare of the full-length mirror.

Anthony was the golden child, the new face of Axton Records and perhaps the man who would take country music to new levels. He was that hero that was always whispered about up and down the Row, the one all the labels were searching for, the one who would take the genre to the next level and make it even more competitive in an already saturated market. I was the one who had found him, pulled him in and set him on that road to stardom.

Now that part was done. What did I have left to offer him?

I stared at the woman in the mirror. I was going on thirty, at least ten years older than the average woman out there in the parking lot. I was four months gone with a child, and my shape was already changing into that of a more mature, seasoned woman. I had responsibilities, a mortgage and a job that needed my attention. I wasn't wild and free, not like those women out there who were offering him all a man could ever want, with no strings attached.

I had wanted Anthony to fulfil his dreams, and along with that came fame. Now he had it, and he also had the perks that went with it. I felt as though I might be left behind.

I stared at my own eyes until they started to blur in the mirror. Then I took a deep breath and reminded myself that I was here with him, I was the one on the bus, and it was his child in my belly. I reminded myself of the first time he told me he loved me, and of the plans we had for making a life together, and of the house he was planning to build for us to share.

None of those groupies out there had that, did they? None of them even had an inkling of his plans, his devotion, and his desire to be the best father — and partner — he could be.

I reminded myself of that and waited for it to make me feel better.

I thought about it all as I removed every stitch of clothing. I looked at my belly in the mirror, at the new, gently rounded shape. My breasts were heavier than they had ever been, and the nipples were wider. My hips were the same slim silhouette, but my waist was just a little thicker. My face was flushed with the glow that had become so usual lately. I didn't look like one of those twenty-something women out there anymore. Now I looked like who I was, a woman in her thirties who was expecting a child, who was moving into a new phase of her life, and who was happy to be doing so.

I turned off the bathroom light and looked at my body in the shadows.

In the back of the bus, I felt more secure. The bed was covered with clothes and odds and ends. I dropped them all on the floor and lay down under the blankets just as the screams and squeals started. I knew Anthony was out there, signing autographs and touching hands. Within minutes he was on the bus, the door closing with a whoosh behind him.

"Where are you?" he asked, even as he came down the hallway.

I lay back on the pillows and looked up at him. He grinned and lifted the hem of his shirt to pull it over his head. His arms were strong and powerful, the muscles hard from hours of moving around the stage. The little softness in his belly was gone, replaced by ripples of muscle. Though he was still slender and lithe, the shape of his body was changing in ways that made my heart beat a little faster.

"I need a shower," he said, and I shook my head.

"You need to come to bed."

Anthony's grin grew broader. I lifted the blanket and he climbed in with me. His body was hotter than mine, warm with lights and energy and sweat. I ran my hands down his back and pulled him close to me as his mouth came down over mine. He kissed me lazily, as though we had all the time in the world and there wasn't a crowd of people outside the door. His hand slid from my breasts to my belly and lingered there while he nibbled on my lower lip.

"I like knowing you're pregnant with my baby," he whispered. "It's sexy as hell to know I put that child inside you. It makes me want you more than I ever did."

His words were the perfect antidote to the doubts I had experienced just moments before he walked in. I arched into his hand and lifted a leg across his hip, giving him access to whatever he might want. Anthony recognised the invitation and slid his hand between my thighs. His fingers pushed hard against the wetness he found there.

"You're mine," he said. His lips found my neck and his teeth bit down, leaving a mark and making me gasp in surprise. "Mine."

Anthony moved over me. All ideas of foreplay were forgotten as he pushed into me, filling me completely. He was hard and thick, his whole body tense, every muscle primed to move. He thrust once and rocked the bed. I put my hands on the headboard to hold myself steady, then he was moving hard and deep, with a single-minded purpose.

I lifted my hips to accommodate him and ground against him as he pushed harder and harder. Soon he was going at me so hard that the line between pleasure and pain had blurred. Just when I thought I couldn't take another moment of it, my body went over an edge I hadn't even realised was close, and I bit down hard on his shoulder while my whole being exploded from the inside out. The throbbing reached all the way to my toes. I had time to take a few deep breaths before Anthony pulled out and pushed me onto my knees.

I braced myself as he entered me from behind, his hands in my hair, his breath on my back. I pushed against him, taking more. When I whimpered with the pressure of it, he slowed down just enough to whisper, "Am I hurting you?"

"No."

"Should I stop?"

"Don't you dare stop."

He pushed my head down into the pillow. He moved forward, almost under me, and thrust at an upward angle. It hurt but it felt good too, and I cried out into the pillow with every thrust. I reached under my body and played with myself as he stroked harder and harder.

"I'm going to come."

I wasn't there yet, but that was just fine. I focused on the way he filled me, on the feeling of his body, so hard against mine, and the way I had to brace myself on my hands to keep from falling to the mattress. His hands tightened in my hair and his thrusts became jerky. He paused, thrust twice, then pushed as deep as he could.

I rose up to meet him. The rush of heat inside me was almost enough to send me to my own climax. Anthony held very still, holding his breath, until he had given me all he had inside him.

Then he collapsed over me, sending us both to the mattress. A tiny twinge of pain from low in my belly reminded me that it wasn't just the two of us in bed, and I shrugged Anthony's weight to the side. Spooning against me, he nuzzled my neck and his hands were everywhere, all over my sides and back and legs. He grabbed a handful of my hair and pulled me around for a kiss. His tongue slid out of my mouth and made a trail down my throat.

"More," he murmured. "I want more."

I rolled onto my side. Anthony pulled one leg up over his hip and pushed against me. He was still just as hard as he had been when he first slid into me. I turned my head and watched his eyes as he moved – those wild, bright, beautiful eyes that were now filled with desire. The motion of his body into mine made a private, crude sound of wetness. I grabbed him by his hair and led his mouth to one of my nipples, which he sucked hard enough to make me gasp in pain.

"Too hard…"

Anthony eased up. His tongue made circles on my flesh. His body kept moving into me, until the heat between us made me forget where I ended and where he began. The scent of sex filled my nose. Anthony was covered in sweat, and his breath was harsh against my skin. I lifted my leg higher, trying to take him deeper, and he responded by turning me onto my back and lifting both my knees over his shoulders.

The first thrust made me wince. "Can we do this?" he asked.

"Careful. I don't know how much I can take."

Anthony smiled as he slid in, taking his slow, luxurious time. "Your body is changing."

"Yes."

"I like that."

"What do you like about it?"

"I like that every time is a surprise. I never know what is going to be new this week."

"I like that, too."

"I like how your breasts look now. They're full. Ripe."

"Yeah?"

"Beautiful."

He pushed harder and harder, gauging my reactions by watching my face. When he knew I wasn't hurting, when he was sure I was enjoying myself, he thrust with all the power he wanted to use.

My hips burned. My thighs ached. A small twinge announced itself in a low corner of my belly. My back hurt from being bent almost double. But he was hitting that spot that made me go crazy, and my body told him so. My voice did too, in long moans that seemed to turn him on even more.

Anthony whispered naughty things into my ear as I started to come. It made the feeling last longer, made me cry out instead of moan. I throbbed around him, even as I watched him throw his head back and grit his teeth. He flooded me a second time, pushed as deep as he could go, claiming me in the most important way either one of us could imagine.

When he collapsed over me this time, it was with a satisfied sigh. Neither one of us spoke while we tried to get our breath back. I was almost surprised to hear the voices from outside the bus—I had completely forgotten where we were, or that anyone else existed at all.

"Did I hurt you?"

I smiled and cuddled into his arm. He was covered in sweat. My hair was damp with it. We would have to change and wash the sheets.

"You didn't hurt me."

I reached down to play with him. Anthony was still hard. The surprise of it moved me to stillness. We lay together, breathing in counterpoint, while thoughts raced through my head.

"I want it all the time," he said, his voice filled with what sounded for all the world like an apology.

I eased up and sat facing him. The wetness he had left spilled out of me and onto the sheets underneath us.

"That isn't like you," I said.

"I know."

"You don't go that often. It's just not the way your body is made."

Anthony didn't say anything. He reached out and traced an invisible line on my thigh.

"What's going on?"

He sat up with me. "I thought you might like the fact that I want to go all night long. All day, too."

"Depends on what you're using to get there."

His face was carefully blank.

"Who says I'm using anything?"

"The fact that you didn't deny it outright says all I need to know."

I kept my voice soft and careful. I didn't want a fight. I wanted him to be able to talk to me, not to get defensive, even as my own heart was racing with something very close to fury.

"I can't keep this up, Janey."

128

"Nobody can," I soothed. "You're working at a pace that is unreal."

"But I can't stop it." Anthony ran his hand along my arm. "It's moving too fast."

"We have to stop it."

"Janey, it's not that simple."

"Right now." There was a note of near panic in my voice.

"I'm all right, honey."

Anthony stood up. I reached out for his hand and he clasped mine with enough strength to hurt.

"Anthony…"

"Be there for me. That's all I need right now."

"You can't handle all this."

"I'm handling it. It isn't much longer. We've got a baby to consider, and a house to build, and a life to create. Just let me get through this part of the tour and then we'll make good on those plans."

I started to doubt my own thoughts on the matter. He seemed to be handling things all right. Even if he had a little pick-me-up to do it, that didn't mean he was addicted, did it? I wasn't even sure what he was on, or if he did it every night, or if it was something he did occasionally. Hell, I had done a line or two in my time, and it didn't make me an addict, did it?

I looked at our joined hands until he leant down to kiss me.

"Get a shower with me," he said.

The shower was small, a very tight fit, especially with my growing belly between us. I watched as he washed his hair, then he turned to me and I closed my eyes, leaned my head back and let him wash mine. It had become one of our little rituals. I let the sweet scent and the firm massage of Anthony's fingers wash away the doubts and fears.

I knew this man so well—I would know if the problem got out of hand, wouldn't I? I would know when things got to a point where he wasn't handling them anymore, but they were handling him.

When the shampoo was all gone and the bubbles washed away down the drain, I kissed my way down his chest. He chuckled when I nibbled at his belly button. He drew in a harsh, hard breath when I dropped to my knees in front of him and took advantage of the fact his body was still primed and ready to go. He leaned against the wall as I did all the things he loved. His hands trembled when he touched my hair. The water was running cold when he jerked, called my name and gave me what I wanted. He leaned against the wall of the shower and tried to catch his breath.

"Three times," I murmured.

"Do you like it?"

"I do," I admitted.

He pulled me up to him, turned off the water and wrapped us both in thick towels. He fluffed my hair as tenderly as if I were a child. Then he pulled me tight against his naked body. I could feel his heartbeat against my ear.

"You love me more than I deserve," he said.

Chapter Nine

The house was magnificent. It was over seven thousand square feet, three stories and more than enough garage, all settled in the center of twelve wooded acres. The six bedrooms were huge, but the master suite put them all to shame. There were Jacuzzis and a wraparound porch. The house boasted two staircases and a kitchen twice the size of my old one. It had big gates, a long and winding driveway and an impressive security system.

It also had a treehouse and a swing set in the back yard, both brand new, built especially for our child.

We had planned on building a house of our own, but when our chosen realtor told us about a home that was halfway finished, we decided to give it a look. The potential owners had backed out of their contract because the husband was transferred overseas, and now the house was sitting in limbo, waiting for an owner to swoop in and make it a home. When I saw the big staircase and the beautiful skylights, I was lost. When Anthony saw the enormous bedrooms and the back yard that provided plenty of privacy and room to romp, he didn't bother asking how much it would cost.

"When can we move in?" he had asked.

Now I stood at the foot of the stairs and looked up to the skylight in the center of the building, three stories up. The building was now finished, and only the small details remained. It still smelled of fresh paint, sawdust and the sweet aroma of promise.

The furniture was in place, most of it still covered by clear plastic. Parts of a ceiling fan lay strewn across the living room table, waiting for assembly. The new refrigerator hummed a single low note. The fireplace in the front room was enormous, imposing, and the mantel that surrounded it was built specifically with award statuettes in mind. It would be not only our home, but also a testament to how far we would travel down the road of fortune and fame.

Anthony's boots made hollow thumps on the hardwood floors. I listened to him approach while fluffy white clouds drifted across the skylight. His hands curled around my waist—what was left of it, anyway. Somehow sensing his father's touch, the baby inside me kicked.

"It all ours," he whispered.

"Just what we wanted."

"Can you believe it's been a year since we met?"

The clouds drifted slowly away. "Is that all?"

"Did you ever think that we would come to this?"

I closed my eyes and rocked back and forth with him. Had it been only a year ago when I saw Anthony Keenan sitting on a stool in a smoky bar, playing his guitar and drinking Jack Daniels?

A year ago I had been reckless, full of myself, with no goal in life other than the next talent, the next contract, the next award on a mantel. I thought of how hard I had been, how difficult to get to know, how closed off and jaded by the whole separate world that was the music industry. I didn't recognize the old me anymore. And I wasn't sure I wanted to—I wasn't sure I liked who I had been, but I was sure that I liked who I had become. I had grown into my own when I fell in love with Anthony.

"I love you," I said.

"Ditto, kiddo."

Outside, a horn honked. It was a brief reminder we couldn't close ourselves up behind those doors just yet. I turned in his arms and watched him look around the house. His gaze landed on the mantel.

"Nervous?" I asked.

"Of course not. This is a *great* house."

"That's not what I meant."

132

"About the baby? Of course."

"Silly man."

"Do I really have to watch the delivery?"

I kissed his nose. "You know what I'm talking about."

"What, pray tell?"

"About the press conference."

"Oh. That."

"Well?"

"Well, they aren't going to ask me anything new."

I rolled my eyes at his forced nonchalance. We both knew better. "A platinum record," I said, and laughed.

Anthony dropped to his knees and spoke to my belly. "Did you hear that, kid? Your daddy's hit the big time!"

The week the record was released, there were people standing in line to get it when the stores opened. Radio stations had frenzied crowds when they held giveaways. The first shipments sold out. It shot to the bestseller lists for Internet sales, and downloads skyrocketed. By the end of the week, we knew Anthony's self-titled debut had sold well over half a million copies—he had a gold record. Within the next week, sales had slumped but were still stronger than the vast majority of releases in their second week. By the end of the third week, Keith had called us into his offices and popped open a bottle of champagne. A poster of Anthony's album cover stood five stories tall on the building across the street. We looked at it through the window and waved to passersby.

"Our first platinum record," Keith said, as the three of us toasted each other.

"It's just a stepping stone," I reminded Anthony now. "Things only get better from here."

"Yeah. Next come the awards shows, where I will sweep them all."

I smiled. "Let me guess. You've already written your acceptance speech?"

Anthony took a few steps back and threw his arms out wide. "I would like to thank God, whoever that may be.

133

The fans! Without your stalker tendencies and homemade brownies, I would never be where I am today—"

"Oooh, that's bad!" I teased.

"To my family," he continued. "My daddy taught me that blood is thicker than everything but currency ink, and my momma taught me that appearances mean everything. And to all those at the record label, who didn't try to change me, and look what it got them!"

"Ooooh…"

"And most of all, to my dearest friend-who-shall-not-be-named," he intoned, touching his heart. "You shall have the best sex of your life when I get home with this award. Thank you, Music City!"

I laughed. The sound echoed down from the skylight of the huge house. Outside, the car horn sounded one more time, a long peal of impatience.

"I don't want to go," Anthony whined, sounding for all the world like a little child. I straightened his dress shirt. He unbuttoned another button, opening it halfway down his chest. I buttoned it back up, and he unbuttoned it again.

I raised an eyebrow at him, and he waggled a finger in my face.

"Sex appeal is the same," he reminded me, "whether I've got a kid on the way or not."

I grinned and left the shirt alone. I brushed his hair back from his face. A little gold hoop in his ear caught the light coming from above. I stepped back to look at him. The months had been good to him, and though he still looked a bit tired, his body looked honed and hard, better than ever.

"You're so handsome."

"And you're so beautiful."

"This kid is going to be gorgeous."

"There's not a chance of anything else."

Anthony cradled my belly in his hand. At over six months along, there was no doubt I was pregnant. Some women started out with a cute little bump, but not me—the day I started showing, it was all at once, and more than obvious to anyone. Anthony loved the feel of my bigger belly, especially at night, when I curled up to him and he wrapped his body around mine.

"And the kid is going to be famous," Anthony said. "Don't forget that part."

As if putting an exclamation point on the statement, the kid in question kicked against my belly. Anthony nodded with satisfaction.

"See?"

The horn honked again. This time it was a long bellow, one that would brook no more stalling. We made our way out of the house, locking the door behind us, and climbed into the back of the long, black sedan. The limousine moved soundlessly down the driveway the moment the doors closed. I turned to watch the house disappear into the distance, and I grinned when I saw Anthony doing the same thing.

"I feel like a little kid with a new toy," he admitted when he saw he had been caught.

I laced my fingers with his. "I know."

In the weeks following Anthony's tour, the requests for his time had remained almost overwhelming. Anthony had appealed to the publicist, the managers and everyone else who had a hand in his career to help him tone things down. He knew it was getting to a point where even he couldn't keep up, and he told them so. The furor would die down for a few days, then it would start back up. It was a constant struggle to balance the time Anthony needed with the time his public demanded.

I watched Anthony at the press conference. I sat in the back, hiding from the cameras, while Anthony sat front and center with Keith, who was beaming with pride in his young talent. The reporters asked questions, most of them the usual drivel, but there was a tension in the room that said this was not a usual kind of press conference. They saw the makings of a star in front of them, and they wanted to make as good an impression as possible. Landing an interview with Anthony might be easy right now, but a year from now he would be almost impossible to catch, and everyone in the room knew it.

Anthony had an air about him that was different from the one he projected a year ago. Back then he was defiant, determined to make his own way and damned if he would play the Nashville game to do it. Now he was smiling for the cameras, schmoozing with the big leaguers and taking business cards like he was an old pro at getting to know complete strangers. He was much more open and likeable than he used to be. Those in the press room adored him.

I hung on his every word until the conference was over, then I slipped out the back door to wait for him. I sat in the limousine and enjoyed the view of people passing by on the sidewalk. Many of them glanced over and tried to see in the windows. I was very aware of being out in the middle of the city, being watched by those who walked by, but not being seen by anyone at all.

I flipped open the center console. There were all sorts of drinks to choose from. I found a bottle of water and sat back to look at a magazine while I waited for Anthony to come back out to the car. I flipped through a few pages before I got disgusted and put it aside. All the glossy ads were of skinny models, and now that my pregnancy was very obvious, I wasn't in the mood to look at those perfectly trim and slim bodies.

Getting ready for bikini weather? Choosing the best little black dress? Give me a break. Even my feet no longer fit into my high heels.

I drank my water and brooded until Anthony came out and climbed into the car. As soon as the door closed behind him, the driver moved smoothly away from the curb and headed in the direction of our house.

"You were good in there," I said.

Anthony leaned back in the seat and closed his eyes. He stretched out with his feet on the opposite seat. "I'm such a fake, Janey."

"You're not a fake."

"Why not?"

"You just have a persona."

"That's a nice way to say I'm a fake."

"Part of the game, honey."

I looked out the window and saw my own reflection superimposed over the buildings of downtown. The limousine turned a sharp corner and my belly lurched.

Anthony leaned up to get a bottle of soda from the console. He popped the top and sat back. I felt him watching me but I didn't turn around. He gently caressed the inside of my arm with one fingertip.

"I love you being pregnant," he whispered, a kind of reverence in his voice.

I looked at him then. He was smiling at me, but something about him seemed a bit strange. Something about his smile, his eyes, even the way he was sitting in the seat, almost as though there was a part of him that was a stranger to me. I tried to shake the feeling but as his smile grew broader, I felt an uneasiness that had nothing to do with the motion of the car or the baby inside me.

"You look different," I said.

"Gee, thanks."

"I mean it. There's something."

"There's nothing." Anthony sat up and put his feet on the floor.

"What's wrong with you?"

"Nothing is wrong with me."

"But you look…"

"What?"

I suddenly knew where I had seen it before, and exactly what it was that I was seeing. I looked back out the window to try and collect my thoughts. Anthony obviously knew what I was thinking, because he took a long drink of his soda and didn't say a word. I stared at the scenery as the city changed to the country. My heart was pounding so hard, I could feel the blood pumping through my arms and legs. My head felt like it would explode with the throbbing. I wondered if my face was as hot as it felt.

"Has it been going on all this time?" I asked.

"I don't know what you mean."

"Don't do that," I snapped. "Don't you dare play me for a fool, Anthony."

There was silence in the car for a long moment.

"I am handling it," he said.

"You're addicted, aren't you?"

"I don't know."

The shock of his admission silenced me. The car turned onto an older road, one the city had forgotten, filled with potholes and the occasional spots of gravel. There were farms on either side. Our new home was only minutes away. I wondered how I would feel when I walked into it again, now that everything was different than it was when I left.

Now that everything had changed in the span of a single car ride.

"You don't know," I said slowly.

"No."

"Have you been on it all this time?"

"Since the tour?"

"Yes."

"Yeah."

"Were you on it when I got pregnant?" I asked, knowing if he had been, I would never be able to forgive him for what he might have done to our baby.

Anthony looked just as horrified as I was by the possibility. "My God, Janey! No. Absolutely not."

"Are you sure?"

"It started way after that, Janey."

"Were you on it the day I told you?"

He answered carefully. "You were already pregnant. You waited several weeks to tell me, you know?"

I closed my eyes in relief. "How often?"

"Does it matter?"

The urge to slap him was suddenly overwhelming. I had to clench my fists in my lap to keep them under control. I felt like a jealous lover who had just discovered her man's girlfriend. I wanted to know everything and nothing at all.

"It matters," I said simply, when I thought I could speak without lashing out at him.

"Every day," he said, and there was an edge of defiance to his voice that caused me to look at him in amazement. "More than that. It's been a way of life for a while now."

"But…"

I didn't know how to respond. I put my water back in the console, then took it out again. I looked out the window, at the partition that separated us from the driver, at the long leather seat along the side of the limousine. I didn't know where to park my gaze. I didn't know what to do.

Anthony sat back in the seat, cool and collected, while he watched me struggle. A part of me hated him for how aloof he could be at a time like this.

"I didn't know," I said, realizing how lame that sounded. Would I be such a mess right now if I had known? I wiped away a tear and berated myself for daring to cry at all.

"No," he said. "You didn't know."

"You're an addict."

Anthony said nothing.

"Cocaine?"

He nodded.

"Other things?"

He simply looked at me, refusing to answer.

"Who gave it to you?"

"It doesn't matter."

"Where do you get it?"

"You don't need to know that, Janey."

My hand snaked out of my lap before I realized what I was about to do. I slapped him once, hard. Anthony's head slammed against the window, and he let out a little yelp of surprise. The fact I had caught him by such surprise sent a surge of power through me. It felt a little bit like retribution for the shock he had given me.

He looked at me with such unmasked fury that I could hardly breathe. I immediately drew back to my side of the car, my heart pounding, my hands going to my belly, that protective instinct kicking in. The look in Anthony's eyes frightened me to my core.

What had I done?

Then that anger was gone almost as quickly as it had come, replaced by contrition. We looked at each other over the fine leather seat, and Anthony looked entirely normal, but I had seen that look he gave me—I had *seen* it, and it had scared the fuck out of me, deep down, where it really counted.

"Who?" This time I heard the shrillness of anger in my own voice. I knew I had pushed things too far, and I wouldn't be able to back down. I might as well take it all the way.

"Why?"

"Because I want to know."

"Obviously."

"I have a *right* to know, dammit."

"What difference would it make?"

"It would tell me who to blame for this," I said, but even as the words came out I knew that wasn't true. Anthony was the only one I could blame for this.

"You already know it's my fault."

"If you don't tell me," I said, "I'll talk to Keith. You won't have any choice but to go into rehab, Anthony. You need it anyway."

Anthony gave me a look that said he was angry enough to cut me, and the words he chose to do it were like a dagger with a jagged edge.

"What makes you think Keith doesn't already know?"

The shock of that sent the fight right out of me. It was replaced with a tiredness that I had never known before. The baby moved inside my belly, kicking hard, and I winced as I shifted position in the seat. Anthony's eyes drifted to my belly then came back to meet my own.

"You have a child on the way," I said.

He was silent.

"You have a child," I repeated.

That was all I could think to say.

Anthony looked at me while tears welled in his eyes. It was a crossroads of emotion that would leave us both damaged, and at that moment, we both knew it. How badly it damaged us was up to him, and he knew that, too.

"Will you help me, Janey?"

I closed my eyes. Jesus Christ, I could handle anything but that note of sadness in his voice, anything but that pleading that told me he needed me, despite what he had done to us, to his child, to himself. I almost longed for that fury in his eyes, for utter contempt, for anything else but the way his gentle, apologetic voice could split my heart in two.

Anthony reached over to take my hand. We sat in silence on the ride home, and when our house loomed at the end of the long, imposing driveway, I wiped away another tear.

We went into the house, closed the door and locked it behind us.

* * * *

That night I lay in bed awake while Anthony slept beside me. He hardly moved, and sometimes I could hardly hear him breathe. I stretched out my hand and placed it on his chest, feeling the strong, steady heartbeat under my palm.

The room smelled like sawdust and paint, a comforting smell, one of good things to come. The moonlight streamed through the high windows, creating gentle shadows on the floor. The ceiling fan above us whirled lazily without a sound. It was such a big place, so new and full of promise, but tonight it felt like an echoing tomb instead of a refuge.

I crawled out of bed. Anthony didn't move. I watched him for a moment before I went to the kitchen and got a glass of orange juice out of the brand-new refrigerator. I drank it as

I wandered the house. I covered every room on the lower level then stood in front of the fireplace, where the mantel held a single photograph—that of me and Anthony from many months ago, when everything was wild and free, before we had so many decisions to make.

I rubbed my belly and felt the baby move. I didn't know whether it was a boy or a girl, but my intuition told me it was a little boy. It was something that just felt right, to think I was going to have a son. It probably defied logic, and wouldn't I be the surprised one if I had a girl instead?

Anthony wanted a son. He wanted a boy to carry on his family name. As I stood there in the moonlight and rubbed my belly, I hoped that family name would be synonymous with honorable and honest men, not with anything less.

When I padded back to the bedroom, Anthony was awake and waiting for me.

We studied each other in the shadows, our gazes locking over the expanse of satin sheets. Finally Anthony looked away, and in the light coming from the windows, I saw every moment of the last year bearing down on him. He didn't just look tired—he looked exhausted.

"I can't do this anymore, Janey."

I nodded even though I didn't know which part he meant. I just knew that something had to change. Something had to give, because we had both been pushed to our limits. I thought of that look in his eyes in the car, the utter fury, and I shuddered with the memory. "What do you want to do?"

He stared out the window for so long, I wondered if he had heard me. I lay down on the bed and stared at the ceiling fan. It went around and around, constant, never changing, hypnotic.

"I think it's time I got some help," he said.

I blinked back tears. I knew it was the right thing, so why did it make me feel so sad? "That's a good decision."

"I'm scared."

"I know. I am too."

"I don't want to go into rehab. I don't think it's gone that far."

"Just how far is too far?"

"I don't know."

"If not rehab, what other alternative is there?"

"I want to try it myself first."

"Yourself?"

"Go to a meeting. Talk to someone."

I sighed and rolled over to face him. "Do you think that's wise?"

"I don't know. I won't know until I try."

We held hands and looked at each other for a long time.

"You know, when I start going to meetings, the press will find out," he said.

"Probably."

"They will make me sound like the second coming of Keith Richards."

"But that doesn't matter much now, does it?"

"I guess not. What will it do to my career?"

"I'm sure we can turn it into a positive. Spin is everything, you know?"

"How could I forget?"

We both lay in silence while we thought about what the press would say. They would probably eat him alive. His rise was too monumental, his image too good, to not make an addiction a top story. Rumors would fly like hurricanes. They would cash in on every one of them. Anthony would go from being the golden child to being tabloid fodder.

"How bad is this?" I asked. "Really, Anthony. Don't lie to me. I want to know what we're up against here."

"You want to know how much I'm doing."

"That's a good place to start."

Anthony's voice was hard, as though he had trouble saying it all out loud. "I'm addicted, Janey. Do you have any idea how much effort it takes to say that?"

"No," I admitted, trying not to cry.

"I wanted to wait until there were more signs, or until I had problems that would force me into rehab." His laugh was bitter. "Can you imagine? Waiting until I hit rock bottom?"

"Most addicts do just that."

"I know. But if I wait, I'm going to lose you."

It was something he had never said aloud before, recognition of just how bad things could become. Our idyllic life was held by a thread, and only Anthony knew just how thin that thread was getting. If he said he needed help, then I believed him.

"We'll start looking into it in the morning," I said.

"Okay."

"I don't know how to go about it."

"Neither do I."

"I guess we can make some phone calls. Start there."

He didn't answer for a long time, and when he did, his voice was tinged with the slightest edge of hope, like a child who might have just found a way out of trouble.

"Do we have to do it in the morning?"

"What do you mean?"

"Is there a better time?"

"How long do you want to wait, Anthony? Another day? Another week?"

My voice was rising. I took a deep breath and struggled to keep my emotions under control. Was he really trying to find a way out of this, now that he had admitted how big the problem really was?

I spoke quietly, though I wanted to scream. "Then it turns into another month, then the baby is here, and then what?" I asked. "You won't want to leave while you're getting to know your child. Then that's another year, then another tour, then it just gets worse...and then you wind up in such bad shape, it takes a miracle to pull you out of it."

Neither of us spoke after that. Anthony slipped his hands over my belly. He kissed me with a desperation that said much more than what his words could convey. Tears blocked our throats and made us breathe harder. When the kisses weren't enough, Anthony pulled me against him and showed me what he wanted with the movement of his hips against mine. I rolled onto my side and he moved behind me, then into me, pushing hard even as he pulled me toward him with his strong arms. His hands cradled the life inside me while he buried his face against my shoulder.

Anthony made love to me slowly, with more passion than I had ever felt. The fear was there between us, as alive and vital as we ourselves were, and the words that we both needed to say were lost somewhere in the madness of it all. So we simply moved with each other and let the desire carry us away, like it so often did, to a place where the only thoughts were of the way we made each other feel.

Anthony didn't stop until I came first. He played me with his body, his hands and his lips until I arched into him and cried out into the silence of our bedroom. Only then did he pull out and move away from me.

"Anthony?"

"Watch."

He lay on his back in the bed. I watched as his hand moved up and down, his hips moving with every slow stroke. His breath was ragged, and there were trails of tears on his cheeks. I kissed them away as he pushed himself closer to the orgasm that I so badly wanted him to have. I wanted to share the pleasure with him.

I moved down on the bed. I watched, just a few inches away, at all the things Anthony did when he was doing it for himself. I studied how long his strokes were, how firm his grip was, what places he paid the most attention to, what gave him the most pleasure. I watched the way the moonlight fell over him. I listened to the way his breathing sped up then slowed down, depending on what his hand was doing at that moment.

It was somehow more intimate than anything else we had ever done. Anthony was completely vulnerable, letting me see a part of him that was usually reserved for his own private world, and watching him made me feel more connected to him than ever.

He moved faster, and I moved closer.

"I'm going to," he murmured.

"Good."

Anthony's breath hitched once, and his hand faltered. He cried out my name. This time it sounded entirely the same and yet somehow different. The display was a gift he had given me, a show of trust. It was another door into Anthony, this one thrown wide open in the shadows of our bedroom, and watching him there made me want to cry and laugh at the same time.

He hauled me up to him and kissed me. He kissed me until neither one of us could breathe, then fell back to the bed, pulling me with him until I was almost lying on top of him. I tried to move and he wouldn't let me.

"I'm too heavy now…"

"Never. Hush."

Anthony held me in the waning light of the moon. He kissed my forehead. He ran his hands through my hair. When he cried harder than I had ever seen him cry, I held him and did the same for him. The sobs eventually quieted to the occasional tear, then the tears were gone, replaced by an utter exhaustion. He gave in to it for the first time in a long time, and I watched him sleep, his face finally clear and unlined, the tears healing everything as best they could.

When the sun came up, we were both sound asleep, wrapped in each other's arms.

Chapter Ten

The weeks since Anthony's decision were difficult ones. We made a phone call to Keith the morning after our discussion on what to do. Keith then made a call or two to the appropriate people and by noon Anthony was meeting with a very discreet counselor for lunch. By the end of that hour, he had a list of contacts and a place to go. That night he went to a meeting, and the people he met there were a comforting surprise.

"I saw people I knew, Janey. People I never dreamed would have an addiction. They were there, and they gave me a lot of support. I feel stronger right now than I have in a long time."

He didn't look very strong. He looked pale and ragged. His hands shook. He paced the floor. He was starving but he couldn't keep anything down. He couldn't sleep. Sometimes he threw up, and sometimes he flew into a rage that sent him out to the back yard, where he tried his best to tear apart a tree and not risk hurting anyone else. As the drugs left his body he needed more, and without his fix he became at turns a loose cannon, at others a sobbing mess.

He needed constant reassurance that he could do what he was setting out to do. We both knew he was going through withdrawal, but neither one of us said it aloud.

"You know what bothered me the most about that meeting?" he asked the next day.

"What?"

Anthony looked out the window, into the distant field. "They weren't surprised to see me."

The days turned into weeks, and even as we prepared

for the birth of the baby, Anthony had moments when he needed care just as much as our child did. He made calls to his sponsor in the middle of the night. He paced the house and sometimes broke down into tears for no apparent reason.

The tabloids had a field day with him. They had already reported what they believed was a scandal—Anthony's pregnant girlfriend, the one he hadn't bothered to marry yet. Though we had talked about marriage from time to time and certainly weren't opposed to it, the fact that we hadn't jumped into a quickie wedding caused a stir. Anthony's image took some tarnish.

The news that he was now kicking a drug habit was enough to send the vultures into a feeding frenzy.

Their lust to get the story brought them right to our doorstep. In the past we heard about the terrible stories from friends, usually with a laughing remark about how untrue the stories were, and that was the extent of how deeply it touched our lives. But once the latest scandal broke, the cameras were everywhere, and most of the time they were in places we didn't expect. We were photographed at odd moments, while driving to the grocery or walking into a bookstore. Someone was tailing Anthony's truck every time he left the house. It was unnerving enough to make us stay at home most of the time, and we sometimes resorted to hiding behind the black-tinted windows of the Axton limousine, but even that didn't shelter us from the invasions of privacy.

"Jesus Christ, look at this," he said one day as he was flipping through the channels on the television. He was the subject of a popular talk show. We watched as the women on the screen worked through one rumor after another and didn't get their facts straight on any of them. Anthony turned the television off in disgust.

Then he unplugged it, just in case either of us had the insane urge to watch more of that drivel.

"I think we should raise our child without television," he

said.

"Without magazines, either. Or newspapers." I was trying to cheer him up, and it worked. He grinned at me.

"Without Internet access."

"In a very posh private school where everybody is a celebrity."

"So it's all a moot point, right?"

"Right."

He stared out the front windows, at the direction of the gates we now kept locked at all hours, the ones that kept the world away from us. "I see a camera and have the urge to smash it. It comes out of nowhere. I'm like one of Pavlov's dogs."

I made a barking sound, and Anthony laughed.

A few weeks after that, with my belly about to burst and his long break over, he went back out on tour. I went on with my life as well as I could while I waited for the arrival of our child, putting the finishing touches on the nursery, seeing the doctor more often and waking up often in the night with the tightening in my belly that said the baby would come, and soon.

Anthony's schedule was as crazy as always, but he had people around him who could help him stay clean. Those who had offered drugs in the past were summarily dismissed from the entourage. Anthony was determined to kick the habit and keep his career going full throttle at the same time.

That was where he was now, somewhere in Oklahoma.

I was in a labor room in a Nashville hospital, looking at the cheery wallpaper and beeping monitors. When it was time, babies didn't bother to wait around. The first contraction came around noon, and brought me to my knees. The second contraction came five minutes later, before the limousine had a chance to arrive, before I had a chance to get accustomed to the fact that this was really happening.

Now I looked at the big clock on the wall and I wondered which would get here first... Anthony or the baby?

"Breathe, honey," Kristin said. "Just breathe. I know it's hard, but that's all you have to do. Let your body do the hard work, and you just breathe to stay on top of it."

The light above me was too bright, glaring, showing the whole world my pain. I looked away from it to the monitor beside the bed. The little green lights said everything was fine, and so did the little number on the screen—one-five-four—the heartbeat of the baby that was trying to make its way into the world.

Kristin sat beside me with a cool washcloth and a steady hand to hold onto. She had been there with me through the last five hours of labor—was it only that long?—but her eyes were clear and happy. She looked fresh, as though she hadn't been dealing with a hurting and demanding woman for hours on end.

"I want this over," I moaned. I was tired of the constant ebb and flow. I was on the verge of asking for an epidural, despite all my promises to myself and the baby that I wouldn't. I wanted to sleep. I wanted to get the baby out. When another contraction came, I wanted to die and get it all over with.

"It will be over soon," Kristin soothed, and gripped my hand hard. She could see the contractions on the monitor long before I could feel them. When this one came to its full force, it took my breath away. All my breathing techniques, all the good things I had learned in the birthing class, none of it seemed to matter. If I couldn't catch my breath, how could I possibly breathe the right way?

I held onto her hands until it was over, then burst into tears. It wasn't the first time.

"It's all right," Kristin murmured. "Rest for a minute."

"I want Anthony, dammit."

"He's on his way."

"I'm going to fucking kill him."

Kristin tried not to laugh, and I tried my best not to burst into tears again.

"Where is he?" I asked her, though she had already told

me half a dozen times.

"He's in the air, honey. He's trying to get here."

Just then, another contraction started.

"Let's place bets on which one gets here first," I muttered through gritted teeth.

There was no question that the paparazzi had beaten him to the front doors. Security had been called numerous times, always with a tense voice over the intercom system. One of the nurses had whispered to me about big news vans and cameras with large lenses. The medical staff was sometimes enthralled and sometimes annoyed by the intrusion, but no one ever seemed to harbor any blame toward me.

"Can we turn that light off?" I asked, and Kristin took care of it. The only illumination came from the strip of lights above the headboard of the bed. It was enough to see the monitors and Kristin's face while she talked to me. I stared at a little red dot on the monitor and used it as my focal point—another trick I learned in birthing classes—as another contraction started. I fought to breathe through it, but again I failed. I wanted to cry again, but I fought against that, too.

"Where did they say Anthony was when you called?"

"At a radio station."

"I should have called him earlier today. I should have known that backache wasn't just a fluke."

"This is your first time. Besides, it's different for everybody. You didn't know."

"I should have known, dammit."

"Yeah, well. You aren't superwoman."

"No shit. If I were I wouldn't be whining like a fucking baby."

"You curse like a sailor when you're in labor," Kristin said with a grin.

"Sorry, I'm not much for decorum right now. I would dance naked in the streets if only this baby would hurry up and come."

She laughed and kissed my forehead. "Give those

paparazzi a show, huh?"

"I guess it's too much to hope they went away."

"It's insanity out there."

I was glad the little labor room didn't have any windows. A nurse swished by on quiet feet. I could hear another woman's baby monitor beeping from the room next to mine. Someone laughed from a distant hallway. Within the quiet confines of the hospital, it seemed the crazy tabloid world didn't exist.

"Anthony will be furious," I said.

"I don't blame him."

"What do they expect to see, anyway?"

Kristin shrugged in commiseration.

"Anthony should be here," I pouted.

"He will be."

"He's in the air, you said?"

"I'm sure he's on a plane right now."

"It's not fair that men get all the pleasure and none of the pain."

"I'm with you there, babe."

"That's why killing someone during childbirth should be legal."

Kristin laughed.

"Seriously."

Another pain hit, this one stronger than any of those before, and I couldn't think, much less laugh.

"That was a good one," Kristin said as I came down from it. She looked at the monitor. The nurse came in and looked, too. She smiled and said all was going well, then checked between my legs.

"You're at eight centimeters," she said. "Things get tougher from here, but they won't last much longer."

"I want an epidural," I said.

"It's too late, honey. If we give you one now, it will slow things down."

"Damn it!" I almost hollered.

"Not much longer!"

She whooshed out with a cheery smile.

"I hate her," I hissed.

Kristin held onto my hand and smiled down at me. She watched while I rode the wave of three more contractions. My body was threatening to come apart at the seams. Any sense of modesty left me, and I said anything that came to mind, most of which would have been shocking if I had been in any mood to care. The nurses took it all in stride, and I realized they had probably heard much worse.

Ten minutes later I was fully dilated. Nurses suddenly flooded the room, each of them doing something different. I was helped to a sitting position and part of the bed was taken away, leaving a birthing chair. Gravity would work to help me.

The doctor stepped in, dressed from head to toe in sterile garments. I couldn't see his smile, but I could hear it. "Let's get this baby out!"

"Anthony isn't here yet," I protested, and a nurse patted my shoulder.

"He's going to miss the big show, honey. But you can hold it over his head for the rest of his life," she joked.

Kristin kissed my forehead. "Here we go."

My world narrowed down to nothing but a mission — to get that baby out. I forgot about Anthony, about the nurses, about anything other than what I had to do. My body took over, and now the contractions didn't feel like pain without a purpose, but pain for a cause. I could feel the change with every one of them, the way my body bore down of its own accord. Pushing was a natural response, not something that I had to be taught.

I suddenly knew how women had given birth alone for centuries. We were born knowing what to do. It was knowledge as natural to our bodies as breathing. The pain was secondary, a distant thing. The only thing that mattered was going along with my body and letting it do what it was made to do.

I was aware of little else. I heard a growl, one that had to have come from me. I felt a sudden rush of wetness and a burn that seemed to seep through my very bones. My mind told me to scream but my body told me to conserve my energy. I turned that scream into power instead, used all of it to push down hard. My body became hard as iron.

I could do this.

I *would* do this.

With a sudden rush of pain, something gave way. I did scream then, not in pain but in the sheer victory of it. I knew, even before I heard the baby cry, that I had done it—surrounded by people, yet all by myself, I had done it. I collapsed back onto the bed and cool hands soothed my forehead, my arms, my cheek.

The baby cried, a long and reedy sound, uncertain. The second cry was lusty and full.

"It's a boy," Kristin said. I opened my eyes to see the tiniest being imaginable, covered with red and white, cradled in the arms of a smiling nurse. She was doing something to his belly button.

I watched as the nurse handed a pair of scissors to Kristin. My best friend stepped forward and cut the cord, freeing the little boy from me. She turned to me with an expression of absolute awe.

"You did it. You did so well!"

"Is he okay? Everything is fine?"

"Perfect," a nurse called from the corner. They had taken my son over there, to a small table that was set up just for that purpose. He was flailing his tight little fists and screaming at the top of his lungs. It was the sweetest sound I had ever heard.

"We've got some work to do," the doctor said to me, but I hardly heard him. I suddenly couldn't keep my eyes open. My whole body throbbed with the aftermath. There were cool hands on me, soothing voices around me, and I just let myself drift for a while, listening to the sound of my newborn son.

Soon after I was back up on the bed and covered with a

clean sheet, they laid him in my arms. Wrapped in a blanket and weighing hardly anything at all, he looked up at me with his father's eyes. I touched his forehead and kissed his nose. The nurse stepped out of the way and left me to hold him for that first of countless times.

Kristin sat on the bed beside me and freed his little hand from the blankets. She held it against her fingertip and marveled at how small it was. She catalogued every feature of his face and exclaimed over how much he looked like Anthony. Then she grew quiet and wiped a single tear from her eye.

"I got to cut the cord. I didn't expect that."

"I'm glad you did. I would much rather you do it than the doctor."

She smiled, but there was sadness there. It seemed so out of place with the joyousness that was coursing through me.

"What's wrong?"

She shook her head and then buried her face in her hands.

"It should have been Anthony. He should have been here."

For the first time during that long, hard day, Kristin started to cry.

* * * *

"Hey, gorgeous. Wake up."

There was a hand on my shoulder. I opened my eyes to see Anthony standing over me, peering down into my face. His had a wide smile. In his arms was a little bundle wrapped in blue. I pushed myself up on the bed and winced at the soreness.

"Are you okay?" he whispered.

"I'm okay." I reached my arms up and Anthony laid our baby in them. He sat on the edge of the bed. "When did you get here? What time is it?"

"It's about midnight," he said. "You had him two hours ago."

155

"You missed it."

Anthony touched my cheek with the back of his hand. "I'm sorry, honey."

"Did you see?" I unwrapped the baby until his hands were free. Anthony reached out and touched one. The little fingers jerked once, but the baby slept on.

"The nurses waylaid me as soon as I came in. They told me you were fine. You were sleeping. They took me to the nursery. I hope that's okay?"

"That's okay."

He stared at the baby, as though he couldn't tear his eyes away. I smiled at him and watched as he drank his fill of the child he and I had created.

"You haven't named him," he said.

"No. I wanted to make sure with you one last time before I signed anything."

"Are we sure?"

"I still think Stephen sounds good. Don't you?"

He smiled down at the little being in my arms. "Stephen. Hey, Stephen. You've got a name."

Anthony leaned over both of us. The baby shifted, annoyed by the movement. Anthony wrapped his strong arms around us and kissed me slowly, tenderly. I could feel the tremble in him that said he was on the verge of tears.

"He's so beautiful," he whispered against my lips. "Can you believe he's ours?"

"Stephen Anthony Keenan," I whispered.

"In the morning, the whole world will know," he mused. "Right now, it's just us. How strange does that feel?"

"Was it really bad outside?"

Anthony sighed. "Not as bad as you might think. Half of them were asleep, I guess."

"I don't want any of those vultures near our baby." The surge of protectiveness was fierce. The mere thought of someone trying to capture pictures of our child made me lightheaded with anger.

"We'll be careful," he assured me. "But it will happen

eventually."

I took a breath and looked back down at Stephen. This was a child born into a celebrity-crazed world. With his father's popularity going nowhere but up, we had no choice but to take it all in stride and find a way to coexist with it. I decided not to think about it tonight, when there were so many good things that were more deserving of our attention.

"Stephen Anthony Keenan," I repeated.

"Something's not right about that," Anthony said pensively.

"What do you mean?"

He leaned back in his chair and studied me for a long while. "He's got my last name."

"Of course he does."

"But you don't."

I stared at Anthony, thinking of the right thing to say. *It doesn't matter. I'm happy with us anyway. Marriage isn't a necessity. Our commitment is the same.* But none of those things sounded right on my tongue, perhaps because in all the changing I had been doing, that had changed, too. My convictions had been shaken, and things that didn't matter before seemed to matter a great deal now. The little boy in my arms had made sure of that.

I settled with saying what I knew was true. "I love you, Anthony. You're the father of my child. That makes us as much family as we will ever be."

He smiled. "Yes. But I would love the rest of the world to see it the same way."

I had thought all the tears were used up through the pain of childbirth and the emotion of the day, but they weren't. I started to cry as Anthony reached into his pocket and pulled out a tiny black box. He smoothed my hair back from my forehead and kissed my nose.

"This is why it took me so long to get here," he whispered. "I wasn't willing to face my son for the first time without a special something to give his mother."

157

I looked at our child, sleeping soundly in my arms, the baby who looked just like Anthony yet somehow a little like me. I had never thought being his mother would come along with being his father's wife, but it was something I was surprisingly ready for, something that felt like a missing piece of a puzzle.

Anthony said the magic words.

"I want to be your husband."

He opened the box and I gasped aloud. My tears ceased in the light of those diamonds shining up from the black velvet.

"Anthony, that's—that ring is too much!" I blurted, and Anthony laughed loud enough to wake Stephen. The baby stretched in his blanket and screwed up his little face, preparing to let out a wail. He waved a tiny fist in the air. Anthony waited until he had calmed down, watching as his son went back to sleep with a sigh and something that sounded for all the world like the coo of a dove.

Anthony and I looked at each other in the dim hospital light. He had tears in his eyes, but his lips were smiling. He pulled out the ring again, and this time the diamonds sparkled even brighter than before. It seemed as though the light came from within, as if it would go on forever.

"I know this isn't the most romantic time or place," he said. "But it seems like the most fitting one. Janey—will you marry me?"

I nodded, not trusting myself to speak. Anthony took my hand and slid the ring onto the appropriate finger. I was surprised by the weight of it and by the way it made my hand look different from what I had always known. When I lifted my hand to his face, the light flashed in the diamonds again, proclaiming without words exactly what that ring meant.

"When?" I asked, and Anthony laughed at my eagerness.

"As soon as you are out of here."

"As soon as I get my figure back," I corrected. "I want a dress. The whole nine yards."

Anthony kissed my palm. "Then you shall have it."

We rested there together in my hospital bed, our son curled up between us. Nothing else mattered—not the cameras outside or the record label down the street, nor the platinum records on the walls or the songs on the radio. The only things that mattered were right there in that bed. The world at that moment was bright and shiny as a brand-new nickel, waiting for us to take hold of it and make it ours.

Chapter Eleven

Six months later, I did the one thing I had once sworn I would never, ever do.

I walked down the aisle.

The church was filled with candles. The scent of vanilla mingled with the scent of sweet, aromatic smoke. White silk ribbons decorated everything from the doors of the church to the pews to the train of my long, luscious dress. The aisle was a carpet of white rose petals, dotted with red — the color of passion.

My family was there, having flown in from all corners of the country for the occasion. Seeing them all reminded me I had always been surrounded by love, and though sometimes my decisions were not the best, I was never looked down upon for them. Even my stodgy old Aunt Mae, who had been known to go on and on about the shames of having children out of wedlock, took one look at my little boy and melted.

"Oh, look at that boy," she whispered as she took him into her arms for the first time. Stephen was six months old on our wedding day, and his smile lit up the room. Aunt Mae kissed his forehead, smoothed down his fine dark hair and gave him a look of such love that I knew all the lectures about children out of wedlock had already been forgotten.

"Your mother would be so proud," she said. "Your father, too."

When the crowd was seated and the ceremony was about to start, I looked out into the crowd from my vantage point at the top of the stairs. Where my parents should have been, there was an empty space and a pair of white roses. I had promised myself I would not cry as I walked down the aisle, but the sight of those roses did me in.

"Oh, God," I murmured, wiping away a tear and trying not to mess up my carefully applied cosmetics as I did it.

Keith kissed my cheek and took my arm. There had never been any question of who would walk me down the aisle. Keith was as much my family as anyone out there in the crowd, and though I would have loved to have my father walk me down the aisle, I was proud to have Keith beside me.

"You have never been more beautiful," he said to me as I clutched his arm.

Anthony's family was conspicuously absent. He swore it didn't matter, but I knew it hurt him more than he would ever admit. Whenever I brought it up, he insisted Stephen and I were all the family he needed.

My nieces served as flower girls, and dropped more crimson-red petals over the white carpet as they walked forward. The crowd oohed and aahed appropriately, and all the young ladies blushed becomingly.

Kristin, my maid of honor, kissed me on the cheek and walked down the aisle with tears in her eyes. Anthony winked at her when she got to the altar, and Kristin impetuously reached out to clasp his hand in one long, hard squeeze.

The music began and Keith took a deep breath. "Time to go," he said.

We slowly approached the man I was to marry, and my vows to keep the tears at bay fell to the wayside as I gazed at him. He looked like a prince in his deep-blue tuxedo, and the way he looked at me as I walked down the aisle toward him was something I knew would stay with me for the rest of my life. Under his gaze, the whole world fell away, and there was nothing there but the two of us, surrounded by such love it was hard to breathe.

"Who gives this woman?" the preacher asked.

Keith's voice hitched on a tear. "On behalf of her father,

I do."

Anthony's hand was warm on mine as he smiled at me and Keith found his seat.

Our Stephen sat in the front row and squirmed in the arms of Auntie Mae, and once disrupted the short service with a resounding cry. Laughter from all of our guests came right after it, and thus Anthony and I ushered in our new life together on the wings of laughter and our son's little voice.

It was as intimate as I had dreamed it could be. Our vows were said without a single thought to the rest of the world, and with our friends as witnesses, we solidified what we had started almost two years before. The doors were tightly closed and the ushers doubled as security guards, but we didn't mind that small intrusion. Our privacy was kept intact by those friends who wanted all the best for us.

But life as Anthony Keenan's wife was not always going to be one of quiet privacy.

When we opened the doors of the church, the paparazzi went wild. They had camped outside, waiting for what they were sure would be a magnificent wedding. Imagine their surprise when the guests numbered in the double digits instead of the hundreds. We spent thirty minutes giving them what they wanted—shots of the bride and groom looking happy—and with our openness we prevented any one photographer from getting an exclusive deal with a tabloid, thus making our nuptials a nonissue for those who wished to turn it into a moneymaker.

Three limousines departed from the basement of the church. Nobody was sure which one we were in. Each limousine went in a different direction, and the paparazzi were plunged into confusion. After a long roundabout drive, we found ourselves at a private airstrip, climbing into a private plane. Within minutes we were aloft, full of ourselves for our ingenuity, and finally able to enjoy the weight of the new rings on our fingers.

We made only one call before we shut out the rest of the world for the honeymoon. As Auntie Mae assured us

Stephen would be fine with her for the week, we could hear his happy babbling in the background.

"What a beautiful wedding," she said. "What a lovely baby, and what a husband you have! You're a lucky girl, Janey, and don't you ever forget it."

"I won't," I promised her.

The island villa was one of those discreet places that never used your real name and assigned one person to be at your beck and call during your stay, so as to reduce the possibility of outsiders finding you. Our attendant was a lovely young woman who moved through the rooms as quietly as a mouse and made sure we wanted for nothing.

As soon as she was out of the room and the door was closed behind us, Anthony picked me up. My belly was flat again, and though my hips would always be a little wider than they were before the baby, the extra weight did me a world of good.

Anthony showed me just how much he liked it by hastily removing every stitch of clothing I had on. There was very little finesse that first time as newlyweds—the thrill of being together, alone, starting this new phase of our lives, was enough to make us forget the romantic conventions. Five minutes later he was standing on the bed above me, holding my legs high in the air as I braced myself, almost standing on my head. The change of scenery had made us adventurous.

Once we got our breath back and made sure my back was not permanently damaged, we ordered something for dinner. The fruit cups for the appetizer were as far as we got—soon we were dipping strawberries into unmentionable places and doing naughty things with the whipped cream. Sticky with the sweetness and drunk on each other, the second time we made love was slow and easy, a benediction to the delicious weight of the ring on my finger and the fact that my last name was now the same as his.

"Janey Keenan," I mused, and he smiled down at me, our

bodies joined.

"I love the way that sounds," he whispered.

Anthony took my hand and traced my fingers, then kissed each tip. He then kissed my wedding ring, running his tongue along the gold edges.

"We're married," he said.

"Yes."

"This feels good, Janey. Really, really good. It feels right."

I smiled. "Yes, it does."

He wrapped his arms around me and smiled against my shoulder. "I already love being your husband."

"Good. You're stuck with me."

Anthony stood on shaky legs. He pulled me up with him and we ambled toward the shower, arm in arm, entirely comfortable and happy with the new world of marriage.

We stepped outside the next morning and headed for the beach. The brisk ocean wind felt heavenly, just a little cooler than expected, and the water was perfect. We dived into the water without a moment's hesitation and came up wrestling, dunking each other under the waves, trying our best to wear each other out. After only a few minutes of frolicking in the tide, we saw it—a camera with a wide lens pointing at us from an unassuming beach house.

Much to my surprise, Anthony didn't get upset. He took it all in stride. "Might as well show them we're happy," he said, and dunked me under the water again.

I found his foot under the water and down he went.

We thought we had outsmarted the system, but our honeymoon in the Virgin Islands was filled with unwelcome intrusions. Paparazzi camped out on the grounds outside the resort. Though we were often alone while in the hotel itself, any time we ventured outside, someone caught a photograph of us with their long lenses. Unflattering shots appeared on the Internet and on the cover of tabloids. We were determined our time alone would not be ruined, but even so, it was hard to truly relax when we knew our every move was subject to documentation. By the time our honeymoon was over, we were more than ready to get back to our son and our home behind the iron gates, locked away from the world.

But once we were back home it was more of the same. As we settled into life with Stephen and worked hard on becoming the best parents we could be, we dealt with being followed at every turn. Anthony's fame had skyrocketed, and while that meant all horizons were now open to him, it also destroyed so many of the simple things we had taken for granted. Going to the grocery store became an exercise in exasperation. A trip to the movies required renting out a whole room in the theatre just to have enough peace to watch the film. We once tried to go to the mall, and a near riot ensued when the young women there realized Anthony was in their midst. After that close call, bodyguards became a necessity.

Early one morning, not long after we had come back to the States, I stumbled into the kitchen to make morning coffee. When I happened to glance out the window, I saw a sight that made my blood run cold. There stood three women, all giggling in the early morning light, all holding cameras, pointed toward our kitchen window. They had to have climbed over the fence, walked through almost a mile of wooded terrain, and sought out the one window in our home that gave them a clear view inside.

The audacity was stunning. I held tightly onto the counter, staring out the window at the image of fans gone crazy. My hand shook as I reached for the phone and dialed the police.

At this point we had called them so often, I had memorized the number.

After that, we wasted no expense on security. Guards prowled the grounds and manned the gate. We rarely left home by ourselves, but opted for the limousine instead. I learned the value of personal shoppers and had our groceries delivered. It seemed a small price to pay to have our family safe and secure, though I often chafed at being locked away from the world.

Anthony was everywhere, on the radio, on the television, on the stage in front of thousands of fans. His hard work over the span of almost twenty years was being billed as an overnight success. The disregard for all those long years of struggling would have bothered us if we let it, but we chose to make light of the situation. After all, we had learned that any story had a spin, and that spin would be at the whims of an editor who knew nothing at all about us.

As Anthony's concerts went from small venues to college towns to large arenas, the frenzy continued to build. Women came out of the past like ghosts revisiting the living, telling tales of wild times with Anthony. His ex-wife received a six-figure advance on a novel she hadn't written yet. Old high school friends came forward with childhood tales of theft and vandalism. Nude pictures surfaced of a young Anthony with a former girlfriend, and they made the rounds on the Internet while the most diehard fans covered their salaciousness with indignation, said they didn't want to see them, but secretly saved them to their hard drives.

As his wife, I was not immune to character attacks. My former relationship with David was dragged through the mud, and since none of the principals would talk, mysterious "sources" told wild tales that were far from the truth. My business relationship with Keith was questioned. Stories were fabricated out of thin air. When it came to Anthony, I was painted as a gold digger who kick-started his career, took him away from a loving wife, then got pregnant so he would have to marry me. None of it was true, but it made for good sales, so the lies just kept on coming.

Sometimes the tabloids hit on something that seemed legitimate—such as the photographs of Anthony with a girlfriend from fifteen years before—and those things were always a product of the past, something that didn't hurt my relationship with Anthony. Everyone had a past, and I had no problem with the fact that my husband's had been a little wild. After all, I had quite a few skeletons in my own closet, didn't I?

Then came something I couldn't ignore.

I was feeding Stephen when Kristin came to visit. She was one of the very few people who could pass through the gates on sight. The bodyguards trusted her as much as I did. When she called to me from the front door, I hollered from the kitchen and fed Stephen another spoonful of pureed sweet potatoes. He gurgled happily and slammed his hands down on the messy top of his high chair.

Kristin turned the corner and looked at me with haunted eyes. One look at her said something was very, very wrong.

"What's wrong?" I asked, coming up out of my chair. Kristin didn't say a word, but her hug was so tight it made it hard to breathe. I knew it was bad.

"Your kids," I said, and she immediately shook her head.

"They're fine."

"You...are you hurt? Was there an accident?"

"I'm fine," she said. "It's not about me."

"Okay...okay."

I took a deep breath, relief turning my knees to jelly.

"Sit down," she said. "We've got something to talk about."

"Okay?"

"Where's Anthony?"

My blood ran cold. I glanced at the silent radio on the counter, thought about his schedule, worked times in my head. Where was he? Was he okay?

"What's wrong?"

"Is Anthony here with you?"

"He's in Atlanta. He'll be back tonight."

She nodded. I pulled a chair up next to mine and Kristin sat down. Her eyes were watery and her nose was red. She sniffled then uttered a short, harsh laugh.

"I've been crying for hours," she said, and shook her head.

"Will you *please* tell me what's wrong?"

The panic made my hands shake so hard, I could barely feed Stephen. She picked up the spoon and took the jar of baby food out of my hand. Stephen smiled at her as she gave him another bite. He spat it out, getting it all over his bib and even on his shirt, and laughed out loud. She gave him another one and this one went down where it was supposed to go.

"Kristin?"

"I got a phone call today from a reporter who wanted a quote."

That was a typical thing. She got calls like that at least once a week. I breathed a sigh of relief. "Is that all?"

"He had something, a big story, he said. There was something about his tone, Janey. It seemed like he was arrogant about it, excited, in a way the others usually aren't."

"What was the story?"

Kristin gave Stephen another spoonful before she answered.

"They have pictures," she said.

"Okay?"

She sat back in the chair and took a deep breath. "Pictures of Anthony and some woman. They were taken a few weeks ago."

I nodded, still not understanding what this meant. "Pictures of what?"

Kristin stared at Stephen as if she hadn't heard me. "I told him he was lying. The reporter, I mean. He asked me if I would give a quote. I said I had to see the pictures. So he sent them to me through email."

"And?"

Kristin wiped her eyes with the back of her hand.

"They're real, Janey. It's Anthony. And this woman, I don't know who she is, but what they're doing is real, too. They're going to publish those photographs, honey, and I wanted you to hear it from me before you heard it from some reporter or from that television in there."

I sat perfectly still, not quite believing what I had just heard. Pictures of Anthony with another woman? Was this another one from his past? I could handle a man with a past, but good grief—just how many women were stuck in that closet?

Then the reality of it hit me, and with it came a rush of shock that made me sick to my stomach. I sat there for a long moment, thinking I would be all right, willing myself to be, even as my heart kicked into overdrive. There was an overwhelming metallic taste in my mouth, much like blood.

I lurched to the bathroom and threw up everything I had eaten for lunch.

When there was nothing left in me, I sat down hard on the floor and grabbed blindly for a towel. In the distant kitchen, Kristin talked to Stephen while the water ran in the sink. A keening sound built up from deep inside the middle of me, from the place where it really counts. It spiraled up, the pressure built, the sound threatened to escape. I found myself rocking back and forth on the floor, clutching the towel as though it were a lifeline.

With sickening clarity, I suddenly understood what insanity felt like.

I dug my nails into my palms. The fresh pain of it cleared my head. I wiped my mouth and leaned back against the wall as Kristin appeared in the doorway, Stephen on one hip.

"Janey."

I closed my eyes. "Okay. I'm okay."

"Do you want to see them for yourself?"

The thought of it made me feel sick all over again. I shook my head. "You wouldn't tell me if they weren't real. You wouldn't do that."

Kristin boosted Stephen up higher on her hip. He grabbed a handful of her golden hair and she worked to free it as she watched me there on the floor. "I'm sorry."

"When did it happen?"

"Two weeks ago."

"You checked it all out, I assume."

"I called the photographer. I had to pry it out of the editor, but he finally gave the number of the scumbag who took the shots. There's no doubt, Janey."

"What show? What city?"

"Phoenix."

I stared at some point on the wall, seeing Anthony in the back of my mind. What was I doing while he was in Phoenix? The days blurred, one after another, and I wasn't sure where I had been. It was suddenly important to me, for reasons I might never understand, to know where I was and what I was doing at the moment he was doing intimate things with someone else.

I remembered a time, soon after I met him, when he put a wedding band on his finger and said, '*It keeps the groupies away.*'

And what had I said in return? Something about groupies being good for business? Jesus, how maniacally determined I was to be right. I had no clue about such things back then.

Nobody could ever say I hadn't been warned.

"Who was she?"

"I have no idea." Kristin put Stephen down on the floor. He immediately started to crawl off to the living room, where his toys were scattered all over the floor. There was the sound of a rattle, along with a satisfied giggle.

"You're taking this too well," she said.

"I'm not taking this at all. It hasn't sunk in. It isn't real yet."

Silence descended, and in that time I thought back to the last two years, to the way things had started, to the man he used to be. I wondered if he was high when he was fucking that other woman. I wondered if it mattered. I thought about things until the sun moved enough to come at that odd angle through the bathroom window, blinding me until I got to my feet.

"What now?" she asked.

What now? That was the biggest question I could imagine, and I had no idea what the answer might be. My husband had cheated on me. That was all I really knew, and even that seemed as distant as a dusty road sign over a vast horizon. The knowledge of it was there but the emotions were suspended, waiting for some clue as to how to proceed.

Stephen cooed from the living room floor and banged one of his toys against another.

"He has a son," I said to Kristin, as if that was any sort of reason or comfort. I looked out the door at my little boy. He was trying to stick his whole fist in his mouth. When he failed at that, he tried to eat one of his toys. He was perfectly content, safe in the cocoon of love around him, and he had no idea that an earthquake had just rocked his world.

"He has a son," I repeated, and waited for tears that did not come.

* * * *

When Anthony walked through the door that night, I was sure he was expecting everything to be the same as it had always been. He brought a small bag with him, filled with the most basic things, since he would be home for four days between gigs. I watched him close the door. The moonlight washed over him from those high rounded windows, brilliant light that turned his hair to the color of smoke. He headed straight for the bedroom, and finding it dark and quiet, turned to the living room.

"I'm in here," I called softly from the couch. Anthony stood in the wide archway and waited while his eyes adjusted to the dim light.

"Why are the lights out?" he asked.

"I like them that way right now."

Anthony dropped his bag onto the floor beside his feet and came toward me. I took a long pull of the bottle of Jack Daniels. I wasn't drunk, not even close to it. The liquor was simply to relax me, to keep me calm enough that I didn't try to kill him.

"Where's Stephen?"

"He's at Kristin's house for the night."

Even before the sentence was finished, Anthony's whole tone shifted. I could feel it from across the distance between us. *A night alone*, he was thinking, *she planned this*, and he was more than ready to accept it as a romantic interlude between two overworked parents who were overdue for some private time.

"Why did you do that?" There it was, the teasing note in his voice.

"Why did you?"

Anthony paused, suddenly uncertain. He leaned against one side of the archway. I could make out his face now in the moonlight, could see he was confused. But he wasn't confused enough, and the way he cleared his throat in the silence proved everything.

"Janey?"

I swirled the liquor in the bottle. "Don't play dumb, Anthony. You're a lot of things, but you're not dumb, and neither am I."

He didn't speak for a long time. I was teetering on the brink of emotional exhaustion. Only so many things could go through a person's mind before all her resources started to wear thin. I knew what he said in the next few minutes would determine whether my reaction would be sane or flat-out violent.

"I know what you've done," I said, making things very simple and clear.

He saved us both a lot of anger by resigning to the situation. He sighed heavily and dropped into the nearest chair. He buried his face in his hands and would not look at me.

"Tell me what happened," he said.

I took a deep breath. "Kristin got a phone call from a reporter. She got the pictures and she came here to tell me, before anyone else had a chance to do it."

Anthony nodded. "She's good to you."

I said nothing, and the silence drew all the comparisons Anthony needed.

"Was it just once?" I asked, needing to know this above all else. A one-time indiscretion I might be able to handle.

More than that and I would have to rethink things, perhaps even the trajectory of my life.

"No."

My reaction came out of nowhere. I upended the liquor bottle. Alcohol sloshed out onto my wrist. I flung it as hard as I could into the moonlit darkness. It hit the fireplace stones and shattered. The rain of glass sounded like hail on the roof.

Anthony stood up but made no move to go anywhere. I shoved the coffee table with my foot and it moved across the hardwood with an ungodly screech.

"How long have you been fucking around behind my back?"

My voice was disjointed, not my own. My whole body throbbed with my heartbeat. My hands shook so hard I had to put them between my knees and squeeze them there to keep them under control. I was on the verge of attacking him, right on the brink of physically assaulting my own husband, and he knew it. He stood his ground and let his voice do the calming, if any calming could be had.

"I'm so sorry, Janey. I know it's late to say that, I know it might not matter, but I'm so damn sorry. I don't have any answers for you that will make it better."

"I asked you a question," I hissed.

"I don't know. Really, I don't. The days and weeks all blur together. The only times on the calendar that make any sense are the days when Stephen turns one month older. Honest to God, Janey, I don't know how to answer that question."

The mention of our son made me so furious, I could no longer trust myself to speak. The silence drew out hard between us.

"Maybe a few months," he said softly. "Not quite that. It hasn't been anyone in particular. It's been someone after a show every now and then. That's all."

"That's all," I repeated. The pain in my chest was starting to dim again. The numbness came as a relief.

"Groupies," he said.

"I know what you meant."

"Janey..."

His eyes were wet with unshed tears. His whole body was tense in a sad kind of way, as if he wanted to cry but wasn't sure it was appropriate to do so. He wanted to come to me, that much I knew, but the thought of him touching me right at that moment made me want to scream.

"Were you high?"

The question rocked Anthony back on his heels. He sat down again in the chair and looked at the floor, at the fireplace, at the door – anywhere but at me.

"And how long has *that* been going on, Anthony? How long have you been back on it?"

"A long time," he admitted softly. "But never at home, Janey. Never here. Not around Stephen. That's why you never saw it. It wasn't anything you missed."

"Well, that's obviously not true."

"It wasn't your fault. It was me being a good little addict and covering my every track."

The fact that he admitted it all so fully made me believe him.

"I know you hate me," he said.

"Probably."

My agreement stopped Anthony from the apologetic questions of forgiveness. He fell silent and for a long time we just looked at each other over the space of the living room.

"Come to bed," he finally said.

Was he absolutely insane? "I'm not coming to bed with you."

"Come lie down with me. In the morning we'll decide what to do, when we can both think. Right now anything we say can't be taken back."

"I don't want to be in the same bed with you, Anthony."

He ran his hands through his hair and walked to the fireplace. Glass crunched under his shoes. "I won't touch

174

you, Janey. I know I don't have the right to do that tonight."

"If ever," I amended.

"If ever," he agreed.

I was as tired as if I had run a marathon. The emotional turmoil had beaten my body like nothing physical ever could. When I rose to my feet, I stumbled. Anthony reached out with a lightning-quick hand and caught me before I fell against the crooked table.

His touch burned my skin. I pulled slowly away and walked to the bedroom. I stared at the neatly made bed, at the fresh, crisp sheets, and I was suddenly slammed by mental images of Anthony with someone else. How was it done? Up against the bus? In the bed in the back? Or on some forgotten stairwell, covered with dust, the secrecy heightening the pleasure?

The thought of what he had done made me shudder with pain. I was suddenly lightheaded. I sat down heavily on the bed, spread my knees and dropped my head between them. I took deep breaths until the world stopped spinning, until things seemed more under control.

I crawled under the covers and Anthony did the same, careful not to touch me unless I wanted him to. We lay in the wide bed and looked at each other from our matching pillows.

"We've been married for three months," I whispered. "Three months this week."

Anthony slid a hand across the sheet. His hand hesitated between us, then he settled for something less. He touched a lock of my hair, twirled it around his finger.

"I do love you," he said. "And I am sorry."

No matter how exhausted I was, I didn't think sleep would come. I was certain I would never sleep again. But within moments, I was out.

* * * *

Sometime in the dead of night, Anthony woke me with

the hands he swore wouldn't touch me. They were sliding across my body, the coolness of them in marked contrast to the warmth from hours under the covers. I rolled onto my back to give him more access. My mind raced and fought against his touch, but my body responded as instantly as it always did when Anthony touched me.

"Is this okay?" he whispered.

I didn't speak. I was too busy fighting back the images that popped into my head; too busy trying to fight what my body wanted. It was easier to give in than it was to think, so I did.

I tangled my fingers into his hair and pulled him down for a kiss. When I kicked off the covers and pushed him lower, he went willingly, spreading my legs with his hands and settling between them.

The magic ride of sensation took over all my thoughts, until the only sign of what had happened hours earlier was a distant pounding in the back of my head. I rose up to him and held his head steady with my hands, pushing him closer, determined to get every ounce of satisfaction out of what his tongue and lips were doing. His knowledge of my body was so complete that he could tell the moment I was pushed too close to the edge and could back off just enough to keep me there. He stretched out the promise of pleasure until it shattered with an almost violent shudder and cry.

Then he rose above me to take pleasure of his own. That wasn't what I wanted — not that way. I pushed him aside and climbed on top of him, straddled him and rode him hard enough to make us both hurt. His hands curled around the headboard. My motion made the bed ring and slam against the wall. I was hell-bent on punishment of the most pleasurable kind, a counterattack against those things that hurt from within.

"Damn, Janey," he growled once, and I leaned over him, hissed into his face.

"Take it, you slut. I know you can."

The words were like liquid fire. He thrust up into me and

gave as good as he got, until we were slamming into each other so hard we might as well have been fighting. The lines blurred. I called him names and enjoyed the way it felt.

"Slut. You like that, you fucking slut? You whore? You're nothing but a whore, aren't you? You fuck anything that looks good and then you want to come home and fuck some more, isn't that right?"

His motion faltered. I dug my nails into his chest and he cried out in both pain and pleasure. I stopped when he yanked my hair, but still I kept up the litany of words that had thrown us both into a frenzy.

"Do it, bastard. Fuck me. You can fuck me harder than that."

"Bitch," Anthony growled.

I slapped him.

The sharp sound of it startled us both. Anthony froze for a moment, then rose up with clear intent. He pushed me off. I landed hard on the bed. He climbed on top of me, pinning my arms down over my head. One deep thrust and he was buried completely. I lifted my legs around his waist and rose up to meet every stroke.

"Did that feel good?" he hissed. "Did that make you feel better?"

The orgasm took my breath away. I cried out against his shoulder, teeth bared, hands clenching down on his. He was right behind me, coming deep inside. The name he uttered was mine, over and over and over.

He slowly let me go and moved to his side of the bed. After a long moment of breathing hard, he reached for the bedside lamp. Mellow light flooded the room. The mark of my hand on his face was vivid. He stared at me with bright, wild eyes. His fingers traced the mark.

"I liked that," he said.

"So did I."

Anthony smiled slowly. "Do you feel better?"

"I think I do."

"I'm surprised you let me touch you."

177

"Not any more surprised than I am."

"But I'm glad you did."

I lay down beside him. My body ached. I stared at the ceiling fan until it began to blur.

"Hey."

I didn't answer. Anthony pulled the blankets over both of us and lay there with me, watching me as I watched the ceiling. After long moments of staring, he reached over and turned off the light, covering us in darkness again. Soon his breathing was even and steady, and I knew he was sound asleep. I wished I could go back into dreamland as easily.

I wasn't sure what I was feeling. A part of me wanted him just as much as I always did, but another part of me was horrified by what I had just done. I should be furious with him and kick him out of the house, but instead I was fucking him as hard as I could in the very marriage bed he had made a mockery of with his late-night flings on the road. Instead of packing his bags, I was lying beside him and thinking things through.

I could say that I had known this would come, that the groupies would be too much of a distraction. I had seen it time and time again, and I had been warned more than once, not only by others but also by my own conscience. After all, hadn't he cheated on his first wife with me? I had known all about her and I hadn't cared. The audacity of it came back to slam me in the gut.

What goes around comes around.

But even so, that didn't mean it was all right for him to do what he did. It wasn't. Add the drug use on top of the infidelity and we had a train wreck waiting to happen.

Was I going to sit by and watch?

I toyed with the idea of going out on the road with him. But that would be self-defeating, wouldn't it? Instead of trusting my husband, I would be policing him, which was a sure-fire way to end a marriage even if it was entirely good and aboveboard. At this point I didn't trust him as far as I could throw him, and that was a dangerous place for us to be. How could I ever build trust in him again, especially knowing that his best intentions went out the window when he was high?

I thought about it long into the morning, until the sun came up and Anthony stirred. He woke to find me lying there, watching him.

"What are you thinking?" he asked.

"Thinking about what to do."

"Tell me what you've come up with so far," he said congenially, as if we were talking about the weather or the latest single or how we wanted to decorate a particular room in the house.

"I'm thinking about rehab, for starters."

At the mention of the word *rehab*, all of Anthony's defenses went up. He refused to look me in the eye and moved away to his side of the bed, steering clear of conversation in both the emotional and physical sense. He came up with all sorts of reasons why he shouldn't do that right now, his career chief among them. Then he brought up the fact he wouldn't be able to see Stephen while he was away in a rehabilitation facility, and my response was icy.

"If you're worried about seeing your son now," I said, climbing out of bed and putting on my robe, yanking the sash tight, "you should really think about what it will be like if I divorce you."

The word hung in the air, the threat of it potent as a dangerous gas. Anthony held his breath and watched me as the reality of the way things were started to sink in. Before he started to breathe again, his eyes filled with tears. I recognized it not as the remorse and fear I had expected, but as resentment.

"You're giving me an ultimatum," he said stiffly.

"Yes."

"Just like that? You dictate the path of my life and my career? Rehab or divorce?"

"I don't dictate anything. You've got the option."

Anthony glared at me. His anger broke free when he rose

from the bed and stalked to the walk-in closet. The hangers thudded together as he grabbed a shirt and threw it on, slid into a pair of jeans, all the while cursing under his breath. He came out of the little room and walked right up to me with fire in his eyes.

"How could you ask such a thing?"

"You," I said softly. "You have one *hell* of a lot of nerve, acting like you're the wronged one here. How dare you."

I turned and walked to the kitchen. Anthony was right on my heels. I was shaking inside and out, but my mind was made up. The only way I could ever trust him again was right here in front of us, this ultimatum that I had just given him. He could prove to me he wanted to stop the drugs, then I could accept his mistakes. If he wasn't willing to make a change and preferred instead to continue in his fast lifestyle, he could count me out of it. I wasn't willing to trade my chance at happiness for constant questions about the man I loved, where he was, what he was doing, and whom he was doing it with.

I explained this as best I could. Anthony stared at me until I was finished.

"That's it, then? I go to rehab or you leave me."

"Yes."

"You're giving me an ultimatum," he said again, as if he couldn't believe it.

"You opened the door for this, Anthony. You're the one who brought all this pain and distrust to our doorstep."

"And now I have to pay the piper, is that it?"

I took a deep breath. "The decision is yours."

Anthony turned away from me. He walked through the house, pacing the floors like a caged animal. I watched quietly from the kitchen, holding onto the counter to keep from sinking into the floor in despair. Finally he disappeared into the bedroom and slammed the door hard enough to rattle the pictures on the wall.

I sank to the nearest kitchen chair and stared out the window as I listened to him pack.

Chapter Twelve

The tabloids went crazy with the news of Anthony's affair. The photographs of Anthony with the mysterious groupie hit websites first, and within a week they were in full color on every grocery checkout line. When the more upstanding women's magazines speculated on the issue, it was a reminder of just how popular he had become.

Even Angela couldn't put her usual spin on the situation. She made comments meant to soothe the waters, but no one really noticed. Her press releases went unanswered and often unread. No matter what she said, it was ignored by the tabloid-reading public and their enjoyment of the spectacle.

A week later the news of our separation broke, and life went from barely manageable to completely insane within the span of a day. Vans and trucks parked outside the gates of our house, and anywhere I went was scrutinized by a dozen camera lenses. Now staying at home wasn't a choice—even walking outside to water the plants became a media blitz for those paparazzi hoping to make a buck off the woman scorned. Casual comments to friends somehow found their way to the tabloids, so I learned to be careful whom I trusted. All the entertainment shows were abuzz with the story, so I kept the television off.

It was a very quiet existence that gave me more than enough time to think.

Letting Anthony get away without going to rehab when I was pregnant with Stephen was probably the biggest mistake I had made in the whole situation. That was the time when he was open to the possibility, when with only a little reasoning, I could have talked him into going. I should have insisted. It would have saved us both a world of pain.

But that was hindsight, and this was now. Our choices hadn't been the right ones, but there was nothing to be done about that at this point. There was only what we could do with the place we found ourselves in, and that place didn't look good at all.

Anthony and I agreed to give marriage counseling a try. On the appointed day, the counselor was there and so was I, but Anthony didn't show. He later came up with the excuse of a change in his schedule, but he didn't bother to think about the fact that though I might not be on the road, I still worked for Axton Records, and his schedule was always at my fingertips. He wasn't as busy as he said he was — he just didn't want to be there. When I suggested that, he cursed and hung up on me, proving my hunch to be true.

He didn't bother to see Stephen. He rarely asked about him. It was as if his son didn't exist, but he did put his checks into our joint bank account, and continued to contribute to the account set up for Stephen's college education. I found myself watching the balance in the account, wondering where he got the money to do all the drugs he was apparently enjoying out on the road.

He agreed to attend meetings at Narcotics Anonymous or any other organization that seemed to suit him and his needs, but when the time came to make good on the promises, he refused to go to those either. He suggested taking a sponsor out on the road with him, but plans for that fell through just as quickly as the subject was brought up. The truth was, Anthony couldn't stop what he was doing, and most of the reason was simply because he didn't want to stop. He had the opportunity to get help, but he refused it at every turn.

His world spun away from us, leaving me and Stephen behind, while Anthony dug deeper into a hole of clichés. It would be harder than ever to pull himself from that place when he did get up the courage to do so.

"If you keep this up," I said to him one night, as he talked to me over the phone from backstage in Milwaukee, "you will kill yourself. And if you don't kill yourself, you will wake up one day to find I'm not there anymore, and neither is your son. What will you do then, Anthony?"

"I don't know," he said. "But whatever I do, it will be my choice."

His defiance hung over the house like a cloud long after he had hung up on me again. I resolved not to call him back. When the phone rang late that night, I turned off the ringer.

The silence between us lasted for three weeks. During that time Anthony was seen out and about with different women, most of them models, all of them much younger than he. He didn't bother keeping his conquests hidden from the public. Every week there was another reporter calling with another set of questions, a whole new tabloid story.

Apparently my husband's sex life was very healthy.

His manager, of all people, tried hardest to soothe the wounds. Tom called on a daily basis, telling me where Anthony was and what he was doing. We both knew Tom was only telling half-truths. The photographs had to come from somewhere, and even when I tried to avoid them, I couldn't. They popped up in the most unlikely places, even in the Nashville newspapers—so much for reporting the news and not the gossip. Tom never lied, but he never told me everything, either.

I was offered a tell-all book deal. I turned it down. I was offered representation from the toughest divorce lawyer in town, and I said I would think about it. Kristin offered to babysit so I could spend some time alone, and I took her up on it a few times, always with a bottle of liquor to keep me company. Even the hangovers didn't hurt as much as the thought of my husband in bed with another woman, but at least they gave me something else to think about.

Keith called to ask for my assistance with the label, and I turned in my resignation. That move brought Keith and the full arm-twisting power of Axton Records to my doorstep in an angry fury.

"What the hell are you doing?" Keith hollered.

It was one of the first times we had spoken since Anthony moved out of the house. Keith had known about Anthony's drug addiction and had said nothing. I no longer trusted him, and the friendship that had been so deep before the cocaine came into play had cracked, perhaps irreparably. I was feeling every bit of that loss as Keith stood in my living room, glaring at me with barely controlled anger.

"I'm not comfortable working with you anymore," I said. I knew that wouldn't be the end of it, and sure enough, it was just the beginning.

"You're not comfortable working with Anthony, isn't that what you mean?"

"No," I said calmly. "I'm talking about you, Keith. I don't want to work with you."

The bare-bones explanation rendered him silent for a long moment. He looked around the house, at the records on the walls, the wedding picture above the mantel, then back at me with a haunted expression.

"You blame me for this?"

"I don't blame you for Anthony's decisions," I said, shaking my head. "I blame you for knowing of them, and keeping me in the dark. I blame you for not trying to get help for him. I blame you for becoming so caught up in the fame and the bottom line that you sacrificed the very man who got you there."

Every one of my words was like a well-placed dagger, and there was no protection against the wounds, because each of them spoke the truth. By the time I was done, Keith was pale under his tanned skin and his eyes were wet.

"You were eaten up by the machine," I said. "You let it take over."

Keith could say nothing in his own defense. He sat down heavily in the same chair Anthony had sunk into the night I learned of his adultery. Keith stared at the mantel and shook his head as the last few years ran through his mind.

"I failed him," he finally said. "Worse than that, I failed you. You are the one person who stuck by me and believed when no one else did, and this is how I repaid you for that."

I said nothing.

"You made this company what it was," he went on. "It was me at the helm but it was you driving the ship. Then you moved away from the wheel and we went onto the wrong course. It's not your fault. It's mine, because the buck was supposed to stop with me, and I wasn't paying attention."

I nodded, more in commiseration than in agreement.

"Come back, Janey."

"It's too late for that."

"You're the only one who can set this ship straight. I can't do it myself."

"Yes, you can."

"I came here to talk to you about this. We need you."

I shook my head. "You give me too much credit."

"You don't give yourself enough."

"Axton Records is doing just fine. I can't imagine that train will stop now, do you? It's barreling down the tracks at a hundred miles an hour. You're signing acts left and right. Tell me you're not."

"We are."

"Now Anthony's behavior makes Axton just like the big boys. He screws up and destroys his life, but I'm willing to bet the charts will come out this week with Anthony's album rising up a few notches."

Keith blushed hard, but didn't deny it.

"How much did it jump?"

He shook his head, refusing to answer.

"Come back to us, Janey."

"I can't."

"Full partnership. Your name on the letterhead beside mine."

The offer came out of the blue and shocked me into

complete silence. I sank to the couch and stared at Keith. It was much the same as staring at Anthony on that night that might have ended our marriage, only this time the tables were turned, and I was the one expected to come up with an answer to a question I hadn't seen coming.

I didn't have the first clue as to what to say.

"Think it over."

When he started to say more, I held up my hand. "Stop."

"Anthony isn't the only one who needs you," he said.

Keith rose from the chair and came to me. His strong arms came around me, and I struggled against him, unwilling to accept comfort from the man who had betrayed my husband's safety, my son's future and my own marriage. Keith held on, refusing to let go, and the fight went out of me as quickly as it had come. Tears took the place of my fury, and I leaned against Keith as I cried. He ran his fingers through my hair, kissed my forehead and cradled me like a child until the sobs eased.

"You deserve so many good things," he said.

"Stephen deserves more."

"Let me help make things right, Janey."

I pushed him away. "I'm not sure anyone can do that."

We sat in silence until my sobs eased and he ran out of things to say.

I walked Keith to the door. His hair caught the sunlight, turning it a brilliant blond. His eyes were bright with unshed tears. I looked at him and saw the man who had taken me under his wing and taught me so many things. This was the man who had walked me down the aisle, the godfather of my son, the surrogate father who I had once imagined could never let me down. The truth was I loved him more than I could ever say, and being angry with him was killing me.

He smiled before he disappeared into the car. I watched until the vehicle was a ghost of a shadow in the distance, then it was gone, too.

It was the last time I would ever see Keith alive.

* * * *

The ringing was a serrated edge, cutting jagged lines through my dream. The dream was a good one, one of those that slipped around my mind like warm water flowing through a gentle stream, the kind that infuses a feeling of warmth and closeness for hours afterwards. The phone was an unwelcome intrusion. I tried to ignore it for the space of three rings, but I was already out of my dream anyway, and it was vanishing for good. I picked up the phone right before the answering machine could kick on.

"This better be good."

"Janey?"

It took a moment to realize who was calling.

"Tom?"

"Janey, honey…wake up."

Tom's voice was soothing—too soothing. I glanced at the clock and sat straight up in bed. It was three-thirty-four in the morning. Tom would not be calling me at this hour unless he had absolutely no choice.

A knock sounded from the front door, a hesitant sound. Someone was at the door, someone who had the combination to the gate. Someone who knew us well enough to be trusted with such things.

The knock didn't come again. I swung my legs down to the hardwood floor. The coldness was the final push in waking up, and suddenly I knew why Tom was calling.

"Where is he?"

My voice was steady, even as I fought rising panic.

"Answer the door," Tom said, and that's when I started to shake.

"You're *here*?"

* * * *

The glow of the television slowly filled the room. Everything came into focus.

The news anchor had beautiful raven hair. So much like

187

Anthony, I thought, then closed my eyes to that which I knew was coming, that which I had seen only in my nightmares.

The impossibly early sun glinted off the tail, the only part of the plane that was still above water. The machine bobbed gently with the waves whipped up by the helicopters that hovered overhead. Divers fell backward from the side of long ships. I thought how fitting it was that they were dressed in black.

The urgency in the news anchor's voice was edged with a slight thrill. The woman knew this was a big story, perhaps the biggest of the year. "Just to recap, you are seeing video now of country superstar Anthony Keenan's private plane, which crashed at three-o-eight Eastern time this morning into New York Harbor. Officials have confirmed that Keenan was on the plane, along with an entourage from his record label, Axton Records. Hope for survivors is dwindling…"

The whole world went gray. I heard Tom's voice, felt his hand on my back.

Then there was nothing at all.

* * * *

When the world came back into focus, all I could hear was Stephen's crying. It was jagged, as if someone were pacing with him and jogging him up and down with every step. I blinked once at the ceiling before I sat up, disoriented for a moment until it all came back to me with a vengeance, turning my knees to jelly and my stomach to a knot. I thought I might be sick.

"Take deep breaths," he said. "Stay calm."

"Tom?"

"I'm here. Drink this."

I took a sip of the water. It was cool, not cold, and I could taste the newness of the pipes through which it had flowed. I immediately retched, though nothing came out. The shock hit me again and I started to shiver, at first only a little, then uncontrollably.

"Stephen—"

"Kristin has him."

I nodded, as if this was the most expected thing in the world. When everything else fell apart, count on Kristin to make things better. Tom must have known that as well as I did, and that's why he'd called her.

"Is he okay?"

"He's okay." Tom hesitated. "He heard you crying."

I shook my head slowly, not remembering.

"Janey, they don't know for sure—"

"Who else was on the plane?"

Tom's face looked puffy and swollen. His eyes were red.

"They found Keith," he said.

I waited for more, but that was all.

"Is he alive?"

I watched Tom start to break. It was a frightening thing, seeing a strong man lose his composure by degrees.

"He was," he said.

I heard the past tense. The world began to spin. I closed my eyes.

"We don't have to do this now, Janey."

"Who else?"

"Let's give it some time…"

"Please," I whispered. "I don't want to find out on CNN."

"Angela is gone," Tom said, openly crying now. "So is Victor, the new guitar player…"

"How many people were on the plane?"

"Seven."

Suddenly the rage was a brilliance of pain, an uncontrollable and vicious desperation. This was not happening now, not to us, not this way. This was a mistake, and someone would soon realize that. This could not be about us.

We had a son. Anthony had a *son*. He could not do this to his son, he would not do this, and he would not leave his child.

189

"That son of a bitch," I swore. "How dare he die on us?"

At my angry words, Stephen started crying harder. I was instantly guilty for raising my voice. I listened to Kristin's footsteps as she walked to the other end of the house, bouncing Stephen with every step, cooing to him. I sat on the couch and dropped my face into my hands. The sobs hurt from my soul out.

"I am so sorry," I managed to say. Tom touched my knee. "I know I shouldn't say that, I know I shouldn't be angry with him, but I don't know—nothing seems right."

"You're in shock."

The anger came out of nowhere again. "Gee, you think, Tom?"

"Drink more water, Janey."

"No."

We sat together in the living room, him on the floor and me on the couch, and I thought again of how much this room had seen. The paint still smelled new, but lifetimes of pain had already been lived within these four walls.

"You've got to stay strong right now," Tom said.

I closed my eyes and took deep breaths.

"Stay with me," Tom begged. "Stay on top of this."

The drone of the television didn't get through the haze of pain. It was a jumble of words and images. The important news had already been reported, so what did the rest matter? I stared at the images on the screen, unable to tear my eyes away. The cheery sunlight glinting from that tail and the water moving around it spoke louder than any words ever could. When Tom moved to turn off the television, I snapped at him so fiercely that he jumped at the sound of my voice.

"Janey—damn, Janey."

"I want to see," I said. "I wasn't there with him…"

"Janey, stop. Don't do this."

He tucked a blanket around my legs. It was warm in the house, but I was shivering so hard, my teeth were chattering. He pressed a glass into my hands and the scent of bourbon assaulted me. I took a tiny sip, then another. The heat landed in my center and the shaking seemed to ease. Tom knelt in front of me, his hands on my knees, and looked up into my face until I focused on his eyes.

"Stay with me," he said again, and this time I nodded, though my mind was a million miles away.

Sometime later, Tom and Kristin spoke from the corner of the room. Sometimes Stephen cooed, sometimes he whimpered, but mostly he was silent. I stared at the television screen until a picture of Anthony popped up on it, then I looked away, afraid I would be sick again.

I tuned the television out. I let my mind go elsewhere. It was surprisingly easy to do, and I noted idly that I really was in shock, just as idly as I would note whether the day was sunny or rainy. Nothing seemed as it should be anymore, and that was just fine, wasn't it? Nothing would ever be normal again. I noted this without an ounce of emotion, only a deep weariness, as though I had just traveled a thousand miles.

Lost in my thoughts, I didn't hear the bulletin, or the excitement in the voices coming from the screen.

"Janey!"

"Yes," I said softly.

Tom shook me with both hands. The sudden movement shocked me back into the here and now. "Janey, look!"

On the television, the reporter was so animated it seemed she might come right up off her seat with excitement. She leaned over her desk, shuffling papers, her eyes bright.

"We have just confirmed that Anthony Keenan has been found in the back of the plane, and our reports say he is *alive*. We do not know his condition. For more we are going to our affiliate with WXMV out of New York. Randy, what do you know?"

The wind whipped at the reporter's tie. "Brenda, all we know is that Anthony Keenan was found alive in the plane. They are removing him from the wreckage as we speak. The coast guard has requested a Lifeflight chopper, which you can see in the background — it will be landing any second to take Mr. Keenan to the trauma center, where the teams are on standby…"

I stood up from the couch. The glass of bourbon fell from my hand and thudded on the floor. The liquor splashed over my bare feet.

"Kristin!" Tom hollered, and took off at a run through the house. The two of them talked again, this time in hushed, urgent tones. I was vaguely aware of Kristin standing at the threshold of the room, looking at me as I looked at the screen.

I stood staring at the video, unable to tear my eyes away. The divers were pulling someone out of there, and though there were sheets draped over the scene to keep away prying eyes and camera lenses, there was enough movement to tell that they really were pulling him out — and there was enough urgency to leave no doubt he was alive.

"I've got Stephen," Kristin said, her voice cutting through the fog in my head. "He's fine. You've got to get there, Janey."

"Kristin…"

She shoved me toward the bedroom. "Get dressed," she said.

Tom was already heading for the door. "I'll get the car."

* * * *

When the plane took off, I clenched the armrests and took deep breaths. I remembered Anthony's fear of takeoff, the way he always hated that feeling of lift, that moment when the tires left the ground and he was airborne, for better or for worse. He always said the flight, and even the landing, was a piece of cake.

I wondered if he had known the plane was going down, and at what point did he realize it? Did he have time to be scared? Did he feel it hit the water, and did he think he would die? How long was he in there before they got him out, and was he conscious of what was happening to him?

I tried to pray, but there were no words, just a hollow hope.

I kept my eyes closed and counted to ten. Then I did it again, over and over, until we were in the air and clear of the airport. I was sure I would be sick, but the moment passed. Tom looked up at me from the paperwork he was holding.

"Are you working?" My tone was accusatory, daring him to answer in the affirmative.

"Not really."

"What is that, then?"

"Paperwork," he said with an air of finality.

I could be just as determined. "Like what?"

He didn't answer.

"You're working now? How can you possibly work now?"

"Angela is gone," he said abruptly. "Who do you think is going to talk to the media?"

My breath caught. My heart pounded. I looked back out the window and twisted my wedding band around and around on my finger. I slipped it up and felt the very slight, shallow groove in the skin of my finger, the place where that band had rested since the day Anthony put it there. I hadn't once taken it off, even though there were times I had wanted to, had thought about how it would feel to be without it, just as I was without the man who had given it to me.

"Does Anthony still wear his wedding band?" I asked Tom.

"Yes. He never takes it off, so far as I know."

Clouds drifted in the distance. When I looked out the window, a long and winding length of blue water was below me. The river meandered through farmland. In my head I could see a plane, jet black with gold lettering, the engines whining dangerously high, perhaps a deep boom of explosion that rocked the whole machine, the steep descent.

I tried to focus on anything else, and the first thing in my mind's eye was Anthony standing on the video set, the blue screen behind him. The busy world moved around him but he stood still, as though nothing could touch him.

Images flashed through my head. Was it like this for him? As the plane was going down, what did he think about?

I saw Anthony sitting beside my hospital bed, holding his son in his arms. I saw the tears in his eyes when I walked down the aisle. I heard the laughter as he talked with friends around the dinner table. I tasted the guitar strings on his fingers, the sweat on his chest, the sweet spot underneath his ear. I remembered the touch of his hands on my body, the way he murmured my name, the feel of his hair between my fingers.

I stared at the clouds until a soft bell dinged. We were coming in for landing. I closed the shade over the window without looking down, knowing that I would probably not see the place where Anthony's plane had gone down, but certain I would look for it, whether I wanted to or not.

As we began our descent, Tom reached over and took my hand.

"Do you pray?" he asked.

I closed my eyes.

His words of safekeeping, prayers of protection, whispered all around me as the plane landed. When I opened my eyes, I was struck by the fact that not once in the entire time had Tom prayed for our safe landing. He had prayed for Anthony.

Chapter Thirteen

Machines beeped importantly in the little room. They stood sentry beside the bed, watching over the man who lay upon it. The little lights shone down on his face, turning the white bandages an unearthly green. His lips glistened as I put lip balm on them. The overhead lights were off and all was quiet, save for the steady beeps that reminded me he was still alive after all.

The chair was comfortable enough to sleep in, but I hadn't done much of that. I had spent most of my time simply watching Anthony, listening to the doctors and waiting for him to wake up from whatever hell he was in.

Anthony had been knocked unconscious in the crash. At some point he had awoken and managed to unlock his seat belt—or someone else had done it for him. The fact he was not strapped in allowed him to move with the water as it rose in the cabin.

The impact had killed most of the passengers. The few who hadn't died on impact had expired when the rising water overtook them.

Keith had been found in the same state Anthony was now in—unconscious, barely breathing, but alive enough to fight. Keith had lost that battle right before the ambulance reached the hospital, and nothing the doctors could do would bring him back.

I couldn't think about Keith without incapacitating grief. The first days were impossible, the hellish time when the simple ability to take one breath after another felt like a study in unfairness. Kind nurses had brought pills to take, and I had swallowed them down without asking what they were. Those pills allowed me to drift in a cocoon of emotional distance, and I was grateful for it.

A nurse walked by. Her shoes made a whispering sound. Anthony moved his head but didn't open his eyes. In the five days since the accident he had been moving more and more, but there was no indication of when he might come out of his coma. It could be right now, or it could be months. It could be never. The uncertainty was worse than anything else.

He had surprisingly few injuries from the accident. His arm was broken, his shoulder dislocated – probably from the force of the plane hitting the water – and he had bumps and bruises everywhere. The most troubling thing was his head injury, which didn't appear to be severe, but had put him in a coma nonetheless. The doctors had been straightforward with me, pointed out that Anthony's brain function looked good, but that people in comas were really lost in another world, one their machines couldn't reach. When he woke up was up to him, not up to anything medicine could do.

Tom sat with him sometimes, long enough for me to go down to the cafeteria and eat something, when I found the will to eat at all. The nurses didn't bother me. Here, Anthony was a patient who needed their help, not a superstar who could give an autograph. That might come later, but right now, they were doing all they could to make sure he was comfortable – and they were doing all they could to fight off the media.

The cameras had been camped out in front of the hospital for days. It seemed they never slept, always awake and waiting for the next person to come out of the doors. Reporters were posted at every entrance, watching like military scouts in search of an enemy.

Anthony's family came on the third day – his father, mother and one of his brothers. They stood around his bed as if they were standing around a gravesite, spoke very little and didn't shed a tear. His father never spared a single glance in my direction. Anthony's mother squeezed my hand as they left, a startling gesture in a moment devoid of any other emotion. It gave me good insights into why Anthony acted the way he did, how he could make it seem as though our separation didn't matter.

Thoughts about our relationship were the second thing on my mind, bested only by thoughts about his health.

I had been prepared to let Anthony go, to give him a divorce if that was what he wanted. He hadn't made much of an effort toward counseling or reconciliation, and it seemed his lifestyle was pushing me away from him. Even as he said he wanted to work things out, his time spent with other women made it seem otherwise.

The crash and the days afterwards, the long hours sitting by Anthony's hospital bed, had led me to consider things I hadn't dared think about before, namely the fact I might really lose Anthony for good.

Divorce was something we hadn't discussed, but I knew it would soon enter into our conversations. I doubted he wanted to do what it took to make it work, and sometimes I didn't want to do it, either. I loved him but there was only so much I could take, and Anthony had already handed me enough heartache to last a lifetime.

But seeing him in the hospital bed, vulnerable and needing someone to take care of him, brought back the way I felt when I married him—for better or for worse.

This just happened to be worse.

Taking care of Anthony on a physical level was something I could definitely do, but how would things be on an emotional level when he woke up? I wasn't naïve enough to think his attitude would have changed because he had been injured, but I hoped we would be able to reach some sort of compromise. The fact he had almost died, that we had lost so many people we loved, might be enough to make us take a second look at what more we could lose if we kept going down the path we were on.

As I thought things through, Anthony slept.

The days went by, ticking off the calendar with maddening slowness. Anthony moved much more often, but he still did not open his eyes. The doctors were almost certain he could hear the things around him, so I made a point of talking to him as much as I could. I read books and magazines out loud. My voice became hoarse with the constant words. I wrote my own stories and poems, mostly about him, and talked about them out loud as I did it—the talking was good for him and the writing served to distract me.

Kristin came to visit, and she brought Stephen with her. Our son was too young to understand, but was fascinated by the beeping machines and the little lights. He cooed and tried hard to talk, testing out his newfound babbles, and we hoped the sound got through to Anthony. If anything would get through to him, it would be his little boy.

Stephen giggled and played and sat at the foot of his bed, but still, Anthony didn't wake up. On the day Stephen turned one, his father was deep in a coma, unable to see his son bury his hands into his birthday cake and try to eat the candle. The celebration, held in a tiny room in the hospital, was a harsh reminder of just how much had happened in the time since Stephen had been born. I prayed that for the next birthday, his father would be the one helping him blow out the candles.

Two weeks passed. With the funerals happening during that time, the media frenzy hadn't died down in the least. I left the hospital only to go to the services for those who had worked for us, loved us and died while pursuing a dream with Anthony.

Going to Angela's funeral was hard. Watching her husband drop flowers on her casket was an exercise in torture. Seeing the bright sunlight glint off the gold edging of that casket as they lowered her into the ground started a stream of tears that felt like they would never stop.

But going to Keith's funeral was what almost did me in.

I stood over his casket as it was lowered into the ground. My mind went back through the years, from the time I was a young upstart taken under his wing, to the last conversation we had. I went through all the artists, all the trips, all the times we fought like tigers in the boardroom, all the times we were of one mind and unshakable. I loved him like a father, and he had always taken care of me as though I were his daughter.

I was his best friend. He was my confidant.

He had left a void that could never be filled.

One by one, we stepped forward to say our final goodbyes and sprinkled dirt over the shiny surface. Long after the rest had left, I couldn't walk away. I watched the payloader as it shoveled dirt over the hole. I watched it fill in. I stayed until the casket was covered over. I watched as the flowers were placed over his grave, dozens of arrangements, the scent so full and heady that it almost made me sick. Despite the worried looks from the limousine driver and the pleas of the funeral home staff, I could not walk away.

When the sun started to go down, I knelt before the fresh mound of dirt, my throat choked with the scent of flowers, and dug my fingers into the soil. I stayed there for a long time, long enough for the cold ground to grow warm between my fingers. My tears fell on the dirt, turning it a darker shade. A small breeze rustled the flowers.

"I miss you already," I told him.

* * * *

When I got back to the hospital, security guards led me through paparazzi—but surprisingly, I didn't need them. The photographers and reporters were silent and respectful. They stepped back as I walked through, giving me ample room. A few hands touched me on the shoulder. One squeezed my hand. Shots were taken, but there was no deluge of flashbulbs. When I reached the doors I turned to face them, and for a moment I was taken aback at the sadness on their faces and the tears in their eyes. These very people who had followed us everywhere, the ones who reveled in the very things that had caused me so much pain, were standing respectfully before me, giving my grief its due.

"Thank you," I said. "Thank you for that."

Their condolences came, and I accepted them. For the first time, I stood and answered their questions. I knew they were writing down what I had to say, and that my words would be emblazoned across the front of tabloids before the week was out, maybe even twisted by uncaring editors who were after more sales, but the respectful nature of those photographers demanded more than simply disappearing behind the doors.

Right before I turned to go into the hospital, one of the questions caught me off guard. "I hate to ask this, ma'am," a reporter said. "I know you're not in the mood to talk about things like this, but everyone wants to know."

"What?"

"What are you going to do with the record label?"

At first I didn't understand. My confusion was clear, and the reporter hurried to clarify. He held out a piece of paper. My hands were trembling when I took it.

"Axton Records is yours, ma'am. Or it's going to be. It was announced this afternoon. I guess you were at the funeral then, but I thought you would have known several days ago."

"I haven't left the hospital," I said. "And under the circumstances, there hasn't been any talk of business in there."

I scanned the paper. It was a bulletin announcing the changes in the company, now that the owner and president were no longer there to run it. At first I was angry to read such news from a reporter, but I reminded myself that I hadn't let anyone talk to me about the business — I had shut out all discussion of Nashville and the future of Anthony's recording career. It felt entirely wrong to talk about such things while Anthony was lying in a coma. Besides that, what did the future of his career matter if he wasn't capable of handling it himself?

The missive was long and detailed, but the summary of the story was short and sweet. Keith's final wish was for his baby, Axton Records, to be tended by Janey Mills Keenan.

My knees went weak. I fumbled for words and found none. I leaned against the railing, looking over the small crowd, and I saw the red light blinking on a video camera.

"Turn that off," I said, and much to my surprise, the man holding it mumbled an apology and did just that.

"I'll have a statement about this soon," I said. "I don't know when. I don't know what to say right now. I'm sorry."

One camera flashed as I turned toward the building. I walked to the elevator and rode up to Anthony's floor, numb all the while. The nurses looked at me solemnly but said nothing as I walked through.

Once in Anthony's room, I sank into a chair. Only then did I burst into tears. I cried like my heart would break, in a way I hadn't been able to cry as I stood over Keith's grave. I doubled over in the chair, my hands pressed to my stomach, and fought the urge to scream, to hit something, to fall apart at the seams. I cried until there was nothing left in me, until every part of my body hurt, until I was exhausted with the effort.

When the storm was over, I wiped my eyes and looked up.

Anthony was staring right back at me.

The sudden surprise of seeing him awake brought a welling of fear. It was almost eerie, as if someone had just come back from the dead. The fact he didn't speak, that he had done it so quietly, only added to the ominous feeling.

"Janey?" he whispered, and it wasn't a ghost—it was my Anthony. All fears disappeared in the rush of relief. I came to his bed as he lifted his good arm toward me, and seconds later I was cuddled against him, my arms around him as well as I could manage, my head on his broad chest. The beeps of the monitors had sped up, and I could hear the echo of his heartbeat keeping time.

"I love you," I said.

"I love you, too."

His voice was harsh from weeks of making no sound. I shushed him with a finger against his lips.

"You don't have to talk."

"I love you." It came out in a mere whisper, little more than a noisy breath.

The little beeps were slowing down. He didn't say anything else for the longest time, and I looked up to make sure he was still with me, that he hadn't slipped back to that other world. His eyes were wide and bright, unmistakably alert. Anthony was fully with me, not anywhere else.

I touched his face. His cheek was scruffy against my palm.

"I need to get the nurse," I said gently. "You're in the hospital."

Anthony turned his head and looked at the machines beside him.

"How long have I been out?" he asked.

I poured a cup of water from the pitcher beside the bed and held it to his lips. He drank gratefully, and when his voice came again, it was a bit stronger. "What day is it?"

"Thursday. It's been over two weeks."

Anthony nodded with no surprise at all, as if he expected this answer.

"Do you remember what happened?"

"The engines failed."

"Yes."

"The plane went down."

"Do you remember anything else?"

There was a long moment of silence as he looked around the room.

"Yes." The haunted look in his eyes kept me silent, and he didn't say anything more. He reached for me instead. His arm was weak, but he was still strong enough to hold me there, where we both knew I belonged.

"I should ring for a nurse," I said, and he nodded against my temple.

202

When the nurses came into the room, a small amount of chaos ensued. I stepped back into the corner as they started checking vital signs, responses, asking him questions and smiling when he knew all the answers. Anthony had come out of the coma and though he was a bit sluggish and sometimes confused, by the time the doctor came in and did further tests, everyone was certain he was back for good.

The nurses took turns patting my arm, squeezing my hand or giving me a full-on hug as they walked out of the room. They had seen me there in the chair beside his bed for so many lonely nights — they knew how I had longed for this moment.

After what seemed an eternity of tests and discussions, the last nurse turned out the light. Anthony and I were alone in his room, looking at each other in the dim light from the hallway. The machines were no longer beeping. Every now and then his IV machine gurgled.

"You're here," I said, not attempting to hide the awe in my voice. I wasn't going to attempt to hide anything, anymore — never again. "I thought you were dead."

"So did I."

I blinked back sudden tears. "Did you hear anything? When you were in the coma? I know you told the doctors you didn't. Is that the truth?"

"I think it's the truth," he said. "I know I dreamed a lot. Maybe some of that was you getting through to me, because I remember dreaming about you."

"Anthony…"

I didn't know how to say the things I knew needed to be said. I wasn't even sure now was the time to do it. Why hadn't I paid attention to the hospital chaplain when he came into the room to talk with me? I had tuned him out, sure all he could offer was a long list of platitudes. I could have asked him questions and learned when it was best to tell Anthony exactly what had happened during those weeks he had been in another world.

Anthony took the problem out of my hands. "I know."

"You know?"

The green lights of the machines glinted off the tears in his eyes. He looked at the wide window, where the darkness was tempered by the streetlights a few stories below. It had begun to rain. Lightning occasionally lit up the sky. He watched it for a very long time.

"Keith," he said.

I took his hand. "Yes."

"The engine…it started to miss. Like a car that has water in the gas tank. Lurching, you know?"

I nodded.

"The pilot knew what was wrong. He tried to tell us, but I'm not sure anybody understood. All we really did understand was that we needed to buckle in and get in the emergency positions…like, with our heads down?"

"Yes."

"He said he could make it back to the airport. To just hold on and stay calm. But then the plane just…it just died. No sound. Nothing at all."

I held his hand and waited.

"I could hear the rushing sound as it picked up speed. There was no way to stop it, and there were buildings all around, and I remember thinking he should go for the water. Then it would just be us that got killed, and not the people in those buildings."

I wiped away tears as I listened.

"I don't remember the crash. I remember the moments before and the moments after, but I don't remember a thing about actually going down." He paused, thinking.

"Not remembering it all is normal, I think."

He nodded. "When I woke up, there was water filling the plane."

Anthony was silent for a very long time.

"We were in the farthest seats back," he said. "That's the only reason we made it out."

"Anthony…"

"I know," he said. "I know. He was hurt. We both knew

it."

"You talked to him?"

"We tried to keep each other awake. Then something happened—it felt like that moment right before you fall asleep, when you know you're going to but you aren't there yet—I remember thinking that was it, I was dying. That's the last thing I really remember until I woke up and saw you here."

I wanted to ask about what Keith had said. What had they talked about in his final minutes? But I didn't ask, for the look in Anthony's eyes warned me not to ask anything at all.

"Thank God you're alive," I said simply.

The next morning he sat up in bed and ate. He was ravenous, devouring everything they would let him have. Soon after that he was on his feet, weak and shaky. Every step was assisted by a nurse on either side, and he joked about having so many women at his beck and call. By the time he got back into bed, he was sweating and exhausted. But the time after that was easier, and soon he was walking on his own, his legs gaining strength with every new step.

The time in the hospital stretched for another week. The paparazzi went crazy outside, setting up shop close enough to be bothersome, and the police officers of the town were running full-force to keep them under control. But inside the hospital room it was quiet and serene, a place of healing of not only the body, but also the soul.

"We need to talk about things," he said to me one day, as he sat looking through dozens of cards from well-wishers. "We're still separated, aren't we?"

I knew this conversation was coming, but I still wasn't sure what to say. I finally decided that simplicity was the way to go.

"Yes, I suppose we are," I said.

"I've given it a lot of thought over this past week. I guess I thought about it a lot when I was out, too. I dreamed about you and me, and sometimes I dreamed about us being apart, but mostly it was about us being together. But the most important moment was when that plane started to drop out of the sky."

Anthony took a deep breath. "One of my thoughts was that I could never tell you how sorry I was, and how you would always believe I didn't want you." His eyes welled up with tears. "I never stopped wanting you. I never stopped loving you. I want you to always know that, and no matter how long the rest of my life is, I want to be able to tell you that every single day."

I choked back tears of my own. "Do you think we can make it work?"

"I don't know. Honestly, I don't."

"I don't know, either," I admitted.

"But if I didn't have hope in us, I wouldn't be saying this. I know it's going to be a hard road, and I know we've got a lot of broken trust to rebuild. I know the burden of that is going to be on me, because I'm the one who did the hurting. I also know it isn't just about a marriage—it's about me, too, and getting away from all the bad habits that seem to have become a part of me over this past year or so."

Hearing him admit things in such a stark, unabashed way made the glimmers of hope in my heart sparkle with new determination. If he was willing to be this honest about the way things had to change, then I was willing to listen to what he had to say.

"Tell me," I said. "Tell me where you want to start."

He smiled with such relief, I felt my heart would break. "How about with an apology—how about telling you how sorry I am for the hell I put you through."

Anthony reached toward me. On his finger was his wedding band, the one that matched mine. It still meant something. I went into his arms and he held me against him, not quite as strong as he was before—but the pounding of his heart was just as steady as it ever was.

"I love you," he said.

And in that moment, the worst of the long nightmare was

over.

Chapter Fourteen

Chapter Fourteen

Those first few weeks at home were very hard. Anthony faced not only the struggle of healing, but the compounded difficulty of walking away from an addiction. The temptations were there, but our home became a fortress of safety for him, a haven into which none of those temptations could enter.

Sometimes he would wander the house at night. Sometimes he cried for no reason. The nightmares were frightening in their intensity. The rebellion of his body was over, but the emotional and psychological dependency was still strong. Cocaine had been his way of handling his problems, but now he was dealing with such physical repercussions and emotional grief, he had to forgo what had been his crutch for so long. There was little I could do beyond hold his hand.

"Everything is going to be okay," I would say, but the words often rang hollow, as though I should be doing something more, even though I wasn't sure what that something more could be. I could only be there for him as he went through a hell I couldn't possibly imagine. I longed to be able to take some of the burden away from him.

Anthony's saving grace was Stephen. His son seemed to have gone straight from crawling to running, and Anthony took it upon himself to follow our child around the house, watching him explore everything for the first time. It turned us into children ourselves.

"Nothing makes you see the world differently than crawling around it with a little child," Anthony said one night as he lay in the floor, our little boy cradled on his chest, both of them looking up at the ceiling fan as though they had never seen one before.

Mail from fans and well-wishers poured in. Anthony took the time to read every one of them. Sometimes they made him smile, and other times they made him moody. He would sometimes sit for hours at a time, staring out the window, a stack of letters in his hand.

"All these people love me," he said once. "And they don't have a clue what a jackass I've been to you and Stephen."

"It's what you do from here that matters," I reminded him.

One night I woke up in bed alone. I found him in the living room, surrounded by another stack of those letters. He was strumming on his guitar, and occasionally he would lean forward and write something down on the back of an envelope. Seeing him with his guitar, quietly writing a song in the middle of the night, filled me with a hope that made my heart soar.

I quietly backed out of the room and left him to finish the song.

A week later he composed a letter of his own. He took great pains in making sure it said all he wanted it to say. He read it aloud, over and over, until I could repeat it back to him, verbatim. He then gave it to his new publicist, who sent it out to the media outlets. When the letter was printed, his fans seemed to breathe a collective sigh of relief. Not only was he alive, he was healthy and happy, and there would be new music coming, sooner than later.

That very night he called his old band and offered them their old jobs. Each one of them accepted, but not without reservations. They had dealt with Anthony for a long time, and they weren't willing to put their careers on hold while he went through another stint in rehab. They had families and lives of their own, and bills that had to be paid. Anthony understood, and assured them all he would make their time worthwhile.

When he hung up the phone, he looked at me with the

unspoken question in his eyes.

"You can make it," I said. "I know you can."

My faith might have been shaky, but I never let it show. The last thing Anthony needed was doubt. That kind of uncertainty would hurt him more than help him, so I kept any negative thoughts to myself. I was determined to be a pillar of support, nothing less. The truth was that I was scared to death that he would fall off the wagon and this time, there would be no pulling him out of it. I was terrified that one false move would mean disaster.

But faith meant putting my belief into something I couldn't see, and so I had to give Anthony a chance to prove himself. As time went on, surely my faith would turn into trust. I had to believe he would reward my support by not letting me down.

Sure enough, Anthony came through.

When he felt the need for a hit, he reached out instead. He went to his counsellor, his clean and sober friends and his manager, all of whom were determined to help him through. He turned to me when he needed to talk, and when nothing else seemed to work, he would lock himself in a room with his guitar and our son, writing songs and playing them for Stephen.

The old band came together with tentative smiles, hugs that went on and on, and more than a few tears. They all knew rehearsals would be hard, and they were. Some of those band members had been with him in the old days, and some of them were newer members who had the good fortune of not being on the plane with Anthony that terrible night. There was a lot of guilt hanging around, and they tried to force it away with music. Sometimes it worked, sometimes it didn't, but they kept on going.

"The best way to get to the other side is to go through the pain, not around it," Anthony said, and it became their motto.

Rehearsals were hard on Anthony. Beyond the emotional difficulties, it was a physical challenge as well. His body was still weak, and he tired easily. Even playing guitar for long stretches was difficult. Anthony kept at it, often working late into the night, until his body was aching and his mind was a complete blank. He fell into bed after those rehearsal sessions and slept hard, then got up the next morning to do it all again.

The first concert after his ordeal was in front of a small yet sold-out crowd. The big stage show had been scaled down to simple instruments and no flash. The old-school feel of the show meant the crowd had a more intimate experience. Anthony proved his talent had not suffered through the long weeks of recovery, and the fans were appreciative.

The next day, reviews were carried in all the major newspapers. The comments were all positive, the reviews glowing. The excitement was contagious.

Anthony Keenan was back.

But as plans for a full-scale tour began to shape up, Anthony began to worry.

"I'm not sure I can do this without Keith," he confided. We were lying side by side in bed, talking about anything that came to mind. More and more often we were opening up about the losses we had both suffered, about the pain of remembering and the fear of forgetting.

"We don't have any choice," I said, even as the doubts welled up in me, too. How could *either* of us make it through a tour without Keith? He was the captain, the one always sure at the helm. I had never dreamed of a time when he would not be around to keep us on course.

"I miss him," Anthony said.

"I miss him, too."

"I miss all of them." Anthony sighed and adjusted his pillow. "I miss us, too."

"Us?"

I understood what he meant, but I wanted him to say the words. I wanted to know we were still on the same page.

"We haven't made love since long before the accident," he murmured. His hand reached out and slid along the inside of my arm, the tentative touch of an old lover.

"There have been other considerations," I said carefully. "You've been in recovery in more ways than one, Anthony. I understand what that can do to you."

He rolled onto his side and looked at me in the dim light. His eyes traced every line of my face with a scrutiny that made me blush. "Sometimes it is really hard to think about sex. Not just because of how I feel physically, but how I feel emotionally, too."

"It feels like a betrayal," I said.

Anthony sat up. "You know what I mean, don't you?"

"It feels unfair. Enjoying sex would be like making a mockery of those friends we lost."

"But it's not. It's more of a…affirmation of the life we still have."

I smiled at him. "You've been paying attention in those counselling sessions, haven't you?"

He reached out to take my hand. "I'm learning a lot."

"I am, too."

"It's too soon, isn't it?"

I took a deep breath. I had known this night would come, and that I would have to face the question of whether or not I could make love to Anthony. The infidelity still burned. Sometimes those images of him with someone else would return to the front of my mind, and I would wonder if the pain of it could ever be overcome.

But then I would come back to the way a part of me died when I looked at the television and saw the tail of that plane bobbing in the water. The contradiction of loss and desire was overwhelming.

But, like Anthony had said, the best way to get to the other side was to go through it.

"I'm willing to try," I whispered, even as I started to shake with the uncertainty of what we were talking about doing. Anthony brushed a lock of hair behind my ear and leant forward to kiss me, a tentative touch of his lips against mine, a question in every breath. I ran my fingers through his hair, closed my eyes and remembered our honeymoon, when we had tried every position imaginable and then some, when we had discovered new things about each other with every stroke and sigh.

Why couldn't we rediscover each other again now?

The kiss built until I could hardly breathe. I moved against him, letting my body give way to his, curling into the shape of him until we were pressed together so tightly, it was hard to know where I ended and he began. His arms wrapped around my back and he rolled over in the bed until I was on top of him, looking down into his eyes.

He dropped his hands to the quilt. I looked at him, took my time memorising every line of his face, every change that had been wrought in him. There was a bit more grey in his hair now. The lines in his face were a little deeper, especially those between his eyes, showing quite clearly all the worry he had been through over the last few years. His eyes were bright, no longer tired, and clear of any haze. He was fully present, entirely with me, and I wondered how long it had been since that had happened. How much had the drugs taken from us? How long had it been since I had made love to a man who would remember every last moment?

My hands trembled. Anthony caught them hard between his own.

"I'm scared," I admitted.

"That makes two of us."

"You're scared, too?"

"I'm terrified."

"Of what?"

"I'm scared because it's been so long. I'm scared I won't be able to make up for the pain I've caused. I'm scared that somewhere along the way, you'll change your mind, or I won't be able to do it, or something will be wrong between us or..."

His voice drifted away and we simply looked at one another, finally of one mind, after all those long months of

213

being so much at odds.

"I feel the same way."

Anthony ran his hands up my arms and cupped my shoulders in his broad hands. He pulled me down for a kiss. This one was slow and thorough, with no urgency for more.

"Have we ever had a real date?" he asked against my lips.

I burst into laughter. After a son and marriage and so much to overcome during our years together, he was asking such a question? But when I gave it some thought, I realised with a shock that he was right. We had never once been out on a real date. Our relationship had evolved from a working one, and what happened had been as natural as breathing. It left no room for the conventional.

"A real date," I mused.

"We could, you know. We could date each other."

He was offering a way out, making things easier for both of us. The tension melted out of the room and I laid my head on his chest. "We could."

"What I always took for granted is what I really want to have now."

I looked up at him. His eyes were suspiciously bright, but he had a smile on his face. He cuddled me closer to him and that's how we fell asleep, with my head on his chest and his arms around me.

* * * *

Dating Anthony made me feel like a teenager again. I spent more time in front of the mirror, dressing myself up for him, even buying new clothes to surprise him with when he came home from whatever obligation he had that day. I walked with a new bounce in my step. An excitement I had almost forgotten was now foremost in my mind, and it made the world look entirely different, fresh and new, especially when the limousine pulled up in front of the house at seven o'clock sharp.

Anthony opened the door himself. He watched me walk down the stairs in my new black dress, my hair pulled up in a bun, my feet in high heels and my lips painted with a smile. He wore a suit—without the tie, of course. Anthony would never give himself over entirely to convention. It was one of the things I loved so much about him.

"You look stunning," he said as I stopped at the open door of the long black sedan.

"So do you."

I looked back at the house. Stephen was in there with the babysitter. She had been recommended time and time again, a discreet young woman who understood the privacy concerns of a couple in the public eye. She was to be trusted, but still, I worried about Stephen. With the exception of the time Anthony spent in the hospital, I had hardly been away from him since the day he was born.

"Hey."

Anthony motioned towards the open door of the car. "He's going to be fine. We're going to be fine, too."

We smiled at each other for a moment before we climbed into the limousine. Anthony shut the door behind me. I leant back against the fine leather seat and closed my eyes. Anthony's fingers slid over my thigh, tracing the slit up the side of my dress. His breath was warm against my neck and stirred the ringlets of curls against my ear.

"I love you," he murmured.

There were paparazzi outside the restaurant, proving that even the best-laid plans can be trumped by enough ready cash. Anthony took my hand and walked right through them, pretending they didn't exist. I kept my eyes down at the ground until we were in the restaurant, where we were whisked away to a private table in a very quiet corner.

"We could turn this into a positive," Anthony said as he flipped open his menu.

"What?"

"The constant flashbulbs."

"I'm listening."

215

"How many couples would pay outrageous amounts of money to have their life together photographed? Even wedding albums can cost thousands of dollars to have done by a professional."

"Right."

"They're giving us all the photographs we want, and it's free."

We smiled across the menus at each other.

"If you can't beat the system, you might as well play it, right?"

The waiter came around with a bottle of wine, which Anthony promptly refused. We settled on water instead. We ordered the fish and sat looking at each other over the candles in the centre of the table. Anthony took my hand and toyed with my wedding band, twirling it around and around beside the diamond engagement ring.

"What do you call an engagement ring after you're married?" he asked. "It doesn't make sense to call it an engagement ring anymore, does it?"

The candlelight glinted from the stones. "I've never thought of that."

"I like to think of it more as a promise ring," he said. "The wedding band beside it says I made good on my promise."

He met my eyes without a flinch.

"I stumbled more than once. But I'm going to make good on those promises now, Janey. You deserve nothing less, and you know what?"

Anthony turned my hand over and kissed the centre of my palm. The shiver went all through me, lighting me up from the inside out.

"I deserve nothing less than being a good husband for you."

By the time the meal was served, neither of us cared much about eating. We were too busy talking about what we wanted to do with our lives from this point on. Making plans was something we hadn't dared think about for a very long time. Now that we were considering the possibilities again, the horizons were open and endless, much like they had been when we first fell in love.

"I want you and Stephen on the road with me," he said. "I know we talked about it before and decided we didn't want to do that, but back then, most of the work would have fallen to you. Things are different now, and we can do it together this time. Do you think we could make it work for him? Make the road a good place to grow up?"

"We won't know until we try, right?"

"And I think we should buy a plane."

My train of thought stopped dead on the tracks as I considered this new bombshell. "Buy a *plane*?"

"It makes sense, Janey. We're going to be so busy with the tour, and I don't want to abandon our lives in Nashville. I want to have both. A plane would allow us to do that." When I hesitated, Anthony leant forward, pressing the advantage when he knew he had my full consideration. "We make enough money. We can afford the plane, and it would make life so much easier, wouldn't it?"

"We have the Axton plane," I said.

Anthony sat back in the chair and stared at the candles. The subject of the record label was something we danced around but rarely faced head-on. The paperwork wasn't complete yet, but I was determined to do what Keith had wanted—I was going to take on Axton Records and keep the business booming. Anthony was a huge part of that, and we both knew it. It was awkward for me to be his boss, and it was strange for him to be the anchor on which the whole operation hinged. But together, we were sure we could make it work. In honour of Keith's wishes and memory, we had to give it the best shot we could.

"The Axton plane is not ours," Anthony said. "That's for the label. And if we're going to do this right, we have to keep our personal interests separate from that of the label, don't you think?"

I nodded. "I think you're right."

"What do you think? Should we look into buying a plane?

Give in to the machine and be the hotshots everyone thinks we are anyway?"

I laughed at that. "Do you remember when we first met? You said you couldn't afford to be in Nashville. Now you're talking about buying your own plane so you can fly into Nashville any time you want."

He toyed with his water glass. "Things change."

"They do."

"Have I changed that much, Janey?"

I studied him while I took a bite of fish. *Had* he changed that much? When I met him he was belligerent, focused solely on the music and determined to make it on his own. Over time he came to play the business game, and later he turned to the celebrity game, making the best out of a situation he had no control over. Now he was taking yet another turn, back to the man he used to be, the one who put his heart and soul into everything and took nothing for granted.

"You've come full circle," I said.

Anthony shrugged, suddenly shy with the compliment.

"I like myself again."

"I'm falling in love with you all over again."

Anthony took my hand and held it to his lips for a long time.

"Thank you," he murmured.

* * * *

One date led to another, and another, and another. Sometimes we took Stephen with us, and sometimes we were all alone, just getting to know each other in a way we hadn't taken the time to before. In the past, it was the music that bonded us. Now we were discovering everything else. It was a few years late, but later was better than never.

We didn't make love. Sometimes we would lie beside one another at night and kiss, necking like teenagers until the sun came up. Sometimes we would tease one another until we were both raring to go, then we would find some restraint in the depths of whatever sanity the teasing had left us with. It seemed making love would spoil the moment, would undermine what we were trying to do, which was getting to know each other all over again.

The memories of heartache didn't fade, but they became more manageable as time went on. I learned to accept, not to avoid, and to let myself feel whatever I needed to feel. I learned to remind myself that he was a different man now, a man who had learned from a few very hard lessons. My trust slowly returned, and with it came a new side of me, one I hadn't let him see before — the vulnerable side, the one that needed to lean on my man and let him be strong for me, instead of holding the whole world on my own shoulders.

As our personal relationship shifted, so did our professional ones. Anthony began making decisions with me instead of on his own accord. He was careful about who he chose to go on tour with him, and he never let the shows go overboard. The music was what mattered again, and the stripped-down acoustic shows were evidence of just how dedicated to the music he really was. His old band loved their new gig, and the fans were wilder than ever.

My own professional life took a turn for the better. The business of Axton Records was approached not from a platform of money and records sold, but from a standpoint of keeping the label vibrant and relevant. As a result, we signed new acts that were poised to take off in very different directions. We handled a little bit of everything, and the result of our melting pot was met with a very positive reaction from fans and radio alike. Sales skyrocketed. Tours sold out. Platinum covered the walls. We had to move from the old building to a much bigger one. My office sat front and centre, where I could look out over Music Row.

In April of that year, Anthony got his plane. In May, we hit the road with that plane and a new bus, specifically designed with the needs of a toddler in mind.

That fall, Anthony got the news that would change his life

forever — again.

* * * *

Tom came through the door of the bus that afternoon with a smile on his face and an excited fire in his eyes. I sat up from the book I was reading. Even Stephen stopped playing with his blocks and looked up from his place on the living room floor, anticipating what Tom would have to say.

"I need Anthony. Right now."

"He's sleeping."

"Wake him up."

Stephen definitely understood that. He grabbed the couch and pulled himself up. On wobbly legs, he started towards the bedroom. "Get Daddy, get, get Daddy!" he babbled as he made his way to the back of the bus.

"What's going on?" I asked.

"Everything," Tom said, smiling so hard he looked like a different person.

"Tell me."

"I want to tell him." Tom was practically jumping up and down. "I want to tell him, Janey. My God, I've always wanted to do something like this, but I've never had the chance until now."

"Tell him what?"

Just then, Anthony appeared at the doorway, rubbing his eyes and holding Stephen on one hip.

"Tell me what?"

Tom turned to Anthony, and before the words were out of his mouth, I knew. How could I not have known? I sank down to the couch, the shock of it already hitting, even as Tom uttered the words.

"You've been nominated."

Still halfway lost in sleep, Anthony didn't get it. "Nominated?"

"You've been nominated for the awards in November!"

I started laughing. Anthony stared at Tom. Stephen kicked at him to get down, and Anthony let him slide off his hip to the floor. Our son toddled back to his blocks and knocked them down with one hand, watching them scatter everywhere. His peal of laughter bounced around the room.

Anthony looked at me. "Nominated?" he said again.

Tom shook a paper at him.

"The nominations were this morning, Anthony! Didn't you know that?"

"I guess I did," he said. "But I had no idea…"

"It gets better." Stephen was trying to stand on tiptoe, begging for Tom to pick him up. Tom swung him into his arms like he had done hundreds of times before. Stephen grabbed the paper out of Tom's hand and waved it in his daddy's face.

"Tell me," Anthony said, the shock of it all finally sinking in.

"You were nominated in four categories."

In the wake of Tom's announcement, we all went entirely silent and still. Even Stephen paused and stared around at all of us with wide eyes.

"Song of the Year, Single of the Year…"

Anthony started to laugh.

"Best New Artist."

Anthony stopped laughing.

"And the big one, Anthony — Album of the Year."

I stared at my husband as Stephen started to coo and laugh again. He shook the paper in the air. Tom bounced him on his hip. When I stood up and touched Anthony's shoulder, he gave me a tender look that took my breath away. What he said put it all in perspective.

"Keith should be here."

Then all three of us were laughing and crying and jumping up and down, while Stephen protested at being caught between the three-way hug. I took him into my own arms, freeing Tom to run to the door of the bus. From the steps, he shouted the good news to anyone in the venue who might be within earshot. Cheers of congratulations rang out as the door closed behind Tom. He ran across the parking lot, yelling all the way.

Our little family was left alone in the aftermath.

Anthony sank onto the couch. Stephen went back to his toys. I sat beside Anthony and looked into his wide, shocked eyes.

"There has to be some mistake," he said.

I knew that was coming. Anthony still had a problem with accepting his due. He was good at what he did, one of the best, and the sales of his record proved that. Now the music industry was letting him know, in no uncertain terms, that the movers and shakers considered him one of the best as well.

"There is no mistake," I said. "They know talent when they see it."

"But I haven't been around long enough…it's not time for this yet."

"It's time. You wouldn't have been nominated if it wasn't time."

A slow smile spread across his face. "Album of the Year."

"That's the one that matters, isn't it?"

"It's about Keith," he said.

I wrapped my arms around him and leaned against his shoulder. The album was Keith's baby just as much as it was Anthony's. He'd paid attention to every note, suggested changes that worked like a charm, and put his stamp of approval on every lick before it hit the shelves. Keith even had a hand in the cover art. He had done everything he could to make sure Anthony's vision stayed true to who he really was.

"He didn't change me," Anthony said.

"No."

"You told me he wouldn't."

I smiled, thinking about Keith and the way he operated. He knew a good thing when he saw it, and he never hesitated to go with his gut, no matter what the paper-pushers or the bottom line said he should do. I hoped I could run the label the same way Keith had.

"That's the one I want," Anthony said. "The other nominations are great, but Album of the Year is the one I want. I want it so bad, Janey. I want it more than you can imagine."

I put my arms around him and kissed his lips. I could imagine.

Chapter Fifteen

The frenzy leading up to Anthony's appearance on the awards show was phenomenal. Radio stations were deluged with requests for his songs. Television appearances ramped up, including an appearance and performance on *The Tonight Show*, where Jay Leno asked him how it felt to be one of the sexiest men in the music business.

"As long as my wife thinks I'm sexy, it's great," Anthony told him with his shy smile. The audience roared with approval.

When the show aired that night, I was sitting on the bed with Anthony in a Beverly Hills hotel room. "Do you think I'm sexy?" he asked, raising an eyebrow at me.

"Of course I do."

"How sexy, exactly?"

I looked from the man on the screen to the man beside me. His hair had been cut, but it was still long enough to fall to his shoulders. He was wearing the same clothes he'd worn on the show. His wedding ring gleamed in the light from the bedside lamp.

"Sexy enough to eat."

Anthony quirked an eyebrow at me and moved in to kiss my neck. The show went to a commercial. The way his hands ran through my hair and over my body made his hopes and intentions very clear.

"Am I sexy enough to fuck?"

The show came back from commercial. Anthony was kissing the back of my neck as I watched him on the screen. His hands came up and cupped my breasts as the man on the screen said something that made Jay Leno laugh. By the time the credits flashed, my blouse was open and my bra was somewhere on the floor and Anthony's lips were all over my skin.

It was like the first time, so sultry and easy. At the same time, it was like nothing I had ever known before. The contradiction made my head light and made my heart pound. I stripped the shirt from his shoulders as his lips worked their way down my chest. I unbuckled his belt as his tongue played with my belly button. By the time my own jeans were thrown aside, I was begging to have him inside me.

Anthony held back, even when I pulled on his shoulders and begged harder.

"I want this to last," he panted. "And I can't last right now. I want you too much."

"Who says it has to be just once?"

The sound of Anthony's laughter filled my ears and made his belly jerk against mine. His hardness was hot on my thigh. Even with the blatant invitation, he refused to give me what I wanted. Instead he dropped off the bed and grabbed my legs to slide me over to the edge. The comforter bunched up under me, lifting my hips a little.

"Perfect," he murmured, right before he dived in to taste me.

I gave myself over to the sensation, closed my eyes and arched my back and let him have his way. Anthony's hands were on my hips, pulling me closer. His name was coming out of me, from somewhere deep down inside, from where maybe no one else had ever been before. I twined my fingers through his hair and held him where he was, moved against his mouth and heard his moans of approval from between my thighs.

It wouldn't take long. All those nights of lying beside him and denying myself the pleasure of his body had taken their toll, and now my whole being was a raging fire, consuming everything, even the air in the room. I could hardly breathe.

Anthony held me tight as I bucked and jerked, howling

his name. He was back against me before my orgasm was over, lifting my legs over his shoulders, thrusting down hard. He uttered my name through gritted teeth as he moved, claiming what was his.

His wedding band was cool against the skin of my thigh. I watched his hand tense, watched the ring flash, watched his body as he moved. I wrapped my legs hard around his hips and pressed my feet against his rear, pulling him in. The muscles tensed under me, at first in a rhythm, then the rhythm was gone and his whole body was hard.

When he came, it wasn't with the quiet reverence I was used to. This time it was wild, cataclysmic, the kind of orgasm that threatened to knock him out. He shuddered against me as it went on and on, and when it was over he collapsed in a heap on the bed beside me, our legs tangled up together.

The television droned. The evening news was on—we hadn't been naked for ten minutes yet, and already we were out of breath and shaky, unable to speak. Anthony ran his fingertips across my face until his eyes drifted closed. His hand settled on my throat, over the pulse that was still racing far too fast. I watched him smile.

"Sexy enough to fuck," he murmured.

I stretched on the blankets. My body was still throbbing with the orgasm he had given me. I rolled onto my side. He pulled me back into the spoon of his body, holding me close as he talked, saying nonsense things that meant nothing to anybody else but everything to me.

* * * *

The night of the awards show was hotter than usual for a winter evening, and every bit of that heat was shimmering on the red carpet. The young starlets wore dresses that sparkled like the night sky. Most of the gentlemen were decked out in suits, but some of them wore their usual blue jeans and dress shirts. The reporters were falling all over themselves for interviews, and the stars were smiling for the cameras.

I watched the festivities from our couch at home. Stephen had a terrible cold, and neither Anthony nor I was willing to leave him with anyone else, no matter how capable our babysitter might be.

I watched the stars walk in front of the cameras. Every now and then a peal of joy came from the fans lined up outside the red carpet entrance. It was clear when Anthony showed up – the fans went insane, their screams drowning out everything else, pulling all attention to the tall, dark man who stepped from the dove-grey limousine.

Anthony was stunning in his Armani suit. Up until the last minute, he had considered wearing jeans to the event of the year, in keeping with the bohemian image. His final choice had been the pinstriped suit – with no tie, of course – and it was a good decision. He was more gorgeous than ever. Even the reporters got tongue-tied around him, and the photographers couldn't get enough.

"Where's your pretty wife and that adorable baby?" one of the reporters asked.

"At home. Watching."

Much to my delight, he blew a kiss at the screen. I laughed and Stephen gurgled, pointing with one chubby finger. "Daddy!"

"Doesn't Daddy look good?"

"Daddy come home!"

"He'll come home. He has to do this first."

"No, no. Daddy come home."

"Wanna watch the show with me?"

Stephen cuddled into my side and closed his eyes. His thumb went to his mouth.

"I guess that answers my question, kiddo."

The pre-show cut to commercial, then it was time for the big event. Anthony's name was announced as a performer. The opening act came on the stage – last year's Entertainer of the Year – and I lost myself in the music, just like I always did. For a dozen years I'd watched the show faithfully, then for the next ten I had been in attendance. Now I was at home while my husband was up for an award. I watched the first presentation and couldn't help but think about how everything comes full circle if given enough time.

"And the Song of the Year is…"

Anthony didn't win.

The disappointment was crushing. I buried my head in Stephen's hair as our baby slept against my shoulder. On the screen, the camera panned to those who hadn't won. In years past I had thought that was a really cruel thing to do, but now I was certain of it.

"Single of the Year…"

Again, someone else's name was called. Anthony applauded from the audience, watching as the winner went up to get the award and thank those who had helped make it happen. The next time the camera panned towards Anthony's seat, someone else was sitting there. Anthony was backstage, getting ready to perform onstage in front of all his peers and millions of television viewers.

When the commercial came, I gently laid Stephen down on a blanket in the floor. He stretched once from head to toe, sniffled, then settled in to sleep for the rest of the night. I could have put him in his bedroom, but I wanted him there, where I could look at him. Keeping watch while he was sick was part of it, but an even bigger part was the joy of looking at Stephen and seeing his father in his face.

Since we had made love in that hotel room in Beverly Hills, our life had shifted dramatically. Where we were hesitant before, now we couldn't get enough. We were more attuned to each other than we had ever been, and the desire matched our newfound commitment. We couldn't take our hands off each other. Easing back into the sensual side of our relationship had been the right thing to do, but now I couldn't imagine how we waited so long.

The show came back on the air, and I watched as Anthony's performance was announced. I sat on the edge

228

of the couch, and when that wasn't enough, I got in the floor in front of the television, so I could be as close to my husband as I could possibly get. He strutted onto the stage with his guitar in hand, playing the chords everyone knew by heart, and when he stepped to the microphone, the voice that came out of him was the same I had heard years before in a little bar in the middle of downtown Nashville. But now that voice was known by millions, recognisable in an instant, and the crowd was appreciative. They stood and danced and sang along. When the last chord sounded and Anthony nodded his head in thanks, the applause was deafening. It continued long after the song was over, whoops and hollers from people who were usually more demure than that.

In the quiet of our living room, I applauded right along with them.

When the nominees for the Best New Artist were announced, the tension in the big room was evident, so palpable as to carry through the pixels on the television screen. I sat on the edge of the chair. What I had always dismissed as business was suddenly so much more than that. I was a fan again, cheering on my favourite artist, praying the name in that envelope was the same one ringing over and over in my head.

"Anthony Keenan!"

I jumped to my feet and hollered. The sound woke Stephen, who looked at me with wide, startled eyes. The crowd on the screen went ballistic, rising from their seats as one, laughing and cheering. The camera caught the shock on Anthony's face, a priceless moment before the reality set in. He rose to his feet in a daze while his song played in the background and dozens of people came forward to shake his hand.

Stephen caught sight of the screen. He yawned even as he crawled to it. He slapped a tiny hand at the screen.

"Daddy," he said.

When Anthony was finally onstage and holding the award

in his hand, he stared at it for a long while, too choked up to talk. The crowd looked on with understanding smiles — most of them had been there, and they knew the power of that moment, the weight of that award in a trembling hand.

Finally Anthony looked up.

"I remember," he began, then paused. "I remember making up a funny speech over a year ago, when my wife and I were talking about the awards I might win one day. Now I can't remember a single part of that speech. All I remember is the way she laughed at me, how she looked so happy. I hope I can always keep her that happy."

The camera quickly flashed to the crowd. Anthony had their full attention.

"This is for her, and for all those who believed in me. Some of them are here tonight. Some of the very important ones aren't. But even if I don't see them, I know they see me."

Anthony held up the award. The lights shone from it, turning the crystal prisms into a thousand shades of the rainbow. Everyone in that audience was thinking of the horrible pictures on the news channels, of the day Anthony's life changed forever. I gasped at the brilliance of that prism, at how it seemed to shine so brightly just for those who needed to see it most. The crowd was silent.

"Thank you," he said.

The roar that rose when he stepped away from the podium was remarkable. The crowd rose to their feet again as a beautiful young woman escorted everyone from the stage. Music rose, announcements were made and the cut to commercial came too quickly.

I picked Stephen up and squeezed him. He protested with a loud squeal. I was watching an ad for Clorox bleach while the thrill of the victory still sang through my veins.

The phone rang. I snatched it up.

"Janey?"

Anthony's voice was sure and strong. I knew immediately that something had changed for the better. There was no hesitancy, no question of whether or not he belonged there, no desire to say he didn't deserve what he had. A crowd of his peers had just accepted him with open arms.

For Anthony, the dream had just come full circle.

"I love you," I said.

"I love you, too. I wanted you to know."

"I already do." I was smiling through the tears. I wiped them away as the commercial for Clorox became one for Gerber. I laughed, and Anthony chuckled on his end of the phone line.

"I don't know when I'll be home. Press room and all that."

"I know."

"There's more…"

"Get back out there. You never know."

"Love you."

The phone went dead. I put it back on the cradle and watched as the cameras brought the audience back to the show. Stephen curled up into a ball on his blanket and looked at the television. His eyes drifted closed.

I sat through the performances, gauging them all not through the eyes of a music label executive, but seeing them as a fan for the first time in as long as I could remember. I watched the way the lights glinted from the guitars, the way the women strutted with their microphones, and felt the music in a way that got me deep down in the gut, where it stuck with you and never went away. I remembered the reasons I fell in love with the music in the first place.

When the Album of the Year award was ready to be announced, I again sat on the edge of my seat. The camera panned to each nominee, then moved to a split screen, so all of them could be seen as the award was announced. There was a pregnant pause as the envelope was ripped open.

When Anthony's name was called, he buried his face in his hands.

The crowd went crazier than they had before, something I hadn't thought possible. I watched as Jason stood up and hauled Anthony to his feet. They climbed the steps together, both of them with tears in their eyes as they accepted the award.

Standing in front of the microphone, they looked at each other. Anthony didn't try to hide any emotion. It was all there on his face, naked and raw, and the whole world saw it. Jason, much to my surprise, pulled Anthony into a bear hug. They rocked back and forth until the music stopped, their cue to start talking before the time was up.

"This is for Keith Axton," Anthony said.

And that was all.

When the cameras cut away and the music swelled again, I pressed mute on the remote. I remembered the last time I saw Keith, the way he looked back at me, the smile on his face, the sunlight playing across his hair. In the sudden silence, even as my heart was full of joy and happiness and more love than I thought a human body could hold, I sank to the floor and wept again for the one man who believed with all his heart, even when no one else did.

* * * *

I wasn't in the press room after the show ended, but I heard all about it later. Bits and pieces came out in anecdotes about Anthony, in demonstration of how things had changed in his life, of how much love can do. I heard about the jokes he cracked, the easy manner, the clear-headed vision of a man who had been through hell and back. I heard about the fact he didn't try to hide the tears when Keith's name was brought up, how his vulnerability endeared him to everyone, and how many new fans he garnered before he was through.

Most of all, I heard about the way he cut the press conference short, apologising but at the same time making it clear why he had to go.

"My wife and son are at home," he said. "I should be there with them tonight."

Then he ducked out of the room and into the waiting

limousine. There was no mingling or partying afterwards. The star of the show took the quiet route instead, riding home through the Tennessee darkness to a home whose porch lights were blazing in welcome.

Unable to wait, I rushed out the door as soon as the lights of the limousine splashed across the front of the house. Anthony was out of the car and running before it came to a full stop. He met me on the stairs, picked me up and swung me around, then let loose with a whoop of joy.

"You won! You did it!" I was smiling so hard, my face hurt.

"*We* won," he corrected me.

I wrapped my arms around him, unable to say anything else.

"Let's go inside and celebrate," he whispered against my hair.

As soon as the door closed behind us, Anthony made a beeline for Stephen's room. He looked in on the sleeping child. Stephen lay on his back in his little bed, his breathing easy, his eyes moving every now and then behind closed lids.

Anthony quietly shut the door and turned to me. I was waiting there to be swept up in his arms again. This time he picked me up from the floor and carried me across the house like a new bride. He pushed our bedroom door open with one shoulder, approached the bed and paused for a moment, looking down at me with a crooked smile.

Then he dropped me. I bounced on the cover and let out a yelp of surprise.

"You shit!"

Anthony threw his head back and laughed. "An hour ago I was the hottest thing around, and now my wife calls me a shit. Lovely."

I smiled up at him from the bed and held out my hand, beckoning him to join me. He crawled on top of me and started kissing my neck with a passion that echoed the excitement of the night. I laughed and arched up to him,

233

offering more skin for him to cover. His breath was hot against my ear and his arousal was hard against my thigh.

"Where's your award?" I asked.

"They wouldn't let me bring it home," he pouted.

"Ah, that's right. They have to put your name on it."

He lifted my T-shirt over my head and smiled when he saw I was naked underneath.

"I couldn't help but look at that award and think about fucking with it," I admitted, blushing furiously.

He raised an eyebrow as he looked down at me.

"Fucking with it, huh?"

"It kinda looks like a dildo."

"It's heavy as hell."

"So I could sit on it instead. Ride it while you watch me."

Anthony started laughing hard enough to shake the bed. He laid his head down on the blanket and laughed until his voice was hoarse.

"What?"

"Leave it to you," he accused. "Leave it to you to turn everything into a sexual game."

"Are you complaining?"

"Hell, yes, I'm complaining. I'm going to call whoever is in charge of getting those things engraved and tell him to hurry up, because I've got things to do with that award before it goes up on the mantel."

Soon his suit was lying in a heap on the floor and I was straddling him, doing the things I had envisioned doing to that award. But no award would be so hot, so alive inside me as Anthony's body was. I ran my fingers through his hair and watched his eyes grow dark with desire as I rocked back and forth. I sat straight up to get him as deep as I could, then leant back to let him hit all the good spots, the ones that made my whole body clench and gasp around him.

Anthony watched every move I made. He participated with encouraging words and loving eyes, but he didn't try to touch me.

"How does it feel?" he asked.

"How does what feel?"

"Making love to your award-winning husband."

"The word *husband* is the one that turns me on," I said.

Anthony's body started to tremble. His eyes took on a bright sheen, the look that said he was flooded with both desire and tenderness, and he didn't know which one would take precedence. I watched the battle within him as I moved harder, and finally he closed his eyes and let his body take over.

"I'm going to," he murmured.

I leaned over him and watched his face. He thrust up into me once, then again, then a final time before the pleasure overtook him. Every muscle in his body became hard as stone. The cry that tore from his throat was filled with passion. He uttered my name as he gave himself over to the physical and the emotional upheaval.

That's what I was waiting for. The feeling of him exploding inside me, filling me with what was mine and mine alone, was enough to send me over the edge. I braced my hands on his shoulders and stopped moving. I just let the final twitches of his body push me past that final barrier. When I came it was with an all-consuming shudder, the whole world becoming a distant afterthought to the earthquake that was happening here in our bed.

When I came down from the pinnacle, I collapsed onto Anthony's chest. Even as the thrill of the night coursed through us like live electricity, the ghosts of the past crowded around, waiting to receive their own due. The memories swayed around us, comforting thoughts that reminded us of who we were and just how far we had come. We lay together and let the silence wrap around us, creating a place of homage for whatever would come next.

"You did it," I said, awed again by the man in bed beside me.

"We did it."

"How did I get so lucky?" I rose up on one elbow and

looked at him.

"I'm the lucky one," he whispered.

"You should have seen yourself on that television. You looked the part of the handsome man about town. And you were so genuine! There isn't a single false thing about you."

"Not anymore," he agreed. "But it was a long, hard road to get there. It's always so much easier to pretend than to be who you are, you know?"

"I know."

"Keith knew that lesson long before anyone else around him did."

I looked at Anthony now, and the puzzle piece clicked into place.

"That's what you talked about on the plane, wasn't it? Before Keith died."

It was a bit odd, to talk about Keith's last moments as Anthony and I lay in each other's arms, our bodies still throbbing with passion. But it also seemed fitting. Keith was so much a part of both of us, he was in everything we did — even, somehow, in the moments like these.

"He told me a lot of things. The one thing I remember most is that I already had the best thing in life. I already had you. If I could hold onto that, everything else would come."

I smiled, thinking about Keith and his steadfast belief in me.

"He was right," Anthony said. "The love of a woman is the key to everything else."

"I wonder if Keith knows how good things are now."

"He knows. I'm sure of it. Don't you feel it?"

How could I not?

"Life doesn't get better than this," I said, even as a single tear slid down my cheek. Anthony wiped it away and gave me a wicked smile.

"Baby girl," he murmured as he rose above me, "it *only* gets better from here."

Epilogue

Every seat in the historic Ryman Auditorium was filled. We stood at the balcony and looked down at the crowd. Young and old, fans of new country and the golden oldies, they were all here, together in one place to share in the sound. The Ryman had seen decades of hits played on that stage, and now a new generation of musicians were ready to take their place in history.

It was twenty years, eleven albums and countless awards since that night in November, when Anthony took home the award for Album of the Year. We still lived in the same house. The walls were covered with dozens of platinum plaques. Some of the awards were locked away in the vault, but the most important ones were on display on the mantel, right next to our wedding pictures.

Axton Records was still signing new acts, always on the lookout for the next big thing. We still had a knack for finding them, and the ambition to take them to the top.

"We should go down there," I said.

"I'm not sure I can do this, Janey."

Anthony looked at me with those same dark eyes. The years had been good to him. The laugh lines in his face were clearer. The fine lines in his hands were more pronounced. The little aches and pains of our middle years were becoming bigger aches and pains. His hair was salt-and-pepper now, leaning more towards grey. It was still a shock to look at that sometimes, to realise we had over twenty years behind us. I still found him as handsome as ever.

"You can do this," I reassured him.

"It's so different now." He looked over the crowd. A

237

few people had recognised him, and they were standing hopefully to the side, waiting for an autograph.

"It's just as good."

He squeezed my hand. "It's better."

We slowly made our way to the front of the auditorium. Anthony shook hands, signed autographs and spoke to those who wanted a small moment of his time. We took our seats just as the lights dimmed. The camera panned over to us a few times, and I couldn't help but think of the many awards shows, the many times we had been here in this very room, the moments the camera captured Anthony, again and again and again.

Then the camera turned to the stage.

"The Grand Ole Opry is proud to welcome new Axton Records recording artist—give him some applause now, folks, he's nervous because his parents are here! Please give a big Grand Ole Opry welcome to—Steve Keenan!"

Our son walked out onto that stage for the first time. He carried his father's guitar, my smile and the ambition of a young man who has seen what it took to get to the top, and was determined to make it there.

"Janey...oh, my God." Anthony was staring at the stage while the crowd went wild for the handsome young man who looked so much like his father, it took my breath away. "That's our boy."

That boy stepped to the microphone, strummed his guitar and began to sing. The voice that came out of him reminded me of the first time I had ever seen Anthony, the smooth and sexy growl that had made him famous, the moment I would always remember as the beginning of falling in love with the man who would forever hold my history, my present and my future.

"That's our son," I whispered. Anthony squeezed my hand.

With a final glance of shared love and history, we settled in to watch the show.

A WEEK IN THE SNOW

GWEN MASTERS

A Week in the Snow

Excerpt

Chapter One

"You sound happy. Are you?"

Rebecca smiled and shifted the phone on her shoulder. She stared at the single candle on the mantel. The clock had just chimed midnight. "Yes."

"Tell me."

"This isn't just a want. It's a need. It's like breathing, or my heart beating. I can feel it right now, between my legs." She slid a hand down her naked belly. "I want to lie underneath you and open my legs for your hand, at the same time as you slide your cock into my mouth."

Her own words turned her on just as much as his did, and she let her fingers walk farther down, until she was brushing the neatly trimmed hair at the apex of her thighs. Her nipples were sensitive and tingling, and the cool breeze from the air conditioner kept them hard. She curled her toes against the end of the couch as she listened to his voice, coming low over the phone line.

"You like that, don't you? My cock in your mouth? You like it when I pull your hair and hold you there and make you take it, don't you?"

She touched her clit with her fingertip, then dropped her head back and moaned.

"And at the same time, I'm pushing two fingers into you — no, how about three? — just slamming them in, because you're so wet already, and I'm driving them in and out, and every now and then I press on your clit, right there. You like that? I can hear you panting for it. You wouldn't be panting if my cock was in your mouth, would you? You would be fighting to breathe while you came and came and came."

Rebecca ran one finger on either side of her clit, scissoring it gently, rubbing up and down. The tingles got bigger and her mind started to venture off into the fantasy, the thought of his hands doing those things to her. She imagined her own hands would be on her nipples, playing with them while she bent her head back just so, taking his cock in deep enough to please him, but not deep enough to gag. His fingers would be working magic between her thighs, sliding into her when she needed to be filled, pulling back and teasing her before she could come, making her beg with moans before he slid his fingers in again. That delicious stretching would overcome her and she might forget the motion of her mouth, forget the way she was supposed to move, and he would have to pull on her hair to get her attention again.

That was what did it for her this time — the thought of him pulling on her hair, maybe a little bit frustrated with her, demanding she pay attention to his cock. She imagined the velvet skin sliding between her lips, the tense muscles in his thighs, the way he would look at her as he came. She imagined all of it, except the one part she didn't have to imagine.

"Oh, fuck, Becca—I'm going to come!"

He hollered when he came, his voice loud enough to make her pull the phone away from her ear. He held his breath for a moment, then let it out on a moaning exhale. Rebecca smiled as her own orgasm hit, right in time with his. She arched under her hand, everything but the voice in her ear forgotten, as the orgasm swept from her middle and out to her fingers and toes. Her whole body tingled, her nipples hard enough to hurt, her clit humming under her fingers.

When she relaxed and opened her eyes, she saw the candle. It had burned halfway down, the flame dancing on a small breeze.

"Was it good for you?" he asked, his voice low and dramatic. As if on cue, Rebecca giggled. She always giggled after a really good one, and that was right up there in the top ten. He laughed with her, and that made her feel warm inside. So what if he was thousands of miles away? At moments like this, he felt close enough to touch.

After long minutes of talking about what had just happened, he yawned. She knew he would be going to bed soon, and, even though her time zone put her an hour ahead of him, she would be awake for hours yet, thinking about the coming week and what it might have in store.

He was thinking of it, too. "Have you decided what to pack?" he asked.

"I've already packed one bag with the essentials." She stretched, delighting in the feel of her legs, a little too tense, reminders of what she had just done. The orgasm still thrummed through her now and again. "It's going to take two bags, though—I'm doubling up on everything to survive those chilly temperatures."

"Iowa is chilly in the fall," he agreed.

"You can keep me warm."

"Don't forget the vibrator," he teased.

"Gene," she teased right back. "I thought we were just going to have coffee."

"Of course we are. The morning after."

She giggled again and nestled deeper into the couch. The thought of going to see him was like an adventure. She was always the good girl, the one who was reliable and safe and careful, and this felt like doing something she had always wanted to do, but had never had the nerve. She was going to meet her online boyfriend and she was going to fuck him silly, and then she was going to fuck him some more, and to hell with the good girl act.

"The morning after sounds good," she said. "Are you going to make it for me?"

"You're the woman," he replied. "It's your job."

That was the only thing about Gene that drove her crazy. She always hoped he was joking about the macho way he viewed things; that he really did believe in equality, that he wasn't as chauvinistic as he seemed. But the more time went on, the more she thought maybe he really believed a woman's place was in the kitchen, barefoot and pregnant. Each time the thought came up, it made her wonder: what in the world was he doing with a woman like her, who ran her own business and was determined to make a name for herself?

"Speaking of jobs, mine is waiting on me, and I need to get a few things done before I go to sleep," she said, dangling more bait. "I have to wrap up this latest project before I come to see you."

Gene yawned, as though the project she had going wasn't interesting in the least.

"Okay, babe. I'm going to go to sleep. You might want to get some sleep, too, so you can make that drive."

"I'll be all right."

"Are you sure you won't fly?"

She didn't want to fly, and she had told him that over and over. She wanted to drive her way up from Florida to Iowa, her camera on the seat beside her, ready for good light. She could already imagine all the farms along the way, the old barns begging for a picture, the town squares that deserved to be caught by her lens. The point of the trip was to see

242

Gene, but what was wrong with taking some time of it for herself?

"I really want to take some photographs on the way up." She had said it a hundred times if she had said it once, and she was getting tired of the same old saw. She carefully filtered the note of wariness out of her voice.

"Okay."

His tone was curt, almost hurt, but she stood her ground. "I'll leave tomorrow, and I'll see you on Friday. Want me to call you before I leave?"

"Before you leave, and while you're driving, and while you're at the hotel, and everywhere in between," he said. "I can't wait for you to get here."

No matter their differences, she knew that much was true, and it warmed her from the inside out. "I can't wait, either."

"Goodnight, Becca-girl."

Before she could say anything in response, he hung up. She clicked the phone closed and dropped it on the table, where it slid to a stop against a stack of photo proofs. She stared at the candle until it started to blur, trying to hold on to the good sex and the even better orgasm, but it was already a distant memory. Now she was thinking about the hours of work still ahead of her, the proofs to organise and the mailings to be done. Just thinking about it made her tired.

She sat up on the couch. The sudden wetness between her thighs reminded her of what she had just done with Gene, and what she could expect to do much more of as soon as she got to his house in Iowa. She padded to the bathroom and cleaned up, smiling as she thought about climbing into the shower with Gene after making love, washing away the remnants of him, leaving only the tiny little bruises and love bites that would remind her for days of what they had done.

But first, she had work to do.

Rebecca grabbed the proofs from the living room table and took them to her office, where she sat naked at her desk and pulled out the envelopes. Taking pictures of school kids and dogs and families was the way she paid the overheads, but her real passion was creative photography. In between the shots that took her breath away, she had to do the monotonous jobs—like stuffing four hundred proofs into mailers and getting them ready to drop off at the county school.

She studied the envelopes, glanced at the clock and got to work.

By the next nightfall, she had made it to the Georgia border. It would take another two days of steady driving to get into Iowa, but she felt more than up to the task. As she watched the sun set over the foothills of the Appalachian Mountains, she thought again how good it was to drive the stretch. She pulled over to the side of the road and took pictures until the sun went down, then headed into town for a motel.

She called Gene as soon as she got to her room. He was already asleep, so she quickly told him she was safe in Georgia, and let him go back to dreamland. When she hung up the phone, she crawled under the cool, impersonal covers. She tried to sleep but soon found it impossible—the excitement of the day, the travel, all the new things she had seen, flashed through her head and refused to give her rest. The anticipation of seeing Gene for the first time was the thought that came to her most often, and she finally kicked down the covers, resigned to not going to sleep for a while.

She flipped through the television channels and watched the local news, which was not so different than the news in Miami, though the accents of the newscasters were decidedly different—not as slick and careful, somehow. She watched a bit of a movie, something she vaguely remembered from years ago, but quickly tired of the drama.

She turned the channel again and this time she hit the pay-per-view section. She looked at the listings, and one of them caught her fancy: *Sebastian's Hot Ride.*

244

She laughed out loud at the name, but that didn't stop her from clicking on the title. When it asked if she was sure, she clicked on the button that said she was, though she had no idea what she might find. When the images filled the screen, she dropped the remote on the bedside table and stared.

"Jackpot," she whispered.

The man on the screen was tall, broad-shouldered, unbelievably buff, the kind of man who graced the cover of romance novels. The woman with him was impossibly tiny, her breasts much bigger than God had intended, and she wore nothing but blood red lipstick.

Rebecca watched as the woman lay on the bed and pressed her ample breasts together with her hands, her come-hither eyes making it very clear what the tall stud was supposed to do. He crouched over her and slid his long, thick cock between the white globes. The woman lifted her head a bit, and the camera watched from behind as she sucked his balls into her mouth and worried them with her tongue. The sounds of moans filled the air.

Rebecca's own moan joined in as she slid a hand between her thighs. The movie was unreal, completely over the top, but that didn't stop her from looking at the dick and wishing she had one right now. When the man changed positions and got on top of the woman, lifting her legs high in the air and slowly impaling her with his impossibly perfect cock, Rebecca slid a finger inside herself. She imagined the couple on the bed were really her and Gene, and she watched with fascination as they went through every position imaginable. She played with her clit the whole time, backing off when she got too close to the finish, wanting to make it last.

When the man on the screen held the woman by the hips and slowly pushed his dick into her tight ass, stretching her with it, Rebecca came so hard she felt lightheaded. She watched the movie to the end, hoping to garner some new and interesting positions to use during her time with Gene. When it was over she flipped off the television and lay awake in the darkness, thinking about Gene, and almost wishing she had taken the plane after all.

During the journey, Rebecca stopped often to shoot images that struck her. A field of late-blooming flowers caught her attention, and so did a huge group of wild turkeys. In Tennessee she took pictures of the soaring bridge over the Natchez Trace Parkway. She stopped at a cafe in Kentucky and took pictures of the tractors outside, the farmers at the counter and the waitress who gave her a free scoop of ice cream on top of her apple pie. In Illinois she caught an impressive mass of dark clouds over the flat corn fields while she listened to dire accounts of severe weather on the FM radio stations.

She found old barns everywhere and took enough pictures to create a whole book of them, if she was so inclined. Some of her favourite photographs were those she snapped of the giant windmills. The steel rose imposingly from the ground, at definite odds with the century-old silos and small, squat farmhouses.

She spent the night in a little motel that offered only three channels on the television, no room service and a heater that worked only half the time. There would be no pay-per-view this evening, but she was too tired to care. She cuddled up under the blankets and fell asleep to the buzzing of a neon Vacancy sign outside her window. The new morning dawned crisp and clear, and the neon buzz was replaced with the sound of chirping birds.

In northern Illinois she saw her first snowfall.

Rebecca pulled over to the side of the road when she saw the little white flakes. She stared at the windshield as the snowflakes fell, stuck to the glass for a moment and melted into a drop of water. She was stunned by how pretty they were. She had lived all of her twenty-something years in sunny Miami, where the thermometers never dropped below the fifties. Now that she was seeing snow for the first time, she was utterly fascinated.

Rebecca got out of the car and stood in the cold air, surprised that the temperatures had dropped so quickly. She grabbed her camera, focused on the trunk of her car and tried to get shots of individual snowflakes before they melted. She found it much harder than she had imagined it would be. Finally she put the camera away and simply stood in the softly falling snow, listening to the world around her and breathing deep of the crisp air.

By the time the sun went down, she was crossing the Iowa border. Small farmhouses dotted the landscape, their porch lights shining in the twilight darkness. The snow was falling harder now, and Rebecca drove with her windshield wipers on. The heater in her car had never been used before — why would she ever need it in the Sunshine State? When she turned it on, a burning smell blasted out of the vents. Once the dust was burned away, there was nothing but the blessed heat blowing over Rebecca's face and feet.

The farmhouses became few and far between, and the road was darker than ever without streetlights to help guide her way. The snow came down furiously, drifting across the road, piling up in the ditches. Mixed in with the snow was a hard ticking sleet, the tiny pieces of ice pinging from her windshield. Her headlights shone on a fury of white as she looked for another porch light, and became increasingly worried when none appeared.

When she glanced down at the gas gauge, that worry turned to near-panic.

She pulled carefully to the side of the road and reached for her cell phone. She dialled Gene's number and immediately got a beep, followed by another, louder one. She looked at the little glowing screen.

Call failed.

She tried it again, with the same result. There was no signal.

Think, Rebecca. Think. What's the best thing to do now?

She knew she was on the right road — she had turned on to it several miles back, but she was still a good thirty miles short of where she needed to be. Glancing at the gas gauge one more time, she decided to drive on until she came to another service area. Then she would call Gene, tell him her situation, and ask him to come out and meet her. He knew the roads better than she did, and he knew how to drive on snow. She hadn't the faintest clue.

Comfortable in her decision, she carefully pulled back on to the road. At first she kept her speed at a crawl, but as she grew more confident in her abilities to drive on the snow-covered road, she pressed harder on the gas pedal.

The tyres lost their grip and the car began to skid.

Rebecca tried to remember what she had learned about snow, and whether she should turn into the skid, or away. Before she could decide, there was a dull thud, and the rear of her car bounced. Another thud, and the car slid into the ditch with an air of finality. The engine stalled, sputtered and died.

Rebecca sat behind the wheel, her knuckles white, staring out of the windshield. She took a deep breath. She closed her eyes as the shakes set in.

It had all happened so fast.

Her hands still shaking, Rebecca reached again for her cell phone. She pressed the button and the blue light of the tiny phone filled the car.

No service.

"Damn it, not now!" Rebecca punched buttons on the phone, as if that would make a difference. She threw it on the dash, grabbed the keys, turned the ignition and heard the satisfying roar of the engine. She cranked up the heat, held her hands in front of the vent for a moment, then put the car into gear. Gingerly she pressed on the gas pedal and felt the tyres catch. They gained traction for a moment but almost immediately slipped again, dumping the car back into the ditch. Rebecca put it in reverse and tried the same thing. No luck.

"Damnation!" she hollered.

She shoved open the car door and climbed out. The ditch

was deeper than she had thought and the car was on an angle, so getting to the road was a bit of a struggle. When she turned to look back at the car, she realised it would never come out of there without the help of a tow truck.

The snow was coming down, obscuring everything. It was frigidly cold, like standing in a refrigerator. She got back into the car and slammed the door shut behind her. At least the engine was still running — she held her hands in front of the heater vents, trying to stay warm while she took stock of the situation.

Her phone didn't work. Her car was definitely stuck. It was still snowing, and now the world was so white she couldn't see the yellow lines of the road, though she knew they were only a few feet away. There hadn't been a porch light for miles. She knew which road she was on, but that was all she had in the way of direction.

She was already getting warmer, though. The car's heater was a dragon of a thing, and would probably keep her toasty warm until the gas ran out.

The gas.

She stared at the gauge. It was sitting at just below a quarter of a tank, which was enough to last for a while, but not nearly enough to last through the night. If she were really as stuck as she seemed to be, that gas wouldn't hold out long enough.

"Think," she whispered, fighting against panic. "Think."

She could walk as soon as the snow let up, and try to find the nearest house. She was wearing tennis shoes, two shirts and jeans — not heavy enough to fight the cold of the snow. She had other clothes in her trunk, including a coat. She could layer all of them if she had to.

But first she would wait for the snow storm to let up, so she could see where she was walking when she did venture out of the car.

Rebecca laid her head back against the seat. The engine was still humming along and the heater was blowing full blast. She was warm in her little cocoon of a car, and for a while she simply watched the snow fall outside the window. She even admired how pretty it was, even though she was scared to death of what might happen if it didn't let up soon.

When she looked back at the windshield, it was covered. Panic sliced through her, clean and sharp as a razor blade. She sat up to stare at the white. How much snow was out there? She opened the door a bit and watched as it cut a path through the white drifts, proof that the snow was at least a foot deep, maybe more.

Deep enough to cover the tailpipe?

The sobering thought sent her out into the snow in a hurry. Rebecca pushed the door open all the way, climbed out into snow that now came up well past her ankles, and struggled to the back of the car. The tailpipe wasn't blocked, but it was close. She knelt in the snow, cursed as it soaked through her jeans, and pushed handfuls of it away with her hands. It was still coming down, hard enough to make her efforts seem lost in the blizzard.

"That's what this is," she murmured to herself, her teeth already chattering. "This is a blizzard."

She cleaned around the tailpipe as well as she could, then trudged back to the car, where she leaned towards the heater vents. Her hands were already numb. The cold had seeped through her jeans and now seemed to cool her whole body, making her tremble from head to toe. The heater warmed her quickly, but she knew any chance of finding a house with a glowing porch light was quickly disappearing under the threat of that heavy, wet snow.

She gripped the wheel, leant back against the seat and hollered her frustration at the top of her lungs. The sound filled the little car, but did absolutely nothing to make her feel better. She slammed her fist down on the dashboard, and that immediately made her feel guilty. The car was doing a good job of keeping her warm, after all. She laid her head on the steering wheel and squeezed her eyes shut.

"I will not cry," she chanted. "Will not, will not, will not."

Outside the snow kept falling, turning the landscape into an endless world of white.

More books from
Totally Bound Publishing

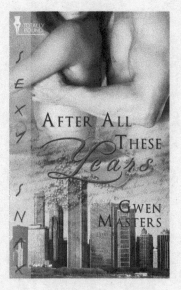

Bobby died over twenty years ago, and Marilyn moved on - but then came William.

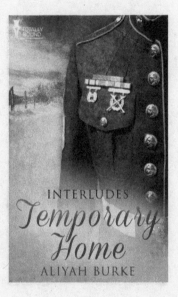

Book one in the Interludes series

Sometimes past demons need to be faced and who better to slay them than a Marine?

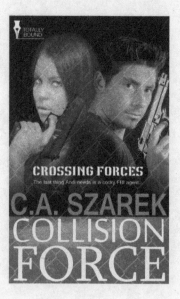

Book one in the Crossing Forces series

*A bad boy FBI agent and a feisty widowed police detective
collide.*

A cop with a mission. A woman with no memory. A killer who hunts them both.

About the Author

Gwen Masters

Gwen Masters has seen hundreds of her short stories published in print and online, and her erotic novels have been translated into half a dozen different languages. When she's not writing smut, she is diving into research on interesting yet obscure topics, hopping a plane every few weeks, and masquerading as a serious news journalist. She splits her time between a home on the Georgia coast and a little place on the outskirts of Philadelphia.

Gwen Masters loves to hear from readers. You can find contact information, website details and an author profile page at https://www.totallybound.com/